PRAISE F(

'*This Way Out* explores th[...] [...]ltural relationships alongside reli[...] [...]nental health, and masculinity in South Asian, Muslim, and LGBTQIA+ cultures, and the power of inclusion and a found family amid love, loss, growth, and change.'

—Booklist

'Adored reading *This Way Out* – deeply-felt and thought-provoking in equal measure . . . It's so fresh and original, I pretty much inhaled it.'

—Angela Chadwick

'It's fascinating, absorbing, and vital!'
—Matt Cain, author of *The Secret Life of Albert Entwistle* and *Becoming Ted*

'A total treat! *This Way Out* . . . is absolutely lovely. I loved its portrayal of the family you are born into and the family you make along the way. It was funny and sad and poignant and heartfelt . . . highly recommended.'

—Bethany Clift, author of *Last One at the Party* and *Love and Other Human Errors*

'This glittering debut is not to be missed.'

—*Hello! Magazine*

'This romantic, honest book is to be celebrated.'

—*Gscene*

BETTER
LEFT
UNSAID

ALSO BY TUFAYEL AHMED

This Way Out

BETTER LEFT UNSAID

TUFAYEL AHMED

LAKE UNION
PUBLISHING

This is a work of fiction. Names, characters, organizations, places, events, and incidents are either products of the author's imagination or are used fictitiously. Any resemblance to actual persons, living or dead, or actual events is purely coincidental.

Text copyright © 2023 by Tufayel Ahmed
All rights reserved.

No part of this book may be reproduced, or stored in a retrieval system, or transmitted in any form or by any means, electronic, mechanical, photocopying, recording, or otherwise, without express written permission of the publisher.

Published by Lake Union Publishing, Seattle

www.apub.com

Amazon, the Amazon logo, and Lake Union Publishing are trademarks of Amazon.com, Inc., or its affiliates.

ISBN-13: 9781542037747
eISBN: 9781542037730

Cover design by Amit Malhotra
Cover images: © Madina Asileva / Getty Images

Printed in the United States of America

For the bold and brave migrant generations
that came before and paved the way.
For the grandmothers, the mothers, the aunts,
sisters, nieces and daughters.

Prologue

SULTANA

Sultana knew she was nearing the end of her life, but this didn't cause her any great pain. She'd lived in her stroke-ravaged body for seven years; that was a long time to get used to the fact that she'd never again be able to walk on her own two feet, that her heart was working harder now to pump blood around her body, and that it was only a matter of time.

What ailed her in her final months wasn't her own mortality, but what would become of her children and husband. Her physical pain was outweighed by the emotional guilt she felt, for she knew that she wouldn't be there, as a mother should, to watch her children grow older and start families of their own. She considered herself fortunate that she had been alive to see her eldest, Imran, marry, mashallah, but the same couldn't be said for Sumaya, her only daughter, in whose fieriness she saw herself at that age, and her youngest, Majid, about whom she felt the most guilt. In her darkest moments, she wallowed in the fact that she hadn't been able to be much of a mother to him, for he had been just seven on that fateful morning when she woke up, unable to feel anything below her neck.

These last months, Sultana had fretted, silently praying – time was slipping away as surely as sand passes through an hourglass, and when the final grains fell, her time would be up. There'd be no resetting the clock. So, even as she felt her body slowly giving up, each thump of her heart more laborious, Sultana's mind remained firm, and she was adamant that she would muster strength one final time to soothe her children's hearts and minds. To leave them not in sorrow, but prepared for what their lives would be without her. Her life was nearing its end, but her children had so much more to live for. Her greatest satisfaction now would be to know that they would have fulfilled lives.

Sultana called each of her children to her bedside, one by one, starting with her oldest child. 'Promise me . . .' she said to each of them, imparting her wishes for their future.

Majid, she feared, would forget her, but perhaps that wasn't such a bad thing. His heart was still young, so he wouldn't be scarred the way her other two children and her husband would be. And she knew that Abdul and her two older children would wrap themselves around him and shower him with the parenting she could not.

Imran and Sumaya concerned Sultana more. She lamented that things were as they had been for the past few years between them. They were once so close. Imran had doted on his baby sister from the moment Sultana and Abdul brought her home from the hospital. Now, the acrimony between them was thick, and mediating between her eldest son and her daughter was as exhausting as her illness.

In the corner of her mind, Sultana questioned whether she had done the right thing all those years ago. Whether the tension between her children was her fault. Even if her husband and children weren't aware of all the facts, she had long borne the guilt of the knowledge she possessed, and the burden it had put on her family.

As much as Sultana yearned for Imran and Sumaya to mend their relationship, she was also wary that if they ever did, it threatened to dredge up memories that were best lost to time. What she had done for her family.

It had been the right thing to do, she had convinced herself in these last weeks of her life.

Her children's fraught relationship hurt her, of course, but she didn't regret what she had done, and she was sure she'd do it all again.

Every mother makes her sacrifices. Every family has its skeletons.

But sometimes, these things are better left unsaid.

Muslim woman's hijab ripped off in shocking viral video

Monday, 10 October 2022 – London Evening Standard

A video depicting the shocking moment a Muslim woman had her hijab ripped off in public has gone viral on social media, as police call for leads to identify the assailant.

The clip, filmed on Saturday in Stratford, East London, shows the unidentified woman waiting for a bus at Stratford bus station when she is confronted by a Caucasian male. The two appear to have a verbal altercation before the woman, wearing a traditional black abaya, is seen trying to walk past him. The man can then be seen reaching for the woman's hijab and pulling it off. The woman can be heard screaming as other bystanders clamour to help her.

The mobile phone footage, first shared on TikTok on Saturday evening by user alimthagr8st, has been viewed over 200,000 times in just 24 hours.

The person behind the camera can be heard saying, 'Yo, he's just taken off her hijab! What the f**k! Stop him! He's just tried to attack her!'

The TikTok user captioned the video, writing: 'Scary scenes in Stratford just now . . . wtf is the world coming to.' The user did not respond to the *Standard*'s requests for comment.

Social media users expressed shock and outrage as the video began circulating on platforms including Twitter and Instagram. Labour MP Shazia Iqbal, who represents nearby East Ham, tweeted: 'This vile display of cowardice is yet another example of how unsafe it is to be a Muslim woman in Britain today. Solidarity with this poor sister. If you're out there, we stand with you. Please find this hooligan and put him behind bars!'

The identity of the victim has not been disclosed, but local police said they attended the scene at 4.38 p.m. following reports of a woman being assaulted at Stratford bus depot.

The Metropolitan Police have released two images of the suspect and ask anyone who may have further information to come forward. One image shows a dark-blond-haired man wearing black tracksuit bottoms with three white stripes down the sides, and a dark blue sweater with a sports logo on it. The second image provides a clearer view of the man's profile. The police noted that the man in the image has a distinctive tattoo on the right side of his neck.

Anyone with information is advised to call 101 with reference 9179/VML32, or Crimestoppers anonymously.

Chapter 1

Imran

It wasn't that Imran wanted to call his sister, although perhaps it had been too long and he probably ought to. It was more that he felt he had no choice. What else could he do? Who else could he turn to? Amma and Baba were long dead and buried, Majid was just a kid, and his in-laws would only rail at him. Tell him that he couldn't take care of his wife. That he had failed her yet again. He felt his back was against a wall. So, he made the phone call he'd never wanted to make.

'It's Fahima,' he told his sister when he finally reached her. New York was five hours behind London and so he had waited for the opportune time – he didn't want to call too early because she'd still be asleep, so he'd waited and waited, until three p.m. It'd be ten o'clock there, he reasoned, not too early, nor too late. He'd changed his mind more than a dozen times before three p.m., of course. *Maybe I don't need her, I can do this*, he told himself. In the end, though, after toying with hitting the Call button and then stopping four times, he finally gave in. *Who am I kidding? I can't do this alone*, he conceded.

Sumaya seemed just as reluctant to get Imran's call as he was to be calling her. The last time they had spoken was when they exchanged pleasantries on Eid day nearly six months ago, and that had been more Fahima's doing than his own – his wife had called his sister in New York to wish her a happy Eid. Imran had merely exchanged pleasantries before handing the phone back. Aside from the odd text to check in on each other, the siblings didn't have much of a relationship anymore, not since Sumaya had moved to New York seven years earlier. In truth, his wife had a closer relationship with his sister than he did, and it was only through Fahima and Sumaya's weekly calls on a Sunday night that he kept abreast with what she was up to. But these were exceptional circumstances, and he had no one else.

'What's going on?' Sumaya said over the phone. She sounded confused.

'I . . . I . . .' Imran stumbled for words. How to explain? The last thing he had expected, or wanted, was to need something – or anything, really – from his sister; and now, pridefully, his request had lodged itself in the back of his throat and he was unwilling to loosen it.

'Look, I'm about to go into a meeting . . .' Sumaya said, sounding impatient at the prolonged silence. 'Shall we talk later?' Even as she said it, it sounded to Imran like a brush-off, and it probably was. He knew that she wouldn't call him back. The intimacy of a phone conversation, each sharing the latest about their lives, like Amma used to do with her sister back home, was an alien concept to them both. Theirs was a more complex relationship – more formal, transactional almost. It was the stuff of polite hellos and how-do-you-dos, but rarely, if ever, deeper.

Imran found it difficult to express his feelings, to articulate his emotions, at the best of times. It was one of the things that Fahima constantly tried to get him to do. With his wife, and before that with Amma, he managed to be softer, loosening himself from the confines of his macho bravado like one might loosen a scarf. But this level of vulnerability – this weakness, as he thought of it – on display to his sister? This was too much. *I've made a mistake*, he thought. He would take the out she had offered him. Yes, talk later, knowing that she'd never call back. He had been foolish to call her. Yet he couldn't hang up either.

'Hello?' Sumaya said on the other end of the line, still waiting for her brother to respond.

'I'm here,' Imran replied. 'I . . . I need you to come here.' His intonation made it sound more like a demand than a request. Maybe it was? After all, she was still his younger sister, and he was still the man of the house – never mind that she no longer lived there.

'Are you okay?' Sumaya said. 'You sound a bit . . . off.'

Why was it so hard for him to elucidate what was going on? Why now, when he needed it most, could he not speak what was in his heart? If he didn't explain, if he didn't try, he'd lose his chance to help Fahima.

'I'm fine. It's your bhabi . . .' Imran finally mustered. 'I don't know how to explain it . . .'

How could he tell his sister that his wife, his Fahima, was the one who was plastered all over the newspapers? Whose humiliation had been captured and shared online for all to see? Tweeted, TikToked and GIFed for the world. The image would forever remain on the internet, like a meme of a celebrity falling over on a red carpet. Except Fahima was no celebrity, this wasn't a funny moment to relive in perpetuity, and she had not consented to her privacy being violated in this way. He felt shame in the pit of his stomach, first at the thought of his wife, helpless, shrieking as her hijab was forcibly removed, and then at the image spreading, as it had, like wildfire. The only saving grace in the whole episode was that no one knew who she was, even as the images of her were published everywhere from London to Chicago to Doha.

'Then try . . .' Sumaya said curtly.

Imran sighed. 'Look at your phone. I'm sending you a link.'

And so, even as he'd just despaired at strangers clicking, zooming in on and sharing articles about Fahima's attack, he opened WhatsApp and did the same, sending Sumaya a link to the *London Evening Standard*. 'Muslim woman's hijab ripped off in shocking viral video,' read the headline. This way was easier than speaking the words. What would he even say? *My wife has been attacked and I couldn't do anything to stop it.* Explaining his plight would only make it worse, give further power to circumstances he very much wished he wasn't in, events that had been embedded in his brain since they had happened. It tortured him inside – and like a monster under a child's bed, speaking of it made it real.

He waited with bated breath as he heard shuffling on the other end of the phone – a muffled 'hold on' as Sumaya moved her phone from her ear, the clacking sound of keys being pressed, and then the audible gasp.

'Wait,' Sumaya said. 'Are you saying . . . this is Bhabi?'

'Yes,' Imran said, deflated. And then: 'I don't know what to do.'

'Fuck,' Sumaya said, her shock permeating through the phone. 'Is . . . is she okay?'

It was a question that Imran couldn't fully answer. He'd not seen his wife this despondent, this visibly apathetic, in their ten years of marriage. He could barely coax her out of bed most days since the attack just over two weeks ago. He'd tried to enlist her overworked and time-poor GP, who simply said she needed time and prescribed some sleeping pills to help her rest. The police liaison assigned to her case hadn't been much help either; the apathy had oozed from her voice even as she said, 'We're here to support you.' Either she was so desensitised to cases like Fahima's or, worse, she just didn't care.

'I could really use your help,' Imran said reluctantly. 'If you can come here . . . I think she'd appreciate it.'

The list of people Imran could turn to was so short that it had only one name, yet he couldn't bring himself to admit that it was *he* who'd appreciate Sumaya's support, for Fahima had yet to be informed of this plan – and so estranged had he become from his sister over the years, and so strained was their relationship, that an expression of his own appreciation felt too much like affection. And despite their blood bond, Imran's affection towards his sister had only further diminished since Baba had died.

It hadn't always been like this. Now, thinking about it, Imran recalled how close they had been growing up. How much he had loved and adored his sister; how protective he had felt over her.

He had been three when Amma was pregnant with Sumaya, and he'd been so excited to become an older brother. He'd rub her belly and make a wish: 'I hope it's a little sister.' His wish had come true and Imran doted on her, gently cradling her in his lap while Amma and Baba prayed namaz, shushing her when she cried, and bringing her his Action Man toy to play with even though she could barely crawl. And Sumaya had reciprocated this child- hood love, screaming the house down when Baba took Imran away each morning to school, and lighting up when he returned home. It would be a decade before Majid, the youngest of the siblings, joined the family, born when Sumaya was ten and Imran was thir- teen. For those ten years before Majid, to Imran's mind he had been Sumaya's favourite person in the world. She'd sneak out of Amma and Baba's bed to sleep beside him.

Once, when Sumaya was nine and had a cold, she was dis- traught that she'd have to miss her friend's birthday party. Imran had saved up the meagre pocket money Baba gave him, and went to the local newsagent's, picking out a colouring book and a pack of crayons for her. Sumaya's face lit up when she saw the gift her

11

brother had bought for her. The light in her eyes, even with a stuffy nose and persistent cough, was that of pure love. She forgot about the party, and the two of them spent the evening colouring in side by side.

So much had changed between them. Life had taken them on different paths. But Imran held on to a little glimmer of hope that his sister might hear his call.

And hear she did. 'I'm coming. I'll try and get there as soon as possible,' Sumaya answered without hesitation, much to Imran's relief. She hadn't raked him over the coals or made him beg for her help, like he had feared she might.

'Okay, I'll see you soon,' he said, again avoiding the words of gratitude or affection that might customarily pass between brother and sister.

As he hung up the phone, Imran exhaled. *That wasn't so bad*, he told himself. Sumaya would come to London and help Fahima recover from the whole ordeal. What his wife needed, he reasoned, was another woman to talk to, a friend, a kindred spirit to share her emotional pain with – a sister. He knew how to help her practically – he'd accompanied her to the police station when she was called in to give a statement, acting as her protector, her guard, a solid, intimidating presence who would ensure that no further harm would come to her. But he didn't feel equipped to support her through the emotional trauma of what had happened to her, and he'd just bungle things if he tried. It was better this way. His sister would be a better companion in this regard, and soon she'd be here, and soon Fahima would return to him, too.

But as Imran basked in the relief of finding a solution to his problem, he had another thought, one he hadn't considered until now. How would he and Sumaya share the same home again? How would they co-exist in the same space after all that had passed between them? Amma and Baba weren't here to act as a buffer, and nor was Majid, who lived in university accommodation in Islington. There'd be nowhere to hide from one another, and there was only so much small talk one could make with someone you shared a kitchen and bathroom with.

Unease crept over him, and a sudden shudder ran down his body.

He didn't know how to hide his resentment towards his sister.

Chapter 2

SUMAYA

As Sumaya ended the call with her brother, a mix of emotions ran through her. Was this why she and Fahima hadn't had their usual calls in the last couple of weeks? Her sister-in-law faithfully called her every week to share news from London. It was their ritual: Fahima would call each Sunday at five o'clock, and the sisters would while away a good hour or so nattering about what each of their weeks had brought – the latest project that Sumaya was contemplating, or the latest baking craze Fahima had discovered on Instagram. Sumaya felt a sudden pang of guilt. She was so consumed by her own life that she hadn't thought anything was wrong, hadn't thought to reach out to Fahima. She should have known that her silence was uncharacteristic. She should have asked if she was okay.

Sumaya looked out of the conference room window at the expansive Midtown Manhattan skyline – the Empire State Building and Chrysler Building towering over the city she now called home. What a vast difference this was, she thought, to the council estates and derelict school buildings she used to see out of windows in London. Here, in New York, she felt hope. There, in Bow, she felt suffocated. But she had told her brother that she'd go home

– though to think of London as home now felt unnatural, like sand in your mouth at the beach. It had been three years since she last visited, for Baba's funeral. She'd been in New York for nearly eight years, and it felt to her as if the time had flown by, immersed as she had been in building a new life. Her own life.

Her phone buzzed with a text message from her friend and former boss, Rachel: *About to go on set – catch up after*. Sumaya had grown to love the breakneck pace of New York life, the dizzying speed at which everyone moved, worked and lived. It was in this very building that she had cut her teeth in the world of television as an assistant, then a producer, then an executive producer for daytime television. Every day had been like hopping on a bullet train. Each day she had to be on the floor, helping produce a live broadcast of *The Rachel Stewart Show*, and then do it all over again the next. There was a relentless energy to the routine that appealed to her – every morning was a chance to start over, no time to dwell on past successes or failures. It made her feel more alive than she had ever felt in London, where life had seemed to grind along slowly, tediously, all the days merging into one as she helplessly watched Amma wither away.

The guilt Sumaya felt over Fahima mingled with a sense of pride at being back in this familiar building. She had learned everything about her craft here, but now she was her own woman, with her own fledgling production company. She had left the show a year earlier to pursue her passion for producing documentaries, but her bond with Rachel and the show was akin to her bond with her sister-in-law. Rachel had taken her in and supported her through this New York life, and aside from her weekly calls with Fahima, there was no friend she spoke to more.

When Amma died, Sumaya had chosen life and adventure. What was her best hope in London? To fall into a monotonous day job, get married and one day die? In New York, she had the opportunity to reinvent herself – and she had transformed into someone the old her might envy. How would she feel going back to London, especially after so long?

Sumaya knew Imran wouldn't ask for her help if he didn't really need it. She couldn't bear to think what Fahima bhabi had been through, and though her brother's choice of words, or rather lack of – not a 'please' or a 'thank you' to be had – was apparent to her, she chose to overlook his caustic behaviour this once.

Bhabi had always been good to her; even when Sumaya's relationship with her brother was tense, they had built their own sisterly bond. How could someone hurt her? Fahima was mild-mannered and caring, and not the least bit offensive. All this because of what she looked like? Sumaya had never known the prejudice that came with wearing a headscarf, having chosen not to wear the hijab when she came of age. Neither Amma nor Baba had imposed it on her either, and so what she'd feared might be an issue of contention in fact wasn't.

The first time she'd met her future sister-in-law, however, part of Sumaya felt envious of how beautifully Fahima wrapped her dark hair in a shimmering burnt-orange poly-satin scarf, tying the ends elegantly into a Parisian knot to one side of her neck. Sumaya, who spent hours straightening or curling her hair to suit the occasion, wished she could be so confident as to hide what she thought of as one of her greatest assets – and still appear so ethereal. She'd never been brave enough to try.

Sumaya sighed and closed her eyes. Fahima wore her hijab so proudly, it was an extension of herself. It wasn't intended as a statement to anyone else – fashion, political or otherwise. How could anyone take such offence at a square piece of fabric that they would violate another's physical being?

And though she didn't consider herself religious, and hadn't prayed in years, here, overlooking her new life, Sumaya tapped into a piece of her old life and offered a dua for her sister-in-law.

◆ ◆ ◆

Sumaya watched from the sidelines, the heat from the overhead lighting rig emanating a glow around her friend. Rachel was sitting in her armchair on set and looked impossibly glamorous in an emerald-green jumpsuit. Next to the eponymous host of *The Rachel Stewart Show*, Sumaya felt dowdy in her black skinny jeans and grey high-neck wool top. Where Rachel's wavy auburn hair caught the light and glistened like she was in a shampoo commercial, Sumaya had her long black hair tied back in a ponytail.

From the edge of the stage, Sumaya watched Rachel expertly interview a reality television housewife, throwing softball questions about her car and jewellery collection before going in for the tough ones about her husband's indictment for embezzlement. This was what made Rachel so good – she managed to make guests so comfortable with breezy small talk that they didn't see the hard questions coming. It was all the more impressive to watch, because Sumaya knew full well that Rachel had never seen a single episode of the housewife's show and likely never would. This was what Sumaya had loved about working with her; no matter what walk of life a guest came from, there was always something juicy to uncover, and watching Rachel dig for golden nuggets of information was akin to watching Serena Williams on a tennis court.

In the three years she had worked with Rachel, Sumaya had grown to admire and respect her – and she was also a gateway to the kinds of events and lavish parties that Sumaya could never have dreamed of in London.

Soon after Sumaya began work on *The Rachel Stewart Show*, she and Rachel had bonded over their humble beginnings. Rachel, who at thirty-five was just a few years older than Sumaya, had grown up poor in Tulsa, Oklahoma, and had lucked into fame fifteen years ago when she won a reality television singing competition and was thus anointed America's sweetheart. After releasing several albums – the last couple of which had failed to meet the chart success of her earlier work – Rachel had segued into daytime television, creating and producing her own show, which was now in its sixth year and growing its audience year-on-year.

Sumaya watched on as Rachel laughed convivially with her guest and the interview came to an end. She again thought of how drastically different her life was now to the one she had left in London – the one that Imran's call had resurrected after all this time. In New York, she was at drinks or a glamorous event every other night, or in business meetings with Netflix to pitch documentary features, but who did she even know in London anymore, except her family? The thought of being so acutely in Imran's presence made her anxious, but she again felt pained by her sister-in-law's trauma, and knew it was only right to see her.

As Rachel signed off the show, Sumaya couldn't help but contrast the reality of Rachel's life – as a celebrity with an entourage and security – with that of Fahima's. No one would dare attempt such a stunt on Rachel, and if they did, their name and face would be all over the papers and their life would never recover.

Yet Fahima's attacker was still free to live their life, and would likely never be caught.

It was unfair, but it was also one of the reasons why Sumaya had broken free from her old life – to live a life that *mattered*.

◆ ◆ ◆

'It'll only be a couple of weeks . . . besides, nothing is really calling to me right now. I need some inspiration,' Sumaya said, taking a sip of the champagne that Rachel had insisted they order after a long day.

'Two weeks! Who am I meant to hang out with if you're not here?' Rachel replied. 'Why the rush to London anyway?'

Sumaya casually took another sip of her drink before replying. 'Just . . . sorting out some family stuff.' She rarely, if ever, discussed her home life with Rachel or her other friends in New York. She wasn't even sure how this evasiveness had come to be. It wasn't something she did consciously, but somewhere along the way she had developed a habit of separating her life back home from the one she had built for herself here. And to transport Rachel and her friends' thoughts from their current location – the opulent lobby bar of The Bowery, with its plush leather sofas and Victorian-style fireplace – to her council house in Bow felt unseemly. All around them, wealthy bankers and celebrities attempting to go incognito in baseball caps and sunglasses clinked glasses and sipped expensive cocktails that certainly wouldn't be available at the local Wetherspoons. Rachel had worked her way up from poverty to be here, to belong in this space – and Sumaya had, too. If only the old Sumaya could see her now.

'A woman of mystery,' Rachel said, interrupting her thoughts. 'Well, if you bump into any eligible British bachelors, send them my way!'

'Oh, the men back home aren't quite like the Hugh Grant types you Americans love to swoon over,' Sumaya replied. 'English guys are more likely to be arrogant, posh assholes, or geezers whose idea of a date is ten pints and a kebab. I don't think that's really your thing, Rach.'

'Besides,' said Mallory, shooting Sumaya an impish smile, 'Sumaya was more into pussy, remember?'

Sumaya nearly choked on her champagne. 'MALLORY!' she squealed.

Mallory was Sumaya's other best friend in New York, and knew how to make her blush. They'd met seven years ago, when Sumaya first arrived in New York, after matching on a dating app. Sumaya had pulled up at the bar and been taken aback by Mallory's beauty; with her model-like gait, chestnut-brown hair and hazel eyes, Mallory was out of her league, Sumaya had decided. Their awkward date, during which Sumaya got giddily drunk after two glasses of red wine on an empty stomach, led to an even more awkward attempt at sex. It was Sumaya's first hook-up in New York, and she had not been prepared for Mallory's forwardness, the lithe way she came towards her and pressed her fingers to her lips, or the way she moved her pelvis into Sumaya's body.

Sumaya had only been with a couple of girls before, and still felt self-conscious about how to navigate sex. Partly because of nerves, and partly out of drunkenness, Sumaya had fumbled out of her underwear, tripping over in the process, and landed face-first on the floor. Thankfully, Mallory had seen the humour in the situation and laughed it off. 'Look, we don't have to do this,' she'd comforted her. 'Maybe the chemistry's just not right, you know?' Sumaya, though hugely attracted to Mallory, had been relieved. They'd resolved to be friends instead, and became each other's go-to person in New York as they were both far away from their families – Mallory's in Chicago, and Sumaya's all the way over in London.

'Oh, yes,' teased Tamera, the fourth and final woman sitting at the round oak table. 'I forgot that Sumaya wasn't always such a heteronormative bore!'

'You're straight!' Sumaya countered.

Tamera was a former colleague from *The Rachel Stewart Show*, running the digital and social teams, but had moved over to a more serious journalism role as social media editor at CNBC six months before Sumaya had left.

'Look, I love Jonathan,' Tamera continued, 'but your stories were much better when you dove into the lady pond.'

'Ew, no one says "lady pond" anymore, Tam,' Mallory quipped. 'But, you know what? She's right . . .'

'Stop, both of you . . .' Sumaya warned them, laughing.

'But seriously . . . are you worried about bumping into your ex?' Mallory asked with genuine concern for her friend.

Although Sumaya didn't share much about her family in London, she had told Mallory all about her first love, Neha, and the way Sumaya had broken her own heart to pursue her dream of living in New York. Neha had played on her mind a lot recently. Memories of her ex had indirectly resurfaced because of Jonathan's proposal. She didn't want to admit it to herself, but the timing of Imran's call was somewhat fortuitous. Her unresolved feelings for Neha had been calling her back home . . . and now she had a reason to return.

'It's a huge city, I really doubt I'll bump into her . . .' Sumaya replied coyly.

'Speaking of Jonny boy, how is he going to cope without wifey for two weeks?' Rachel teased.

Sumaya and Jonathan had been together for five years, first meeting on a night out at a club in Greenwich Village. One minute Sumaya had been dancing with Mallory and her friends, and the next she'd spotted Jonathan walking down the stairs into the dingy club wearing a muscle-fit black T-shirt and had instantly checked him out. Later in the evening, she'd felt someone sidling up to her and gyrating in sync with her to the sound of Rihanna's 'We Found Love'. She'd turned around to find Jonathan smiling at her. He, too, had spotted her from across the dance floor.

After dancing with one another, they'd stepped out into the smoking area to get away from the loud music and get some air. 'I think you're the most beautiful girl in here,' he'd said. 'I can't leave here tonight without getting you to agree to a date. Like, immediately. I don't think I can wait . . . what are you doing tomorrow?'

Sumaya had been stunned. What were the odds that the very guy she had just an hour earlier spotted across the club would be as into her as she was him? She'd agreed to meet the next day, and the day after that, and the day after that, too.

Their first month together, Sumaya and Jonathan had been inseparable. Jonathan had been studying for the bar and neither had much money. But she didn't mind that; she loved that he was just as down as she was to dance the night away in a basement club in Queens, sweat glistening on their foreheads and comingling as they writhed against each other.

Jonathan and Sumaya had moved in together six months after that, sharing a small apartment in Tribeca that neither could afford alone. Thankfully, the building was rent-controlled, and they made ends meet as Jonathan built up his law career and she her television career. The sheen of new romance had worn off over the years as they both focused on their work, but Sumaya felt safe in the companionship their relationship provided. She was convinced that meeting Jonathan was one of the reasons she had been right to move her entire life across the world. It wasn't quite what she had imagined for herself when she'd moved to New York as a young bisexual ready to explore all that the queer scene had to offer, but Jonathan was dependable and kind. The kind of man her parents would have wanted for her – if he were Muslim.

'Enough of this phallic lovefest,' Mallory broke into the conversation. 'Jonathan is a big boy – I'm sure he'll be just fine for two whole weeks. Unless, of course, he needs you to wipe his ass for him after he goes to the bathroom?'

Mallory was joking, but something about this offhand remark bruised Sumaya. Mallory's voice always had an edge to it where Jonathan was concerned. And though she'd never directly expressed her distaste, Sumaya knew what her friend thought of her relationship: that she'd settled. That she'd played it safe. And deep down, she thought maybe Mallory was right.

Sumaya downed the rest of her champagne and shook her head clear of the spiralling thoughts. Jonathan was a good guy, she told herself, and she *did* love him.

Her heart had been broken before. And she couldn't bear to experience that again.

Chapter 3

Imran

Imran sank deeper into his office chair, the mesh of the backrest cutting into him, creating indents in the white dress shirt he had so painstakingly – albeit clumsily – ironed that morning. Fahima usually ironed his work shirts, knowing that her husband was useless at getting out the creases. She even used scented water that made him feel fresh as a meadow. But since the attack, she had stopped waking up early with him and seeing him off to work. And though he didn't mean to feel it or want to feel it, and though he admonished himself, deep inside there was a small slither of resentment towards his wife. When would she be herself again? It had been two weeks. Imran wished he could zap away her sadness, the low mood that lingered in the house every night he came home, and have her return to the bubbly, welcoming presence she had been before she was assaulted. Imran wanted his wife back, wanted things to go back to how they were.

'Ah, Imran, there you are,' said Giles Penry-Smeed, his boss, power-walking into the small office space in a freshly pressed salmon-on-pink shirt, the lines so crisp and sharp that Imran almost envied him. 'Now, I need quarterly sales from Barking and Dagenham as soon as possible . . . which is to say, I'd have much preferred them last week.'

Polite as he was in tone, Giles Penry-Smeed was rarely, if ever, pleasant – at least to Imran. Before the attack, Imran had never truly interrogated why the borough of Barking and Dagenham had de facto become his responsibility, rather than any of the other East London dealerships that Giles and his team were entrusted with running, but he had a hunch it had something to do with the large Asian population in the borough. Joe, who sat to his right, and Martin, whose desk was placed next to Giles's, had never been assigned a specific borough as he had been, and he found this curious too, but he brushed it off whenever Shelly, his other colleague, brought up the office dynamics. 'Don't you think it's a bit weird . . . ?' she'd asked him point-blank once in the kitchenette as they made cups of tea. 'It doesn't seem fair, Imran. I'd have a word if I was you.' But Imran never had raised the issue with Giles.

'I'll have them to you right away . . .' Imran said, making a point of forcefully typing on his keyboard as though he had been tasked with something of the utmost urgency. In truth, though, he had been avoiding sending his boss the sales report from the last quarter because sales were down 40 per cent and he was sure that this would somehow be blamed on him. On top of everything going on at home, which he kept private from his boss and colleagues, Imran felt jittery at work – and so he was putting off for as long as he could the inevitable admonishment from Giles.

'Boss, did you see the game on Saturday?' Martin called out. 'Good result!'

Shelly darted a look in Imran's direction and rolled her eyes. Imran tried to block out the ensuing conversation, reaching for his earbuds and pretending to listen to Spotify. Giles, Martin and Joe often had loud conversations across the office about football or rugby that he and Shelly were ostensibly left out of, and today

24

Imran couldn't bear to pretend that it didn't bother him, and nor could he bear to listen to them droning on when he himself was consumed by more important things and felt as if the walls were closing in.

Fifteen minutes later, an email pinged on his screen. It was Giles. *Don't forget the B&D sales*, it said in the subject line. Giles hadn't bothered to put anything in the body of the email. Imran clenched his jaw, suppressing any indication of anger or annoyance.

When Imran had joined the Celeritas regional office in East London some eight years ago, he had been excited to make his mark on a larger scale after working for a small dealership since university. In a few years, he'd optimistically thought, he'd be running the place. But that optimism had been slowly and painfully squeezed out of him over the years, as he found himself up against a boys' club of ego-driven white men led by Giles.

At first, Imran thought he just needed to work harder to make a good impression, taking on more work than necessary and working through lunch to show Giles what a team player he was. But he'd soon learned that most office business, including staff appraisals, was conducted after-hours in the pub. Twice now Giles had passed him up for promotion to associate regional sales director, each time moving invisible goalposts beyond Imran's reach. It occurred to Imran that both times he'd been overlooked, the promotions went to one of the white guys who joined Giles for drinks down the pub every Friday night.

It had been years since Imran had touched a drop of alcohol – he hadn't drunk since his uni days. He drew a line between work and life, and with a family at home, he'd never been inclined to play that particular game for the sake of a pat on the back. Besides, it wasn't as if Giles or his male colleagues had ever invited him. They'd never asked if he drank, but it was one thing to ask, and another to have his white colleagues reach the assumption that he didn't because of what he looked like.

Although he knew he had more to offer, Imran reluctantly buried his head in the sand and brushed off Shelly's comments that he was being mistreated. He'd never actively sought out another job; he was comfortable with the balance this one provided – clocking off at five o'clock, getting home by six every night and leaving his work firmly behind in the office.

But now, after what had happened to Fahima, the behaviour that he had batted away – such as being asked to speak to an Indian client on the phone despite not speaking Hindi, and the lack of job progression – was becoming harder to swallow.

Perhaps Shelly was right. What had she called Giles's behaviour? *Microaggressions.* 'It's being racist without being blatant about it, but it's racism whatever way you look at it, Imran,' she'd told him once. She'd heard Holly and Phil talking about it on *This Morning*. A staunch royalist, however, Shelly had also added, thus leading Imran to dismiss her, 'But what do they know . . . I wouldn't trust 'em as far as I could throw 'em. Skipping the queen's queue like that.'

The little things that he had accepted as the price he paid for his income now weighed heavier in the context of what had been done to Fahima. If they let the little things go, wouldn't their aggressors just be more emboldened to see how far they could push the limits?

Who had shied away from calling out that man, until he felt so invincible as to put his hands on Fahima?

Imran suddenly felt ashamed. Because he had been part of the problem.

◆　◆　◆

Fahima was in bed when Imran arrived home that evening. Imran deduced, from the still-full cup of tea and uneaten slices of toast spread with a smidgen of butter that he had put on the bedside that morning, that she had not moved since he left for work. And this wasn't the first time.

'Fahima,' he said, drawing closed the curtains, left unattended since morning, even though it was now dark outside, 'are you awake?'

His wife stirred under the covers but didn't respond. This had become something of a daily routine, and Imran was growing increasingly frustrated at Fahima's lack of communication, as well as his own inability to coax her from this mood. Sumaya would be here soon, and maybe she could help Fahima snap out of her melancholy, but until then he was on his own.

'Babe, have you eaten anything? Have you got out of bed at all?' he asked, knowing full well she hadn't.

Again, Fahima didn't respond. He set about clearing the stone-cold tea and untouched toast from the nightstand, worrying all the while about how frail Fahima had started to look over the last couple of weeks – her eyes sunken, her skin, usually emitting a healthy glow, now sallow. He feared she was disintegrating before his eyes, an ember steadily losing its spark.

In the kitchen, he poured the tea away and discarded the toast. He stood at the sink, letting the cold tap water run through his fingers and over the empty mug and side plate. There was something about the chill of the water that soothed him, made him numb to his wife's troubles and the failure he felt deep within. For what felt like minutes, but was in fact only seconds, Imran stood there in meditation until a thought came to him.

When he, Sumaya and Majid were children, Amma used to make them kisuri when they were unwell and during Ramadan. The simplicity of the dish – mostly rice, with some spices, onion and ghee – perfectly lined the stomach after a long day of fasting, or helped settle the stomach when they were poorly. Though he'd

27

never made it before, he'd seen Amma and Fahima make it enough times that he felt confident he could recreate it.

He soaked two cups of rice in warm water before draining it and pouring it into a pot and covering it with fresh water. Then he added some minced ginger, a pinch of salt, a dash of fenugreek and two bay leaves, and let the mixture boil.

Amma had never timed her cooking – she used what she called her antaz, her instinct – so Imran wasn't precisely sure how long to let it cook. When the mixture began to bubble over the sides of the pot, hitting the hob with a sizzle, he turned down the heat and stirred the mixture, adding more water to create the porridge-like consistency of kisuri.

As the pot simmered, he melted some ghee in a hot frying pan, chopped an onion and began to fry it in the clarified butter. Within minutes, the sautéing onions filled the kitchen with the aroma of his childhood. How many times had he walked into this very kitchen, to Amma or Fahima cooking this exact same dish? How many times had the scent of sizzling spices and onion tingled his nostrils and sent reverberations into the pit of his stomach? And how many times had he feverishly shovelled spoonfuls into his mouth, savouring every hint of ginger and fried onion? Food wasn't just food in a Bangladeshi household, but itself a language of love. Maybe this would bring Fahima back to him.

While the onions took on a golden-brown colour, Imran had taken his eye off the rice mixture, and suddenly he noticed it had begun to dry out and burn at the edges of the pot. 'Fuck!' He had been so consumed by the onions that he hadn't thought to check if the pot needed more water. He hastily poured some more boiling water from the kettle and stirred it in, but bits of burned rice, brown flecks bobbing in a sea of white, blemished the dish, and to Imran's eye made it imperfect. How easy it had seemed, when he had watched Amma and Fahima make kisuri. He had only turned his back for a moment . . . Still, it was too late to start over, so he added the ghee and browned onions from the frying pan into the pot, stirring it, and hoped the golden hue of the onions might mask his error.

◆ ◆ ◆

Imran sat on the edge of the bed, the bowl of kisuri in his hands, and tried to rouse his wife.

'I made some kisuri, look,' he said, proudly presenting the hot bowl.

Fahima slowly emerged from under the hefty duvet, her jet-black hair tied back and her eyes reddened. There was a curious look on her face. Had her husband really attempted to make something – even something so simple – himself? She sat up, propping up her pillow behind her, and looked at the bowl of porridge. Whatever was in the bowl looked nothing like the kisuri she made during Ramadan – it looked congealed, inedible, not that she had much of an appetite.

'Here, try some . . . you need to eat,' Imran said softly, as he earnestly scooped up a spoonful and brought it to her mouth.

Fahima's demeanour soured. She made no attempt to open her mouth or accept her husband's offering.

'Please . . .' Imran said. 'Just try . . .'

Fahima remained stoic. Her lips were shut, her jaw firmly clenched, and still Imran sat there, spoon hovering near her mouth, willing her to eat. The silence in the room, the silence between them, was palpable. They were in a stand-off.

'Fahi,' Imran eventually pleaded. 'You can't keep doing this. You need to eat, you need to keep up your strength.'

Still, Fahima stared blankly at her husband, but after several seconds like this she hesitantly parted her mouth, her dry lips cracking as she did. She coughed to clear her throat, and when she spoke – the first time Imran had heard her speak in days – she sounded raspy.

'Please,' she said quietly. 'Please just leave me alone.'

Imran carefully brought the spoon back down into the bowl.

'Do you want to eat it yourself?' he asked. 'Just have some . . .'

Fahima closed her eyes, brought her hands to her face and let out a forceful sigh.

'Why . . . don't . . . you . . . ever . . . listen,' she said through gritted teeth, each word so piercing to Imran's ears that he flinched. This wasn't his Fahima, the softly spoken and sweet wife he revered. To hear her speak in this forcible tone took him by surprise.

'I just . . .' He tried to muster some response, but he couldn't think what to say.

Imran put the bowl of kisuri down on the nightstand and attempted to take Fahima's hands in his. They felt fragile, brittle even, but before he even had a grasp on her, she quickly snapped them away from him. This, too, was unlike his wife, and made him bristle in shock. Perplexed by her coldness, he gently stood up from the bed.

'I don't know what to do.' He whispered the words so softly that he wasn't sure she could hear him. His wife's sudden anger had blindsided him, and he felt like a little boy fresh from being scolded by an adult, wanting to apologise for whatever it was that he had done wrong – if only to placate her.

Fahima looked up at him, a menacing steel in her eyes that he had never seen before.

'*You* don't know what to do?' she screamed at him. '*You* don't?'

A shiver ran down Imran's spine. The scorn in her voice hit him like a thunderbolt. What had happened to Fahima, and who was this in front of him? Frozen to the spot, unable to utter a word, he stood up, stupefied.

'I don't want your fucking kisuri,' Fahima screamed louder, spittle flying from her mouth and dancing in the air. 'I don't want anything. I just want you to leave me alone.'

Then she let out a whimper, suddenly depleted of all energy, like a child after a tantrum. She slid back down into the bed and pulled the covers over her, fading from view.

Imran stayed rooted to the spot.

Confused, and more than a little hurt.

In the darkness of the living room, with nothing but the moon casting a dim glow, Imran lay on the sofa replaying the night's events. In all that he and Fahima had been through, including the losses of Amma and Baba, never had he seen her so vicious. And he had never felt so rejected. What other word was there for it? *I just want you to leave me alone.* He felt the rejection in her words – the uncontrollable way she'd screamed them with a fury he'd never before been subjected to. He'd felt it in her manner, too. He still felt stricken by how cold she had been, as though she had formed a barrier around herself that kept even him, *her husband*, out. It was as if he were a stranger.

The memories of just hours earlier rendered him incapable of sleep as the scene replayed in his head, over and over. He felt hurt mixed with anger; he was hurt by Fahima, not only because he was still smarting from her outburst, but also because she had pushed him away. How could he make things better if she didn't let him? How could he get through to her? He'd tried tonight, he'd tried to comfort her, but it hadn't been enough.

He was angry, too, at the man who had done this to her. To them. It was a fiery hate that had been burning inside him since the attack. What he'd give to just get his hands on that asshole . . .

to put his hands on that man just as he'd seen fit to – dared to – lay hands on Fahima. What kind of pathetic lowlife did something like that to a defenceless woman just trying to get to a bus stop? Imran didn't like to admit it, but there'd been numerous times in the last couple of weeks when he had fantasised about what he might do to the man, given the opportunity for vengeance. The dark thoughts took him down a path that scared him.

But most of all, Imran felt angry at himself. He should've been there in Stratford, by Fahima's side. He should have been able to defend her, protect her. He'd heard horror stories about men following women home, skulking behind them as though they just happened to be going the same way but actually harbouring terrifying intentions. There was always a part of him that worried about this when Fahima went out on her own or with her friends, but he'd never truly entertained the idea of any harm coming to her – she was a native Londoner, she knew her way around. And yet, in a split second, his fears had been realised and there was nothing he could do about it because he hadn't been there. He'd been miles away, at home playing video games. No amount of regret could change what had happened, and for this helplessness he was angrier at himself still, pounding his fists into the sofa. All that they had withstood had gone in that moment.

Looking back, his relationship with Fahima had always had its roadblocks, but each one they had faced down together. When they'd first met, in his final year of university, at an Islamic Society meeting, Imran was immediately entranced by the newcomer to the group. Fahima, a second-year, wore a dark purple hijab and similarly dark purple lipstick. He was struck by the sharp angles of her face – her high cheekbones and pointed jawline. And when she smiled, he felt an instant sense of kinship. He couldn't explain what it was, but he saw a kindness in her smile that felt like home.

After the meeting on campus, some of them went to the coffee shop. Sweaty-palmed and unusually nervous, he psyched himself up and offered to buy Fahima a coffee.

'I don't drink coffee,' she replied, with a cool distance that made Imran think he'd messed things up already.

'Oh,' he stumbled. 'What about tea?'

'I don't drink tea either,' she said, returning to a conversation with some of the other members of the group.

Later, while he was deep in conversation with one of the guys, Ruhel, about the merits of performing Sunnah prayers as well as Fard prayers, he could have sworn he saw Fahima glance over at him, a quizzical look on her face. When they left the coffee shop, Imran felt a tap on his shoulder.

'For next time, I'm more of a hot chocolate girl,' Fahima said, shooting him a smile.

In time, she'd explain that she had been won over by the way he'd talked so passionately about his faith, that she'd sensed he had a strong belief system and that she had wanted to be sure.

Only after several halal dates – coffee shops, bowling, the occasional trip to the cinema – did Fahima feel comfortable enough to accept Imran as not only her boyfriend, but her intended. They laid out a plan: they'd wait until she had finished her social work degree the following year, and then break the news to their families that they wanted to get married. Amma and Baba were delighted with his match, and relieved that with everything else on their plates they wouldn't have to find their son a wife the traditional way. Arranged marriages were the norm, preceded by meetings with friends of friends about their daughters and sons, formal sit-downs between the two families before the marriage was decided. But Imran had taken that burden away from them.

Fahima's parents, however, were less than pleased.

'A car salesman? This is what you want to marry?' Fahima's father had scolded her.

For all their shared culture and heritage, the class divide between Imran and Fahima was apparent. He lived in a council property in East London, while her father, whose family had made its wealth in developing the road infrastructure back home, had afforded Fahima and her siblings a cushier upbringing in Maida Vale.

'Fahima, what kind of life can this man give you?' her mother had pleaded. 'Don't throw your life away. Don't you want your own house? Do you want to be scrimping and saving pennies?'

Fahima knew she'd never be able to convince her parents that her choice was the right one, but she was confident in her match. When she finally threatened to defy them and marry Imran with or without their blessing, they had had no choice but to accept that her mind was made up. But still, they had warned her on more than one occasion that she was making a mistake, that she would see how hard it was to live without the luxuries she had grown up with – a house with its own driveway, her father taking care of her tuition fees. They had wanted to match her with someone of the same social standing as them – a noble doctor or banker – but the girl had made her choice.

'He'll never be good enough for you,' her father had said.

That had been over ten years ago, and still Imran felt their lingering distaste every time he was around his in-laws. The barbed comments about his job and home. The way they gloated about how they spent part of the year abroad in Bangladesh, knowing he couldn't afford to give Fahima the same.

Now, Imran wondered whether they had been right all those years ago, and it bruised him more than anything that had happened tonight.

Maybe he *wasn't* enough for Fahima.

Chapter 4

SUMAYA

Jonathan accompanied Sumaya to JFK Airport. In the departure lounge, she hugged him goodbye without much weight behind her embrace. Something in her felt relief, almost, as she broke free of his grasp and prepared to head to her boarding gate.

Imran's call and her sense of urgency about her return to London was serendipitous, for the longer she and Jonathan skirted around the question he had asked her two weeks ago, and the longer she went without replying, the more awkward things became in their cramped apartment. She felt at a crossroads. Marry Jonathan, and commit to this easy, if unadventurous, routine that they had fallen into? Or walk away? Jonathan was as much a part of her New York story as her career or her friends were, but now, having just said goodbye to him for two weeks, she was almost glad of the respite.

The proposal had come out of the blue – yet as humdrum as asking whether she wanted wok-fried broccoli or steamed greens with her Chinese order. Not that Sumaya had thought much in the past about how she'd like to be proposed to, but she was sure she'd have liked it to have been more exciting than it was. There were no fireworks. They didn't break open a bottle of champagne. There wasn't even a ring.

Jonathan had proposed as Sumaya sorted the laundry in their stiflingly warm bedroom, sweat patches under her armpits. He'd poured them both a glass of red wine and hovered in the bedroom as she folded her clothes and neatly organised them into the drawers.

'I was thinking . . .' Jonathan had said, ever so casually. 'Maybe it's time we got married. What do you think?'

Sumaya had frozen. His sheer nonchalance had startled her.

She had laughed nervously. 'What? You're being silly.'

'No, I really think, you know . . . it's been five years,' Jonathan had said, still playing it cool.

Sumaya had tried to brush it off. 'Where has all this come from? Is it because your brother got engaged?' she had asked. 'I know that it might seem everyone around us is getting married, but that doesn't mean we have to follow them.'

'But . . .' Jonathan had continued. 'I don't know. It makes sense, right? We've been together for so long.'

'Are you actually proposing to me right now?' Sumaya had asked incredulously.

'Yeah,' he had replied. 'Yeah, I guess I am.'

Sumaya had told Jonathan she'd think about his offer. But instead of giving him an answer, she had found herself avoiding the subject; they had spent the last couple of weeks awkwardly sitting on the sofa watching Netflix, Sumaya secretly praying that he wouldn't bring it up again.

She couldn't quite work out why she was reluctant, just that she was. She loved Jonathan, of course, but when she thought about the prospect of getting married and having children with him, she didn't feel sparks course through her body as she'd expected she would.

What she had with Jonathan was easy and uncomplicated. But more and more over the last two weeks, Sumaya had found herself thinking of Neha and the unquenchable thirst that she'd felt whenever she'd been around her. The way she'd felt it so deeply in the pit of her stomach. That was a true love. That was an undeniable love. If it had been Neha asking her the question all those years ago, she would undoubtedly have said yes. Where was that with Jonathan?

All these years later, she still didn't feel she had closure. Why else did her thoughts burn with memories of Neha, when Jonathan was proposing a full life together? Everything that Neha had denied her.

As Sumaya prepared to fly to London, ready to see her brother for the first time in three years, to rush to her sister-in-law's side, she knew, too, that this trip might help her come to a decision. If she could see Neha again, if she could get the closure she hadn't been able to get seven years ago, maybe she could finally move on.

She could finally say yes to Jonathan without anything holding her back.

Sumaya took in the familiar front door to what had once been the family home. The black paint was starting to chip and the brass doorknocker looked as though it had been left to corrode, London's abundant rain slowly turning it copper and grey. Exhausted from her flight and the inordinate wait at baggage reclaim, her head was heavy and her eyes were drooping with fatigue. She'd tried to nap in the Uber from Heathrow to Bow, but too much was on her mind. The anxiety of seeing her brother again. Remembering the way they had left things the last time she was here – her carelessly flinging her clothes into her suitcase, rushing down the stairs, slamming the front door as she left. That had been the day they buried Baba. In the taxi, she'd felt hot with anger at her brother for ruining what was supposed to be a day of sibling harmony. Why couldn't Imran just keep things cordial for Baba's sake?

The rift between them had already opened by that time. It wasn't just because of her going to New York, which she knew Imran resented her for; the chasm had been there long before. Since she had learned the truth about Imran as a teenager, and Amma had made her keep her secret.

A week after Amma's funeral, Sumaya had dropped a bomb-shell on the rest of the family. She was moving to New York.

'What are you talking about?' Imran had questioned her. They had gathered in the living room – her, Imran, Fahima, Baba, Majid – alone for the first time after a claustrophobic week in which the house had been overrun by visiting aunties and uncles with their kids in tow.

'My flight is booked,' Sumaya had said. 'I don't have anything keeping me here anymore – Mum is gone.'

'What about Majid? What about Baba?' Imran had asked incredulously. Surely she didn't mean to flout her duties to her own father and brother? 'You can't just leave them.'

'You're here, aren't you? And Bhabi,' Sumaya had retorted.

'Sumaya, are you sure about this? You'll be away from all your friends and family,' Fahima had reasoned with her sister-in-law.

'I'm sure. I've never been more sure. I don't want to just stay in this East London bubble for the rest of my life,' Sumaya had said, irking Imran. 'I don't want to spend the rest of my life here,' she had continued. 'I don't want to wake up one day paralysed and never be able to leave, never see the world – to end up like Mum.'

'What do you mean, "like Mum"?' Imran had fired back, tak-ing his sister's words as a slight towards their mother, though they had not been. 'You think you're better than her? Better than us?' The veins in his neck had bulged.

'Eré, enough,' Baba had intervened from his position on the sofa.

Imran had stood, towering over his family – who were all seated – and patchy red shadows contrasted with his naturally brown complexion.

'Baba, she can't just leave!' He called out to his father for reason. 'She doesn't know anyone out there! What will she do? What if something happens? And think of Majid . . .'

'Beta, who is the father here?' Baba had replied. 'Majid is my child, as are you, as is Sumaya. If your sister has her mind made up, who are we to stop her? She is a grown woman.'

'But—' Imran had begun, before Baba cut him off.

'But, *fut*,' had said Baba. 'You have all been through a lot, and not a day goes by that I haven't wished that the burden of looking after your amma didn't have to fall on you. You have had to grow up before your time. Now Amma is gone. It is time to live, heh?'

Imran had screwed his face tight in disbelief. He clearly hadn't expected Baba to actually go along with Sumaya's plan. Baba wasn't getting any younger – God knew he looked like he'd aged an extra twenty years from the stress of caring for Amma. And Majid was still just a child. Perhaps somewhere, deep down, Imran still felt that brotherly instinct to protect his sister from harm. How could he do that from 3,000 miles away?

'I have made up my mind,' Sumaya had said, breaking the awkward silence. 'I'm going. I have a couple of job interviews already lined up.'

'Then it is settled,' Baba had decreed. 'Sumaya, if this is really what you want, you will go. Beta,' he had added, turning his attention to Imran, 'you and Fahima will help me with Majid, no?'

Sumaya knew there was no conceivable way Imran could say no. Baba had needed him, so there was no question of him not complying. He'd promised Amma, among other things, that he'd always take care of Baba.

'Yes, Baba,' he had meekly volunteered.

And so, off Sumaya went, only to return after Baba died. Imran had made clear, the last time they had seen each other, how he felt about her. She had selfishly abandoned her family when they needed her most, he'd accused her. She thought she was better than them, with her expensive clothes and fancy job. And what was she thinking, wearing Western clothes to Baba's funeral? The disrespect! Sumaya had worn what she'd thought was a modest long-sleeved navy shift dress and jeans, her hair loosely covered with a scarf. She had shed her Asian wardrobe when she moved to New York, and had had to borrow the scarf from Fahima, who herself wore a traditional salwar kameez and an abaya over her clothing at the mosque. Given the short notice and her lack of Eastern clothing options, Sumaya had deemed this suitable, respectful attire. It was conservative enough to not affront the murabbi – the aunts, uncles and community elders – that had gathered to pay their respects, though they had tittered behind her back nonetheless.

All day, Sumaya had ignored the expected whispers from extended family and neighbours about the return of the prodigal daughter, and had endured the backhanded compliments that thinly veiled insults: 'New York! Look at you, big shot!' She'd even tried to revert back to who she had once been, dutifully filling teacups and serving freshly fried samosas to guests at the wake, alien as it felt to inhabit the part she had played all those years ago, and to greet people she barely knew as sasa and sasi – uncle and auntie – and hold her tongue when they asked why she wasn't yet married.

But after the prayers were said, after the burial that neither she nor Baba's other female relatives were allowed to attend due to some indiscernible cultural norm, and after the teas had been drunk and the food eaten at Baba's wake, the unspoken detente that Imran and Sumaya had called for the day broke.

Sumaya and Imran had sat alone in the living room. Majid, overwhelmed by the day's events, had gone to see friends, while Fahima had been in the kitchen clearing up after the guests. Though this was the first time the siblings had seen each other in four years, and though their common grief ought to have united them, there had been an eerie silence between them. In this living room that they'd both grown up in, had countless conversations in, quarrelled over the television remote control in, now, in this moment, brother and sister regarded each other with detachment, as if they were complete strangers plucked off the street and forced together.

Minutes had passed like this – Imran casually swiping on his phone, and Sumaya attempting to identify what had changed physically in the room since she had moved. The television she and her siblings had once wrestled for control over had been upgraded, and their weathered chestnut-coloured nesting tables had been replaced by what looked like a basic IKEA coffee table. On the southernmost wall had hung a canvas – deep blue, with ornate white, turquoise and gold decorations bordering the edges, and in the middle 'Allah' written in Arabic in lustrous golden calligraphy. This was new, Sumaya thought. Growing up, Amma and Baba had left the walls bare – no framed photos had adorned them because they might invalidate prayer, but neither had they hung Islamic artwork like Imran and Fahima had done now. Amma and Baba had never felt the need to exhibit their faith. It had been an inward journey between one and one's god. How times had changed.

Like other second-generation immigrant Muslims, it had seemed to her that Imran and Fahima wore their faith like one might a badge – the more pious they appeared to others, the more they felt in touch with their religion. This always struck Sumaya as curious, for it had never been the case with her parents. Their faith and heritage had been encoded in their appearance, their accents. Amma and Baba had been immediately recognisable to

41

their Western neighbours as *foreign*, immigrants, Muslim. Did her generation – Imran's generation – feel the need to compensate for their Western lifestyles by wrapping themselves in a proverbial flag of religiosity? And at what point would they recompense enough to banish their guilt? Sumaya's own faith was more like her parents' – or rather it had been, when she had considered herself practising. She'd never understand why her brother tortured himself with this Western guilt. Hadn't their parents sacrificed their lives back home to come to England so their family could enjoy the benefits of this life? And she *was* enjoying it. She had had a good education, and now had a career in television and lived in New York. Why was Imran so insistent on inhibiting himself with religious standards that had never been imposed on them?

Just as Sumaya thought this, Imran let out a deep sigh and dropped his phone on the sofa with a dull thud. 'So, when are you going back?' he had asked in no particular direction.

Sumaya had snapped out of her ruminative state, realising he was talking to her. 'Tomorrow,' she had said briskly, refraining from saying what was really on her mind. *Why? Can't wait to see the back of me?*

There was a general grunt of acknowledgement from Imran. 'Well, I guess I'll just sort Dad's things myself . . . like always.'

Sumaya had smarted. 'What is that supposed to mean?'

'What do you think it means?' Imran had goaded her.

'Look, I didn't come here to argue,' Sumaya had replied, doing her level best not to be drawn in.

Suddenly, Imran's posture had become rigid. He sat forward on the sofa, back straight, eyes steely. 'Why *did* you bother coming here, hmm?' he had spat. 'You barely cared about Baba enough to come and see him when he was alive. What use are you to us now?'

Sumaya's eyes had stung with the onset of tears at this barb, but she wouldn't give Imran the satisfaction of making her cry.

'Baba told me not to come!' she had said, her voice raised. 'I would have come if I'd known how bad it was . . .'

'So what? That means nothing!' Imran had said, his voice rising to match Sumaya's. 'If you cared at all about him you would have come anyway. I would have!'

'He . . . I didn't know this would happen . . .' Sumaya had spluttered.

'No, Sumaya, you didn't care. You fucked off to New York and you turned your back on your family. You think you're a big woman now, because you post shitty Instagram pictures of your amazing life? Because some rich white woman gave you a job? You're not one of them, Sumaya. You never will be.'

Sumaya had shot up out of the armchair. 'I'm not doing this—'

'Yeah, walk away. *Again*,' Imran had shouted. 'That is what you do, isn't it?'

'What is wrong with you—' Sumaya had started to say, but Imran cut her off.

'*You're* what's wrong with me,' he had screamed at her with such force that she flinched. 'What kind of daughter are you? Leaving Baba when he needed you. *I'm* the one who had to rush him to hospital with chest pains. *I'm* the one who had to clean him because he was too weak to make it to the toilet. *I'm* the one who had to hold him as he died. What were you doing, Sumaya? Drinking cocktails with your white friends like a harami?'

This had fired up Sumaya. 'Oh, poor you, poor *you*. Poor Imran! You don't have a clue . . . You have always been selfish, entitled . . . What were you doing when *I* was at the hospital with Amma? Or have you forgotten everything *I* did for you all?'

Imran had shaken his head, and then fired back, 'Look at you. You're an embarrassment, walking around here dressed like the shaddain. Making a laughing stock of our family. If you had any shame, you'd have stayed away.'

'That's fucking rich,' Sumaya had scoffed. 'Coming from you? Really? *You're* going to lecture *me* about shame?'

'No one wants you here,' Imran had said, his voice now cold and impassive. 'We don't need you anymore. As far as I'm concerned, you walked out on this family years ago. Go back to New York, Sumaya. Go back to your perfect little life . . . go back to pretending you're something you're not . . .'

At that, Sumaya had stormed up the stairs to her old bedroom, grabbed her suitcase and left for the airport, even though her flight wasn't until the next day. It was all she could do not to say something she'd regret. Because if she did, she'd break her promise to Amma.

If only Imran knew the truth.

Chapter 5

SULTANA

Whether it was mother's intuition, or perhaps some cosmic enlightenment the closer she got to death, Sultana instantly knew that something was troubling Sumaya. Her daughter sat by her bedside, as she did every evening, but on this particular night they didn't pray together as they usually did, and Sumaya didn't try to handfeed her orange slices, the citrusy smell filling the room and temporarily masking the scent of her own decay. Although Sumaya sat beside her, at least corporeally, her mind was somewhere else entirely.

'What's wrong?' Sultana asked breathily in Bengali; her once-booming voice, too, had been lost in recent years.

Sumaya shook her head, not wanting to burden her mother, but Sultana wasn't about to let her daughter's sullen demeanour go unquestioned.

'Eh, I may be stuck in this bed, but I'm not stupid, beti,' she said, lacing her words with the signature caustic humour that, thankfully, she hadn't yet lost.

'I'm fine, Amma,' Sumaya replied quietly. 'There's nothing wrong.'

'You think I didn't raise you?' Sultana countered. 'You think I don't know every single one of your moods? When you're happy, when you're sad, when you're angry?'

'Amma . . . don't worry . . .'

This only served to rile Sultana further. How she wished her children and her husband wouldn't treat her as if she were completely feeble! She was still as sharp as she had ever been, and she wouldn't be placated by *don't worry* or *it's okay*, as if she might expire on the spot if they dared burden her. Sultana knew there were things that her family kept from her about her condition – she wasn't naive. From the concerned looks on their faces after speaking to her doctors and the placid *it's nothings*, she was certain they were coddling her – that they believed they were sparing her any more than she could bear. But who were they to tell her what she could and couldn't bear, at least mentally?

So Sultana pressed on. 'If you're just going to sit there sour-faced like a lemon, I'm better off staring at the wall.'

'Amma,' Sumaya said reticently. 'How do . . . how do I . . . how do I know whether I'm making the right choices?'

'What do you mean, beti?'

'I . . . I've met someone, Amma.'

Sultana turned to her daughter, elation on her face. *Alhamdulillah!* Perhaps she would live to see her daughter marry, to see her off into the next chapter of her life. But why wasn't Sumaya joyful? Why was her forehead creased with consternation?

'Sumaya, what is it?' she prodded.

'I . . . I don't know if what I'm doing is wrong . . .'

Sultana's eyes remained fixed on her daughter. She wished she could peer inside her brain, extract whatever it was that Sumaya found so difficult to express. Had she met a boy that she and Abdul wouldn't approve of? One of those gundas – ruffians – that stayed out till all hours of the night doing god knows what. Drinking and smoking and gambling. Had she met a white boy? Or a black boy?

Gently, she asked her daughter: 'Does it feel wrong?'

'No,' Sumaya replied emphatically. 'It feels . . . right.'

'Then what is the problem? I know the daughter Baba and I have raised, and I know that whoever this man is, my good and intelligent daughter will make the right choice. I have no doubt.'

All of a sudden, Sumaya broke into a sob, tears pouring down her face, as though she had held them back for so long the dam had finally burst. Seeing her daughter cry, and unable to move her arm towards her to offer a comforting hand on hers, made Sultana's eyes well, too.

'Amma . . .' Sumaya whimpered through her tears, and this seemed to go on for at least several minutes. 'Amma . . . Amma . . .'

Whatever the matter was with her child, Sultana sensed from her anguished wails that this was bigger than she might have expected, and inside she, too, felt anguished. What kind of mother was she that she couldn't lift herself out of bed and wrap her arms around Sumaya? Rock her back and forth as her daughter cried. Wipe her tears away with the sleeve of her dress. All these things that a mother should do, but Sultana was helpless to provide, and so mother and daughter wept together. If only Sultana were healthy and able-bodied, if only she had more time to help her daughter through this matter of the heart . . . if only, if only, if only.

Eventually, Sumaya stymied her tears – a brief moment of resolve. 'Amma,' she said again, soft and childlike, and this transported Sultana back to when her daughter was just a little girl, full of innocence and sincerity, unblemished by the world and in need of a mother's love and protection. She saw her daughter not as she was now, a grown woman of twenty-four, but the little girl whose hair she used to braid, lacquering her thick, black mane with amla oil to keep it glossy and healthy. How Sumaya had loved to brush

47

her doll's hair as Sultana had brushed hers, her vivid imagination bringing to life whimsical games of castles and tea parties. And, seeing this return of innocence in her daughter, Sultana was all the more determined to protect her one more time. Maybe the last time.

'Whatever it is, beti . . . say it,' Sultana said. 'Who is this man?'

Tense silence followed before Sumaya spoke. 'That's the problem, Amma . . . it isn't a man.'

Sultana's confusion was written on her face – the creased forehead, the startled eyes. She didn't understand, couldn't immediately gauge just what her daughter was telling her. If not a man, then who?! She wondered, for a split moment, whether Sumaya was unwell. Perhaps she had a fever that had struck her incomprehensible – but no, the girl didn't sound congested or appear ill in any way.

It still hadn't occurred to Sultana what Sumaya was telling her implicitly, what she wasn't reading between the lines. It took her what seemed like minutes to compute her daughter's words, not only because all the religion ever instilled in her from childhood up to now told her that homosexuality was incompatible with being a Muslim, but because she had never encountered a situation like this before. Of course, she knew that gay and lesbian people existed, she wasn't naive – they showed men kissing on television nowadays and she rather liked that Elton John fellow, who she was vaguely aware was gay – but knowing of their existence was the extent of her understanding of homosexuality.

Sultana had never met a gay couple, or had anyone in her family, to her knowledge anyway, come out as gay or lesbian. It wasn't something she had ever confronted. And now, her own daughter was sitting before her, admitting to . . . to what? Being in love with a woman? Having relations with someone of the same sex? It didn't seem possible, and yet she couldn't deny what she was hearing, and

48

to see her daughter so pained by the weight of her secret left her feeling conflicted.

Again, Sultana took in her daughter's visage, drinking in her brown eyes, the wide bridge of her nose, her rounded features, all of which Sumaya had got from her; and she again saw the little girl – innocent and wholesome – that she had once been, in need of nothing more than her mother's love and protection. And though she didn't completely understand it, and though she feared the ridicule and scorn her daughter might face for her sexuality, she simply said: 'Tell me everything.'

Sumaya did as her mother asked. She explained that she'd always felt attracted to both men and women, how she had tried to bury her feelings for other women, and how she had met this girl, Neha, who had made it so that she couldn't keep her true nature buried any longer. Neha had studied at the same university as her and they had been close. There had always been something between them, a frisson that neither could quite explain. Sumaya told her mother how, after graduating, she'd felt a piece of her was missing but she couldn't identify what – no longer seeing her friend every day made her days less bright, less colourful. She'd realised that what she felt wasn't just the intense bond of friendship, but something more, and Neha felt the same.

'I'm in love with her, Amma,' Sumaya told her. It was Neha that Sumaya turned to whenever her mother's health declined, after the hospital appointments that would exhaust mother and daughter, after the grave discussions with her mother's doctors about her long-term prognosis. Neha had given Sumaya the consolation Sultana could not, for her daughter's heartache was rooted in Sultana's downturn. As her daughter talked about this girl who had embraced her so wholly, who had given her the second-best thing to a mother's love, how could she blame this Neha for wrapping her daughter in love? A part of her was even grateful to this stranger for taking the mantle of being her daughter's confidante and carer, for she herself felt her illness had robbed her of being adequate for the duty.

Who was she to deny her daughter her happiness? Sumaya had been so dutiful and patient in caring for her all these years, when it should have been *her* taking care of her child. In that instant, Sultana resolved to provide Sumaya what little solace she could, knowing her time would soon be up. She may not fully comprehend it, but her daughter had her whole life ahead of her, and no life worth living was lived in shadows. Sumaya deserved happiness, and Sultana would feel all the more content in the afterlife in the knowledge that her child was happy.

Sultana thought, too, about her own life. A life determined for her in 1960s Bangladesh. She hadn't had choices the way her children had. Her own mama and baba hadn't been able to afford to give Sultana and her siblings the education or instil in them the ambition that she yearned for for her own children. They had been poor fieldworkers who had struggled to keep the hearth lit, who hadn't been able to afford electricity and had forgone meals to ensure their children's plates were full.

This, for the first time, Sultana explained to her daughter. She rarely talked about her own childhood to her children – about her life before their father. She kept those memories locked deep within, because what use were they to her now? Her path had been forged for her. The truth was she had been a commodity, like other girls of her era, to be married to a man who could afford a handsome dowry that would keep her parents and her siblings fed.

'We didn't believe in romance,' Sultana said. 'There wasn't all this dating, these butterflies . . . I met your father once before my wedding day and that was that. That is who I was expected to be with. I wasn't just born your father's wife or your mother. But I didn't have the luxury of ambition. I remember when I was a small

50

girl, your uncle had a small black-and-white television that barely worked, and all the kids from the village would crowd around it, mesmerised.'

Sultana closed her eyes and composed herself, the memory that she was about to reveal reigniting hurt in her that she thought she had long ago pacified. 'I was maybe nine . . . on the screen there were these American men in big suits and helmets . . . they were walking on the moon! Imagine! Men were walking on the moon, and there we were, holes in our dresses and sand in our shoes. I had never seen anything like it . . . I remember saying to your uncle, "I want to be just like them!" I wanted to be one of those spacemen! And your uncle . . . he just laughed at me . . . he said, "When you're old enough, you will find a good husband and have babies." And he was right.'

Sumaya reached out to her mother and tightly held her hand. 'It's not fair . . .' she said.

'No, it wasn't fair. And now I'm here, stuck in this bed . . . and I know, my sweet daughter, that I won't be here forever. And that is unfair, too. I want to see my children grow old, I want to meet my grandchildren . . . But that is life, Sumaya. Life isn't fair.'

'So, you're saying I should accept that I can't be with who I love?' Sumaya asked.

'No, beti, you misunderstand me,' Sultana said, shaking her head. 'Your baba and I came to this country to give you and your brothers the lives we never had. Maybe it wasn't fair, but I sacrificed so you could live. I want you to live, Sumaya. I want you to follow your happiness, whatever that is. I don't know that I understand, but you must live your life *for you*. That is all I want. Your health and your happiness.'

Sumaya reached forward and rested her head on her mother's arm, and a new flood of tears soaked Sultana, but she knew these weren't tears of distress but of relief. She had given her daughter her blessing to be herself, and that was the greatest gift she could give.

'But,' Sultana added cautiously, 'I need you to do one thing, Sumaya. Listen to me carefully.'

Sumaya raised her head, mascara streaking down her face, and looked her mother in the eyes.

'Remember what I said . . . life isn't fair,' Sultana said, her tone more subdued. 'Not everyone will understand what you have told me, Sumaya. Your baba, Imran . . . they are devout men. I fear that they won't accept you as you are and I won't be here to do anything about it. The society we come from, Sumaya, is still hard for us women; some people still see a woman's place as a wife and mother, like my uncle did. What men can do, we cannot.' Her voice was almost a whisper. 'Don't tell them,' she warned her daughter. 'Your baba, your bhaiya . . . please. It's the only way I know you'll be accepted and happy. Go. Go away from here, find your happiness elsewhere and be free.'

'Amma—' Sumaya tried to protest, but her mother cut her off.

'It's the only way, Sumaya. I need you to be careful. This isn't something they will understand. Live your life, be whoever you want to be, love whoever you want to love . . . just promise me this one thing. Promise me.'

Tears in her eyes, her heart made heavy by her mother's request, Sumaya did the only thing she felt she could in that moment.

'I promise,' she said.

Chapter 6

SUMAYA

Imran opened the front door as Sumaya waved off her Uber driver. He looked to her to be a bit rounder than she remembered, his cheeks more filled out and his belly carrying a paunch. In his dark beard, she spotted flecks of white that signified the passage of time. Did she look older to him, too? A moment of self-consciousness. Was there grey in her hair? Lines and grooves on her face that hadn't been there three years ago? It seemed silly to doubt herself this way – she was only thirty-one – and yet standing in her brother's gaze it was as though she were standing under a microscope.

'Sumaya. Come in,' Imran greeted her, and this invitation into what was by right her home as much as his stung. He was treating her as a guest, as though she had given up the right to call this place home by virtue of her absence. Maybe she had. She tried to look past this strange welcome and walked through the door, entering the small hallway that extended out into the living room. Directly in front of her were the stairs she had hurriedly run down three years earlier with her suitcase packed. The ones she, Imran and Majid had run up and down so many times as children, causing a racket. She took off her shoes and placed her suitcase near the banister. Imran watched but said nothing.

'So,' she eventually said, turning to her brother. 'Where's Bhabi? Is she okay?'

'She's in bed . . . she barely comes out of her room these days,' Imran said, and Sumaya sensed a tinge of anguish in his voice, and she almost felt sorry for him.

'Okay, I'll go up and see her,' she said.

Imran simply nodded in acquiescence. Strange, Sumaya thought. How subdued he seemed, as if the fire in him had been extinguished. How unlike the Imran she had last encountered. Perhaps he had changed? After all, he had called her of his own accord, asked for her help. Well, he hadn't so much asked, she reminded herself, but to make the call must have been difficult for him. Maybe she ought to give him the benefit of the doubt?

Up the stairs and across the landing, she walked past the bedroom she had once occupied, the one nearest the stairs. The door was closed and she wondered what, if anything, had changed inside. At the other end of the landing was the small box room that was Majid's, past the bathroom, further away from the other bedrooms. She walked past the empty room that had once belonged to Imran, located next to hers, and stopped in front of the door to the master bedroom. She took a deep breath. Imran and Fahima had taken over her parents' old room. This was their house now, she reminded herself. It made sense. But still, she almost expected to see or hear Amma and Baba on the other side of the door.

The thought of Amma and Baba made her eyes water. How much she had missed in her time away. She would always live with the regret of not being here for Baba in his time of need.

Without Amma's various needs – the prescription runs, the appointments, the running up and down stairs with her meals – to provide structure for his day, Baba himself had deteriorated, spending more and more time stationary in front of the television, when he wasn't cooking spinach bhazis and chicken curries in too much oil or ghee. His own ailments became more prominent – angina, diabetes, and chronic back pain from carrying his own weight. Sumaya wondered whether Baba had slowly given up on himself without Amma.

Baba had had his first heart attack four years ago. Amma had been gone for three years by that point. His inactivity and unhealthy diet had caught up with him. Sumaya had called her father regularly, but Baba had insisted she shouldn't come home, because of her hectic job. Her hours were long and hard, and any time off would invariably lead to a pile-up of more work upon her return. Baba's second heart attack came a year later, and this time he didn't survive. Sumaya regretted not coming home earlier. She'd missed his final moments.

Sumaya gently knocked on the door before opening it. The room was dark; the only light illuminating the shape of her sister-in-law in bed came from the landing. Sumaya carefully stepped into the room, leaving the door ajar so she could see, and gingerly crept towards the bed, centred against the wall opposite the door. A feeling of déjà vu came over her. How many times had she come into this room and sat by Amma's bedside? Here she had fed Amma, given her sponge baths and watched over her as she slept, fearing that one of these times her mother might not wake up.

'Bhabi,' she called out gently to the mound under the bedcovers. 'It's me . . . Sumaya.'

A rustle under the blankets, and then a head peeked out over the top of the duvet.

Sumaya was startled, not only because Fahima looked confused by her presence but because she had never seen her sister-in-law look this dishevelled. Fahima always looked effortlessly put-together, her hijab and lipstick complementing each other, her make-up flawless and her clothes carefully considered. The Fahima before her looked unkempt – hair frizzing all over the place, her eyes sunken and her cheeks hollowed.

Sumaya took a seat on the edge of the bed and leaned in to give her sister-in-law a hug, but Fahima still wore an expression of puzzlement even as she accepted the arms around her. In her embrace, her sister-in-law felt bonier than she remembered, her shoulder blades protruding to the point of digging into Sumaya's hands.

'How are you, Bhabi?' she asked, pulling away and taking in the sight of her; a shell of the woman she knew. This didn't feel right. Her sister-in-law was generally a jovial, warm person – perhaps too kind sometimes and, at least with Imran, too submissive. To see her this way, listless and drained of colour, sent a shiver down Sumaya's spine.

When Fahima spoke, her words came out slowly, her voice cracking. 'Sumaya . . . what are you doing here . . . ?'

'I'm here to see you,' Sumaya said. 'Bhaiya called me and I got a flight as soon as I could.'

'He . . . what?'

'Wait. You didn't know?' Sumaya asked.

'No . . . no, I didn't,' Fahima replied.

Now Sumaya was confused. For all the empathy she had for her sister-in-law, she felt a spark of anger at hearing this.

Typical Imran. Not even bothering to consult his wife before he acted. Thinking he knew best for everyone.

And yet again unwittingly drafting in Sumaya to clean up his mess . . .

Sumaya walked into the kitchen to find her brother serving up bowls of pasta in tomato sauce, a jar of Dolmio on the counter.

Really? This was the best he could do? Sauce out of a jar? No wonder he had gained weight.

'It isn't much,' Imran said sheepishly as he placed the bowls on the kitchen table – one for her and one for him. 'But I thought you might be hungry.'

'Thanks,' Sumaya replied, sitting at the table in front of the bowl of bright red pasta. How many additives did this sauce have to make it such a colour? And to her eye, the pasta looked mushy. Imran had obviously boiled it for too long. Still, not wanting to appear rude, she took her fork and helped herself to a mouthful. The overwhelming taste of salt and sugar in the dish made her wince.

'So,' she said carefully, setting her fork back down on the table. 'I just went to see Bhabi. She doesn't look well at all. Has she spoken to anyone? A doctor? A therapist?'

'You know what doctors are like . . . useless, just gave her some sleeping pills.'

'Really? They didn't try to get her to speak to someone?'

'No.'

'What about the police? Surely they must have, like . . . a therapist . . . or something . . .'

'What do they care?' Imran spat. 'To them she's just another Muslim who probably deserved it . . .'

'Come on,' Sumaya said. 'I'm sure it's not like that.'

'They don't care about our people, Sumaya. A white girl goes missing and it's all over the news, and the whole police force and bloody MI5 are on the case. Something happens to one of us and it's just another day. They're probably laughing at us.'

'That's not true,' Sumaya said more forcefully. 'And you didn't answer my question – what have they said?'

'Nothing.'

'Well, when was the last time you spoke to them? Have you tried calling them?'

Imran went quiet.

'Well, there you go. Don't you think you ought to call the police and see if there's any update?'

'What's the point . . . ?'

Sumaya sighed. Talking to her brother was like hitting her head against a brick wall, and she didn't want to get drawn into yet another debate about how the government and all public officials were against Muslims in this country. They'd had this argument more times than she could count when she'd lived here, and they'd never seen eye-to-eye on the subject. How was it that both she and her brother could be born here, raised British, and still have such different viewpoints on the culture? Imran saw himself as an outsider, even though he wasn't the one who'd had to uproot his life like Amma and Baba had! He had been afforded all the opportunities that England had to offer. And yet he still acted like a persecuted minority. It was exhausting.

'Okay,' she said, changing tack. 'Has she spoken to you at least? She should try to talk to someone.'

'No,' Imran replied, and Sumaya sensed again the sorrow in his voice. 'She won't speak to me either.'

'Oh,' was all that came out of her mouth in response. She racked her brain, to think of something encouraging to add. 'I guess it's still really traumatic for her. Maybe she needs more time. It can't be easy . . .'

'I don't know what to say sometimes . . .' Imran confessed, and for the second time tonight Sumaya almost felt sorry for her brother, seeing him so small, so retreated into himself.

'Imagine how she must feel. I can't even imagine it,' she said. 'To feel so . . . violated. Like your body isn't your own, that some man feels he has some right to touch you . . .'

Imran looked up, and for a moment the siblings locked eyes. Sumaya saw what appeared to be tears forming at the edges of her brother's eyes.

'It isn't just that,' Imran said, his voice low. He sighed. 'There's something you should know . . .'

Sumaya tensed in her chair. Oh god, what was her brother about to tell her? Had something else happened? A chill ran down her spine.

'Something happened a few years ago, and that was tough on her,' Imran said. 'And now this.'

'What?'

Imran placed his hands on the table, fidgeting with his fingers. 'I haven't told anyone this. Majid doesn't know either. When Baba died, she was pregnant,' he said. 'She . . . we . . . lost the baby . . .'

Sumaya's mouth opened in a silent expression of shock. She brought a hand to her chest as if clutching her heart. 'Oh my . . .'

'She had a miscarriage a couple of months after Baba's funeral. Maybe it was the stress of everything, I don't know . . . but she was really depressed, and now . . .'

'Poor Bhabi,' Sumaya said. This latest revelation made her heart ache even more for her sister-in-law. When she had last seen her brother and Fahima for Baba's funeral, they had been expecting a baby! For her, a niece or a nephew! And she'd had no idea. All those times she and Fahima spoke on the phone on a Sunday, and her sister-in-law was hiding such a heartbreaking secret. In the space of just a few seconds, she, too, felt the loss of it – she could have been an aunt, but the opportunity had been snatched away. And that didn't even compare to what Fahima must have felt. 'I'm so sorry,' she added, offering Imran her condolences and meaning it. The frostiness of their relationship paled compared to this.

'So . . . that's why I guess I needed some help . . . After losing the baby, she was so . . . it was like she was a different person, a zombie. She didn't take it well at all. Moping around, not wanting to go outside, just sitting here in the house – she didn't even want people to come over. It took her months to get back to normal. What happened to her . . . I'm worried it might tip her over the edge. I don't think I can handle that again.'

'It's not just about what you can handle though, is it? What about her?' Sumaya said, immediately picking up on his self-centredness and calling him out.

'Obviously . . .' he replied. 'That's not how I meant it . . .'

'I don't know what you want me to do,' Sumaya said. 'When I spoke to her, it sounded like she had no idea I was coming! Did you even ask her if it was okay for me to come and stay . . . ?'

Imran shook his head. 'I didn't think . . .'

'Yeah, you didn't think,' she said sharply, and then, noticing the severity in her tone, she tried to modulate her voice. 'Look, I'm here for a couple of weeks, and I can try to talk to her and stuff, but I'm not sure how useful I'll be. She needs you and maybe some other support, like a therapist . . .'

Imran bristled at the suggestion of a therapist, which Sumaya took as another objection to Western ways.

'See what you can do, yeah? You have always been close to her; maybe she'll talk to you,' he said.

Now Sumaya was the one bristling, though she tried to keep it inside and bite her tongue. Her brother really thought he could ask her to fly across the Atlantic, wave a magic wand and make everything better for him. What did he think was going to happen? She and Bhabi would spend an evening watching *Titanic*, eat ice cream and cry, and everything would be okay? What Fahima had been through, from the miscarriage to the attack, was so deeply harrowing, so out of Sumaya's own realm of experience, that she didn't feel any more qualified to help Fahima than he did. It felt to her as if history was repeating itself, and she didn't like it.

She tried to swallow down the rising anger and changed the subject. 'How is Majid, by the way?' she asked. She'd texted to tell him she'd be in town, but she hadn't heard back.

'That kid . . .' Imran said, sounding exasperated. 'I swear, he's going to fail his studies if he doesn't knuckle down. All I see on his Insta is parties and going out. He's in his final year, he should be studying.'

Sumaya had seen the Instagram stories, too, but had thought nothing of it. Majid was only twenty-one, still a kid – of course he should be out having fun. Although Majid still had his room at home, he mostly lived on campus at university, where he was studying biological sciences. Even though he could just commute, she didn't blame him for shelling out to get away from Imran.

'I'm sure he's doing just fine . . . he hasn't been kicked out yet,' she joked.

'What would you know?' Imran said scornfully.

'He's still young, come on. He can study and have fun. Just because he likes to go out doesn't mean he's not doing well.'

'And if he doesn't graduate? It isn't going to be you that has to find him a job or have him live with you . . .'

Sumaya narrowed her eyes at this. How did the subject always return to Imran being there and her not?

'I doubt that'll happen, Bhaiya,' she said, trying to ease the tension. 'He's a smart kid. He seems to be doing fine.'

'The only reason he's fine is because I have kept him on the right path,' Imran said. 'I've done everything to make sure that kid gets good grades, gets into uni . . . I won't let him risk his future.'

'Who says he is?' Sumaya said. 'You need to lighten up. There's no reason to worry about him yet, is there?'

'You're not here, you wouldn't know what he's like . . . Always so insolent, never listens to me . . .'

'*Oh my god!*' Sumaya finally snapped. 'Can you stop? Majid is in university, he's on track to get his degree . . . he'll be fine. So what if he talks back a bit? He's still only twenty-one! Do you remember when you were that age? Give him a break. You can't control everything and everyone.'

'I'm just saying, if he thinks he's going to live here for free with no degree . . .'

Sumaya slammed her fists on the kitchen table and rose from her seat. Imran just stared at her, his face hot and eyes steely. She hadn't wanted to lose her cool like this. It didn't bode well to lose her temper so soon either. She still had to spend two weeks with Imran.

'Look . . . I'm just tired,' Sumaya said, offering a mea culpa. 'I think I'm going to go to bed . . .'

She took her half-eaten bowl of pasta to the sink. Her entire body felt heavy – and not because of the jet lag but because she was already fatigued by her brother.

Chapter 7

IMRAN

It bothered Imran to admit it, but he knew his sister was right, and so the next day he resolved to call the police officer investigating Fahima's case for an update. What was the alternative? To remain in this state of helplessness? There was nothing he could personally do to find the person responsible, and this anguished him – what he'd give to just get that guy alone for five minutes and mete out his own justice. But that didn't seem likely to happen, so maybe Sumaya had a point. Something was better than nothing. He'd call Officer Cahill later, on his lunch break.

As pleased as he was to have support from his sister, he couldn't shake the animosity he harboured over Baba's death and her absence during his last year on earth.

After Amma died, Baba had become more and more inactive, and Imran could see the toll losing his wife had taken on him.

'Baba, do you think we should go for a walk?' he'd cajole his father, returning from work in the evening and confirming that Baba had only traversed the square footage between the living room and the kitchen that day.

'Beta, I'm tired,' would come the response.

The more worried he became about Baba's health, the more he thrust himself into the role of father to Majid, ensuring that the boy studied for his exams and completed his essays on time. Perhaps he was too hard on him, but he didn't want Majid to succumb to juvenile distractions, like girls, as he had. He wanted his younger brother to do well in his GCSEs and make it on his own, as he had done.

'Jaan, he's a good kid.' Fahima tried to soothe her husband, but Imran still felt the weight of his responsibilities. Majid needed a father figure, and Baba was too frail.

He needed Sumaya's help with both Majid and Baba, but she was off gallivanting in New York, while he had a wife, an ill father and a surrogate son to look after – while also holding down an all-consuming day job.

And then Baba had died. Imran had awoken startled in the middle of the night to the sound of his father's agonised cries. The noise had been more animalistic than human. Mouth dry, he had run into Baba's bedroom and found his father collapsed on the floor, clutching his chest, still entangled in his sheets from when he'd fallen off the bed.

By the time the ambulance had arrived, it had been too late.

Imran had held his father as Baba gargled and rasped for breath. It was a sound he'd never forget. Eyes closed, rocking back and forth, clutching him in both arms, he had prayed. Then, silence, as Baba's head suddenly felt as heavy as a boulder against his shoulder and his limbs went limp.

He'd held him for as long as he could, until the paramedics, Majid and Fahima had to pry his father's body away from him. As Fahima pulled him away, he'd noticed that Baba's white nightshirt was drenched in his tears.

When Imran closed his eyes, he could still hear Baba's last, desperate gasps for breath.

And for this trauma, which repeated in his mind and from which Sumaya had been spared, he couldn't forgive his sister.

In the office, Imran tried to purge his mind of what was going on at home, but as soon as he opened his work inbox, he saw an email from Giles: *Urgent: We need to talk.* His stomach dropped. He'd still been procrastinating over sending the quarterly sales report for Barking and Dagenham, conveniently 'forgetting' to send it as Giles had requested and ignoring follow-up reminders. As unfair as it was that only his performance would be judged on the results from Barking and Dagenham, he knew that Giles would have questions about the 40 per cent dip, and he didn't have answers. He'd be singled out, of course – this decline a mark of his abilities, though sales across the rest of the region were considered a collective effort.

What was he supposed to do? What was he meant to say? There was no right answer that might satisfy his boss, so he'd avoided the inevitable for as long as possible, hoping Giles might be distracted by other matters and forget again. Now, however, he wondered whether his luck had run out. Giles's cryptic message couldn't lead to anything good.

Imran fretted as he waited for Giles to come into the office, nervously tapping his foot and drumming his nails on his desk. He realised he was being uncharacteristically restless today, and not only because of Giles's email or the phone call to the police. He thought about the exchange with his sister the night before. He'd been the one to call her and ask her to come here, but there was something about her presence that threw him off balance. Already there was tension between them, and he couldn't help the razor-like edge to his voice whenever he spoke to her, and he couldn't help but be pissed off by the disdain apparent in hers. Was this how it would be for her entire visit? And when had they become so antagonistic to one another?

When Giles arrived, he immediately called Imran into the kitchenette. Imran's already frayed nerves now seemed to be trying to escape his body, evident from the goose pimples that sprouted on his arms. As he meekly followed Giles into the kitchenette, he noticed Shelly, Joe and Martin's eyes following them, as if they were watching him being walked to his execution.

Giles closed the door. 'Right,' he said slowly. 'I'm afraid it's bad news.'

Imran tried to maintain eye contact, not let his nerves show, but looking into his boss's steely grey eyes only made his discomfort worse. He quickly darted his glance away, settling on the wall behind him, adorned only by a white office clock. Each tick of the clock reverberated in his eardrums as he waited for Giles to deliver the blow . . .

'I'm afraid, Imran,' Giles continued leisurely, 'that I've had Martin pull up the accounts for Barking and Dagenham and they . . . well, they don't look good.'

Imran tried to keep his composure, his eyes still firmly on the wall, but he felt a piercing pain in his stomach.

'I did ask you for the quarterlies multiple times,' Giles said, shooting Imran a probing glance. 'Nonetheless, the numbers are very disappointing. I'm afraid this puts us all in a very difficult position with the national office, and I can't let this go unchecked. We are a team here, and when one of us doesn't deliver, it reflects badly on everyone. So, I'm going to highly encourage you to make some improvements in your numbers for this quarter. And to ensure you can give your dealerships your undivided attention, regretfully I am going to take you off corporate client work. Martin will take over the Greenr Cars account.'

Imran's expression turned from stoic to shocked. 'But . . . Giles, that's my account!'

'Yes, I realise . . . it's unfortunate . . .'

Imran could feel his cheeks turn red. He hadn't expected this. He knew he'd be blamed for the Dagenham and Barking sales, but this would cost him dearly. Corporate accounts guaranteed higher commission, and he'd convinced his old school friend, Hakeem, to buy a fleet of cars from Celeritas for his new electric-vehicle taxi company. The goal was to revolutionise London's ride-sharing industry by offering an energy-efficient alternative to Uber for the eco-conscious. Riders would be able to book low-emission cab rides at an affordable price, and share their car with other riders on their route. Hakeem's team had developed an algorithm that tracked the emissions per ride and donated a percentage of the cost of each ride to charities challenging climate change. The deal would be a feather in Imran's cap. Hakeem had already secured millions in funding from angel investors in the City, and there was considerable buzz in the business and trade papers already. It had been a real coup for Imran when his old friend had picked him to supply the cars. Now, all of a sudden, he wouldn't even be on the account . . . and he'd lose his commission in the process. Without him, Hakeem wouldn't even have gone with Celeritas!

'No,' Imran said firmly. 'You can't do this. I brought that client in . . .'

'As I said, I can't let this go unchecked.'

'But—' Imran could sense his anger rising, his face getting hotter, his fists beginning to tighten in rage. And then he noticed the expression on Giles's face – was it bewilderment? Or worse . . . fright? Giles was looking at him as though he were a savage, like he might be in danger, trapped in this tiny kitchenette with some sort of animal!

Instantly, Imran tried to temper his anger. As a brown man, he couldn't get away with having an outburst at work – so quick would the white people be to label anyone that didn't look like them as 'uncivilised'. That was the stark reality he lived in. He could only be so much, do so much, without crossing a line that the white people around him never needed to think about inching over. Giles could howl, obviate, scheme and reproach, but he could not.

'This is bullshit,' he said, moderating his tone to extinguish the heat.

As calmly as possible, he left the kitchenette, but his heart was beating fast – and fury coursed through his body. He grabbed his coat from the back of his chair and left the office, every fibre of his being resisting the urge to slam the door behind him.

◆ ◆ ◆

Who had power? What was justice? This, Imran pondered as he stewed in his car, parked alongside the motorway, seething from his encounter with Giles. He sat there, stock-still in the driver's seat, as hours passed and cars rushed by.

It seemed to him that white men had all the power, and he did not. They dictated the norms by which he had to live his life, even though this was just as much his land, his city, his country, as it was theirs. He knew that to live amongst white men, even if he was born here, wasn't to be one of them, and this he was reminded of time and again. Giles had seen fit to punish him, to take from him what was owed to him, where he would not have done the same to others. Fahima's attacker had done it too, brazenly handling her – and by extension, him – with all the innate entitlement that the colour of his skin afforded him and that the colour of Imran's did not. What was just about that? The white man could help himself to his coin and his woman, and he was, what? Expected to silently bow and accept his fate? The notion that all men are born equal was laughable. As was Sumaya's claim the night before that he was controlling. What did he have control over? Not this world – the white man's world. If he had any control, what had happened to

Fahima wouldn't have happened, and nor would Giles be able to deny him the money he had earned.

What Sumaya had dismissed as control wasn't control, but self-preservation. He moved in ways that were methodical, strategic, to ensure he and his family were not consumed by a world that didn't want them. Tolerance wasn't acceptance. He had to push Majid, because he knew what it was to be a man of their faith and colour in a white world – even with qualifications, it was cruel. If Majid had no merits, no degrees, it would be . . . Imran shuddered, not wanting to consider the hardship his younger brother might face without an education to prop him up. Sumaya didn't see this – how, he did not know. They had always had to be twice as good for half as much. She had accepted her lot, had assimilated and fooled herself into thinking she was like the others, but he wasn't fooled. What was earned, not just given, could just as easily be taken away. Sumaya had no idea.

As the sun began to set, dusky red skies overtaking the bright blues and whites that had shone down on his car, Imran composed himself. He still had to call the police officer in charge of Fahima's case and get an update, as he'd planned to earlier.

'I'm afraid there's no news,' said Officer Cahill when Imran finally collected himself enough to dial the number on the back of the card he'd been given. 'We've had no tip-offs or leads as yet.'

'What do you mean?!' Imran reeled. 'It's been nearly three weeks and you haven't done anything?!'

'Sir, I understand you're upset—'

'Don't fob me off,' Imran hissed. 'Some guy is walking free out there after attacking my wife, and you've just been sitting on your arses . . .'

'Sir—'

'This is just typical of your lot,' Imran continued. 'If it was one of us, you'd have armed police bust down the door in no time—'

'Sir,' Cahill interrupted him. 'I appreciate this is a stressful time, but I assure you we are doing all we can—'

Before the officer could finish, Imran ended the call and brought his phone down against the dashboard with thunderous force. This release of pent-up aggression gave him temporary relief.

Beneath the rage, something else stirred that he couldn't quite name. It wasn't helplessness – though he felt that in his bones every time he thought about Fahima, every time he tried to bring her comfort with his meandering words. Helplessness was marked into his skin for all to see, and for himself to revile in the mirror. No, it wasn't helplessness. It was something more. An ache, deep and unholy, that ran from his chest through to his loins, his very manhood, challenging his worth. This was a sorrow that cut deep into his very essence as a man. Who was he if he could not care for his wife as he ought? What kind of man was he to let others trample over him?

He didn't know the answer, and this terrified him.

Evening set in, the moon illuminating the night sky, and yet Imran didn't move. It was now past six o'clock. Fahima would be expecting him. But how could he face her? How could he look her in the eye and explain the truth that troubled his heart and manhood? That another day had gone by and still he hadn't been able to alleviate her pain.

In the past when he thought of Fahima, he'd thought of colour – jewel tones, to be precise. He'd thought of her as deep amethyst silk, shimmering when she caught the light, almost ethereal; he'd thought of her as vibrant chartreuse, bold and ungoverned; ruby red, majestic and kind-hearted. Now, though, he thought of black. The darkness that had drawn over them and extinguished the colour in their lives.

There was little he could say, much less do, to repaint their canvas, but how he wished he could.

In a cruel irony, Fahima would be the one he turned to for counsel if this were anyone else – she was pure, compassionate and rational. She could bring him down off the ledge when anger took him over. She could soothe his insecurities instinctively without him having to say a word.

Fahima had been there to pick him up when Baba died. In the first few months after, he would wake up in the middle of the night, panting, drenched with sweat, reliving those final moments. Baba's last breath in his arms. A nightly horror had laid claim to his subconscious. Fahima would awake with him and, seeing her husband so distressed, hold him, stroke his hair, and curl into his back as he fell asleep again. The comfort of her wrapping herself around him, her hot breath on the back of his neck, reassured him that he wasn't alone, that his nightmares weren't real. That when he awoke she would be there.

And she had been there. He remembered how Fahima had awoken with him at the crack of dawn, the day he returned to work from his too-short bereavement leave after Baba's death. She'd laid out his clothes, freshly ironed, on the bed, and made him his favourite breakfast – paratha and scrambled eggs with onions, chilli and coriander. How his heart had swelled when he sat down at the kitchen table with her. How the dread he had felt the night before, and all through his sleep, fell silent. He hadn't been sure if he was ready to return to work yet – just five days after he'd buried Baba. It was too soon.

'I'll be here when you get home,' Fahima had said, reassuring him by placing her hand over his. 'It's just one day. Eight hours. And then you'll be here, with me.'

When he had returned from work on that first day and parked his car in the bay opposite their house, he saw Fahima fling open

71

the front door and sprint to meet him. She had watched for his return, peering out of the living room window for the sight of his silver Lexus. When he had stepped out of the car, Fahima had wrapped him in her arms, the refreshing scent of her favourite coconut, lavender and ylang-ylang soap welcoming him home.

'I knew you could do it,' she had whispered in his ear, holding his hand and guiding him back into the warmth of their home.

This was how he had got through those first days and weeks. Taking each day a step at a time, closing his eyes at his desk and reminding himself that soon the day would be over and he'd return to the safety of his home, the safety of her.

And how had he repaid her devotion? Perhaps it was the weight of caring for him as well as their unborn child that had caused her miscarriage. Though he'd never admit it out loud, he often blamed himself for needing so much from her then that their child had been lost to them. And he blamed himself for being so grief-stricken that he wasn't able to shoulder the burden of the loss she had suffered: one day a heart beating within her, cells coalescing into a form, and then no movement. He had believed that she understood. That his grief over Baba had made him unable to console her, that he'd be there the next time, that she'd find solace in returning to her parents' home, where her mother could give her the attention he could not.

But he had deluded himself, he realised. 'Next time' had come, and again he could not be the man she needed, the husband she deserved.

Maybe he didn't deserve her at all.

Imran turned the key in the ignition. The car murmured to life. He shook out his legs, numb now from sitting stationary for so long, and put his foot to the pedal.

His heart told him to drive home, but his hands directed the wheel elsewhere – anywhere else.

Chapter 8

SULTANA

Of all her children, it was Imran who had most troubled Sultana as a child. The boy had been a challenge even in the womb – keeping her up all night, somersaulting in her stomach, and making her heave with morning sickness long past her first trimester. 'He's a very spirited boy,' the nurse told her at one of her pregnancy scans. It was almost as if his fate was sealed before he entered the world.

More than once, Sultana and Abdul had despaired at their rambunctious son's antics at school – getting into fistfights, disrupting classes and arguing with his teachers, stealing chocolate from the tuck shop. Once, when Imran was twelve, in his second year of secondary, he had failed to come home from school at a decent time, which was unusual for him and positively distressing for Sultana. By six o'clock, Sultana had been pleading with Abdul to search for the boy, howling, tears seeping into the pleats of her sari. Her mind immediately went to the worst: what if he'd been abducted, what if he'd got into a fight and was lying in a ditch somewhere, what if he had been hit by a car? Sultana banged on the next-door neighbour's door, begging Mrs Sharma to send her sons out to look for Imran, too. By eight o'clock, the search party had returned with no sign of him – not at the school, the mosque or the local playground. When the boy had sauntered through the front door after nine o'clock, oblivious to the heartbreak and worry he had caused, Sultana was so overwhelmed by the sight of him, unscathed and very much alive, that she immediately held him in her arms and wept into his hair. She had chosen to overlook the late hour, the distress he had caused, the search party she had assembled on his behalf, and even the fact that he reeked of cigarette smoke. She had never been so frightened for her son, nor so grateful to see him, so none of that mattered anymore.

'Chill out, Ma,' the boy had said in a cavalier tone.

There had been no admonishment in her voice when she set a plate of rice and lamb curry in front of him, watching as he gobbled it down, no indication that he had set her heart on fire or that her mind had raced, imagining burying her son's cold, adolescent body. What had run through his head she'd never know, but she was simply overjoyed to see him.

That night, Abdul had told her, 'You're too easy on him.'

'He's just a boy,' she had replied, a phrase that would become so familiar as to roll off her tongue without thought or reproach towards her son many more times over the years.

'Perhaps we should send him to Bangladesh to stay with my brother? Maybe he can learn what real hardship looks like,' Abdul had said.

Sultana's eyes had widened but still she said nothing. She rolled away from her husband, a silent tear falling down her cheek. Surely her husband wouldn't send their son away. Even the words made her disconsolate. The thought of her child being ripped away from her, from the comfort of her bosom, scared her.

Although Sultana made excuses for her son and looked the other way when he misbehaved, every night when she lay her head down, she had prayed to Allah to grant her son serenity – for his sake as well as hers and Abdul's. Her husband was not a short-tempered or violent man, but as Imran had grown more unruly in his adolescence, Abdul had also become less tolerant of his behaviour, more exasperated by each letter sent home from the school and by the group of friends he had accumulated. Sultana knew there was a limit to her husband's patience, but her own patience when it came to her children – Imran particularly – was abundant. She was resolute that the boy would grow and mature, that these years wouldn't be what defined him but rather shaped him into a figure like his father. She had barely known Abdul until their wedding, when she was eighteen and he was twenty-four, and so she didn't know what he'd been like in his youth, but she imagined that, like her son, he might have been rowdy – wasn't that what young men were like?

Seeing her husband now, placid and controlled, she prayed for Allah to grant her wish to tame her spirited boy.

As Sultana neared the end of her life, she took stock of her children – their achievements, their unique quirks, the way they each expressed and received love differently. When it came to her first-born, she reflected on the strife that Imran had caused her and Abdul in his early life, how she had prayed each night that he would mature, and how she had feared that his impetuous nature might send him down a path that she could never recover him from. She smiled when she thought about the man he had become, how her prayers to Allah had been answered; for somewhere along the way, her eldest son had matured into a young man she could be proud of. She didn't like to give all the credit to his wife, Fahima, because no man was built without something of his mother's imprint, but she was equally thankful that her son had found grounding and humility in her daughter-in-law. She knew Fahima to be kind and from an upstanding family, and had beamed with pride the day they got married.

She praised Allah that her son had found his way in life, and she thanked him for allowing her to live long enough to see it.

Sultana was not blind, however. She knew that the fire her child carried like a burden would always be there. He had calmed with age and marriage, but there would always be kindling within him, ready to catch alight at a moment's notice. She saw it in the way he interacted with his sister, in the fraught way they argued and bickered. How Imran always seemed to get his way, even if it meant trampling all over his younger sister and brother. How close Imran and Sumaya had once been. It pained her to see them drift apart so, but she did not blame Sumaya for feeling the way she did; in their culture, a woman had to acquiesce to the older men, but this did not quell the hurt her daughter felt, nor did it justify the unfair advantage her son had in life.

Sultana had vowed never to reveal to her son the lengths she had gone to protect him from a worse fate. The lengths that Sumaya had also gone to. And because he'd never know, and because she had made Sumaya promise that she'd never tell, she understood the bitterness in her daughter's heart towards her older brother. There was nothing she wouldn't do for her children, and though she ached for making her daughter complicit, burdening Sumaya with a secret that festered deep inside her and hardened her resentment towards her brother, she knew that the risk to Imran was too great. He had come too far to be derailed now.

'Be good to your sister,' Sultana had urged him in one of their regular late-night conversations before she died. 'She loves you really.'

Night after night, the rest of the house would be asleep, all except Sultana and Imran. Sultana was kept awake nightly by the shooting pains that soared down the left side of her body, the part she had regained feeling in after her stroke; her legs were heavy with pins and needles and her heart was working double time to keep blood pumping throughout her body. What kept Imran awake she did not know – maybe it was the stress of work? How hard her son

76

worked at the car dealership! How proud she was that he'd achieved a degree-level education, something neither she nor Abdul could have dreamed of – something not even possible for them as young people in Bangladesh. She had married by the time she was of university age. But she understood that to be so educated meant to work hard – this was what they had raised and prepared him for: to have a good job, a stable income. And that always required hard work. So maybe it was stress, but stress was a by-product of the opportunity afforded to him, and Sultana was full of pride that her son had not only reached his potential but had also made his ancestors proud.

These nights, when neither of them could sleep, she'd summon him into her and Abdul's bedroom, and they'd whisper into the early hours, comforted by each other's company, their conversations punctuated by Abdul's rhythmic snoring in his bed across the room.

'When you were born, I didn't know what to do,' Sultana confided on this particular night. 'I didn't have any family here to teach me how to raise a child. Just your auntie, Amma's friend, when I moved here, and your father, and he was clumsy. I didn't let him hold you that first day, worried he might drop you! I wish I could have had my ammi, your nanu, to help me . . . that is how it's meant to be with your first. I had to make do.'

Sultana teared up with the memory of these early days of motherhood – the sudden immersion in the language of parenthood. So many times she had worried she wouldn't be able to be a good mother.

'But I would look at you and I knew that my heart was full, that even if I didn't get everything right, if I just kept you alive, raised you into adulthood, that that would be enough. Sumaya and Majid, they were easier because I had you. But when you came along, I was still but a girl myself, younger than you are now. There is nothing like the bond you have with your first-born, beta. I love all my children equally, but what we had is an experience that you can only have once.'

Speaking at length made Sultana out of breath. She gestured to her water bottle and Imran brought it to her lips, allowing her to take deep sips, relieving the dryness in her mouth.

'Everything your baba and I have done, there is reason,' she eventually continued. 'You will always be my first son. Baba and I . . . we may not have done everything right, but we did everything to give you the life you deserve.'

Imran took his mother's hand in his, squeezing it tight. 'I know, Amma. I know.'

'Sumaya, she is headstrong, she is resourceful. Majid, he is gentle, he is kind. I never needed to try with them as I did with you. You were always the one that gave us the biggest headache! Always questioning us, always challenging us, always getting into trouble . . . and still you are full of fire, still you are stubborn – arrogant, even.'

'Amma—' Imran began, but Sultana cut him off.

'No, let me finish. It is both your gift and your curse, this fire. It makes you so uniquely you, my child, my son. It gives you character. But it can also consume you, Imran. I know, for I have seen your mistakes, and me and Baba won't always be here. You must control it. You are a good man, beta, with a good heart but a distracted soul . . . don't let the darkness in you consume you. Think of Fahima, of the family you will have . . . you must be good and true. Be the man we raised you to be.'

Imran let go of his mother's hand and she could see him dab at the corner of his eye.

'I will, Amma,' he said, his voice cracking.

'Promise me this, Imran,' Sultana added. 'That you'll take care of Fahima, your baba, Majid, Sumaya . . . that you'll be the best father one day, inshallah, and that you'll always follow the light. I'll be there in the light, beta, guiding you.'

Through strained sobs, Imran responded: 'I promise.'

Chapter 9

SUMAYA

Sumaya clenched her eyes shut until she saw stars, trying to block out the doubts and unease creeping to the forefront of her mind. Her thoughts blazed with the vision of Neha. She longed to reach out. If she could see her first love once again, get some answers, maybe her heart would be able to settle on Jonathan. Maybe she'd be able to say yes to his proposal.

She had messaged Neha on Instagram the night before. *I'm in town, and I really want to see you*, she wrote. In the long seven – going on eight – years she had been in New York, they had barely spoken. The wound from Neha's rejection when Sumaya had asked her to move to New York with her had taken a long time to heal. It was only in the last couple of years that they had reconnected on Instagram, sending the occasional 'hello' and 'Eid Mubarak' message. They hadn't dared dredge up the past.

Often, in the last two years, Sumaya had swiped through the photos on Neha's profile, trying to glean something about her life since they'd last seen each other. But Neha's Instagram page gave away nothing; there were no photos of her. Just pictures of buildings, flowers and artwork. This made Sumaya even more curious. What did Neha look like now? What was her life like? In the corner of her mind, she'd wondered why she had suddenly taken such an interest in her old flame, when she was settled and meant to be happy with Jonathan. But each time she questioned herself and mentally probed her relationship, doubts began to set in. Doubts that she wasn't ready to address. And so she cast them aside, along with her lingering feelings for Neha, to be examined another day.

Sumaya tossed and turned until finally she gave up any notion of falling back asleep, and rose out of her childhood bed, aggravated by her own mixed emotions. She went downstairs to find her sister-in-law pacing the room in just her nightgown, an expression of concern on her face.

'I don't think your brother came home last night,' Fahima said as Sumaya came into the living room.

'What do you mean?' Sumaya asked.

'He . . . he didn't come to bed last night, and I didn't hear the door open after you arrived. Did you?'

Sumaya took a moment to recollect the events of the day before, but she had been so jetlagged she'd spent most of the day asleep or in a tired stupor. She couldn't reliably say if she'd heard her brother unlocking the door or not. 'No, I don't think I did,' she said uncertainly.

'Where is he?!' Fahima said desperately. 'He isn't picking up his phone.'

Sumaya rested her hands on Fahima's shoulders and guided her to the sofa. 'Look, I'm sure he's just at work. Don't worry, I'll try and call him.'

'What if something terrible has happened . . .' Fahima said, a crack in her voice and fear in her eyes, lines of worry emerging across her forehead.

'I'm sure he's okay, Bhabi. He probably did come home and we were just asleep, and now he's gone to work,' Sumaya said, trying to console her sister-in-law but unconvinced by her own words.

Where was her brother? What was he playing at? How could he leave his wife so alone when she was going through something so agonising? Fahima whimpered next to her and Sumaya wrapped her arms around her, feeling pity for this poor woman who had so much to deal with, and angry with her brother for his sudden disappearing act. It was typical of Imran to put himself first, to not consider other people. She'd hoped he'd changed, but the panic she saw in her sister-in-law told her that there had been no transformative come-to-Jesus moment. He was still a selfish prick.

'Bhabi, shhh,' she said, holding her sister-in-law. 'Don't worry, don't worry . . . I'm sure he's fine.'

If Fahima found little comfort in her consolation, Sumaya couldn't blame her, because she herself was at a loss as to what had got into her brother. Where the fuck was he?

He had better have a damn good answer when she finally got hold of him.

◆ ◆ ◆

After Sumaya had calmed down her sister-in-law, she tried to call and text Imran, but her calls went straight to voicemail. Her messages were delivered, but not read.

In the bathroom, she ran a hot bath for Fahima, adding lavender bath salts and a dash of Dettol to the water, just as Amma used to. She had never understood why her mother insisted on adding Dettol, but she'd sworn that a boiling-hot bath with Dettol could cure all ailments – of both body and mind. As she repeated this ritual that her mother had performed so many times for her in this very bathroom when she was younger, Sumaya felt a stab of pain at her loss. She remembered how, whenever she was ill – whether a cold or simply melancholy – Amma would fill the tub all the way, the water scalding, the smell of the Dettol chemical yet soothing, and tell her that she'd feel better after a bath. And she always did, though now she wondered whether it was because of the bath or her mother's nurturing.

Sumaya gently helped Fahima out of her nightgown and was alarmed by her sister-in-law's gaunt figure; her bones seemed to be protruding from her torso, and as she held her hand and helped lower her into the bathtub, she noticed how brittle her fingers felt and worried they might crumble in her grasp. It occurred to Sumaya how unusual and intimate this act was – to see her sister-in-law naked and vulnerable – but Fahima didn't seem apprehensive or self-conscious about allowing her husband's sister to witness her like this. This was what it meant to be family, to be sisters, Sumaya thought, and felt a rush of sympathy for Fahima, for what she had endured and how it had taken its toll on her physical and mental state.

Fahima rested her head against the edge of the tub and closed her eyes, allowing the water to lap over her body. Her face indicated a sense of calm, and Sumaya wondered if this was the first time in weeks that her sister-in-law had found some semblance of peace. Drawing Fahima a bath was a small act of kindness that took little effort but at least gave her a moment of respite. But beyond this immediate feeling of gratification, Sumaya was sorry that this was the best she could offer. She could not restore Fahima to her former self, no matter how much her brother seemed to pin his hopes on her being some miracle cure. She couldn't take away the pain of what Fahima had gone through at that bus station. Nor could she rewrite history or cast a spell so it had never happened. If it wasn't Fahima, the sad truth was it would have been someone else, and she didn't wish what had happened to her sister-in-law on anyone.

Sumaya allowed Fahima some time like this, watching her deep in repose as steam rose from the tub and filled the air. After twenty minutes, she interrupted her, nudging her to sit up straight. Fahima positioned herself in the centre of the tub, knees drawn into her chest, her arms wrapped around them. Sumaya remembered how she herself used to sit exactly like this while Amma tended to her;

there were parallels, she realised, between her own childlike trust in her mother and the way Fahima looked now, allowing Sumaya to take a jug, fill it with water and gently pour it over her head.

'Is it too hot?' she asked softly.

Fahima shook her head, and so Sumaya did it again, the warmth of the water seeping into Fahima's skin. She repeated the action again and again, imagining the water cleansing Fahima of her bad memories, releasing them from her body like toxins.

Sumaya then took a washcloth and dipped it in the water, lathering it with soap, and gently extended Fahima's right arm out towards her, bringing the cloth down on her skin and delicately stroking it up and down the length of one arm, then the other, like one might a child.

As Sumaya re-lathered the cloth and began scrubbing her back, Fahima startled her by finally breaking the silence between them.

'When you were a little girl, did you ever imagine how many children you'd have?' she asked quietly.

'No, I can't say I did,' Sumaya replied without hesitation.

'When I was a girl, I thought maybe I'd have a whole house full of kids. Four or five, even. I wanted to have them all close in age so that they could grow up together, and then I'd still have time for me when they were adults.'

Sumaya didn't know how to respond. She could not relate to the level of thought that Fahima had given to this subject.

'And when I met your brother,' Fahima continued, 'when we were official, I asked him how many kids he wanted . . . he said four or five too. We both wanted a big family. And I feel like I've disappointed him.'

'No. No, you haven't,' Sumaya quickly assured her. 'I can't begin to understand the pain of what you've been through,' she added, delicately broaching the subject of her sister-in-law's past miscarriage, 'but that doesn't mean it'll never happen.'

'We have tried.'

'Don't give up hope, Bhabi,' Sumaya said. And then, though she didn't necessarily believe it herself but thought it might be what Fahima wanted to hear, she continued: 'If that is what you want, Allah will make it so.'

'I think Allah has cursed me,' Fahima sighed.

'What . . . no,' Sumaya said, turning Fahima's face towards her. Tears streamed from her sister-in-law's eyes, falling into the bathtub. 'You can't think that, surely?'

'How else do you explain it?' Fahima said resignedly. 'Maybe this is my punishment for wanting too much, for being so covetous.'

'What . . . what do you mean?' Sumaya asked, confusion in her voice and on her face.

'After the baby . . .' She began to sob. 'I know it's not right, I know I shouldn't have . . . but losing something I wanted so much, losing the one thing that I wanted more than anything . . . that I still want. It hurts . . . to see other women with what I want. Every time I see my friends on Facebook posting pictures with their children, I know I should be happy for them. I should be grateful that Allah saw fit to deliver them fit and healthy children. But all I can think of is how envious I am. Why them? Why not me?'

Sumaya's face had turned to stone, her mouth slightly agape at Fahima's confession. But before she could neutralise her expression, it was too late; Fahima noticed her dismay and sobbed harder, her eyes downcast.

'I know what you must think of me . . .' she cried. 'What kind of person thinks like that? So selfishly?'

'No . . . Bhabi, no, I don't think *that*.'

'I do,' Fahima continued. 'It's bad, I know it's bad, and I hate myself for it, but I can't help it. Every time I see a little toddler with their mum playing in the park, it just makes me think that my baby would be that age now. That I should be there, waiting for him or her at the bottom of the slide, pushing them on the swing. I see these

mums, so happy, and it makes me want to scream. And again and
again I ask myself, "Why them? Why not me?" I am a terrible person.'

'Bhabi . . .' Sumaya placed a hand on her sister-in-law's shoulder.
'I don't think you're a terrible person. I don't think anyone who knows
you can think that of you. Not one bit. What you've experienced . . .
I don't blame you for feeling angry, or sad, or jealous. I would too.'

'Maybe I deserve what that man did to me . . .'

'No!' Sumaya shouted now. 'No, you don't. No one deserves
that. Listen to me,' she said brusquely, now holding firmly on to
both of her sister-in-law's shoulders. 'What happened to you has
nothing to do with how you feel about the baby, okay?'

'Then why . . . ?' Fahima said through sobs.

This, Sumaya couldn't easily answer. How could she say it was
just bad luck? That she could have been any other hijab-wearing
woman on the street?

'I don't know, Bhabi,' she said, giving her sister-in-law the only
answer she could. 'I honestly can't believe this kind of thing is still going
on – women being criticised or attacked for wearing a hijab. I'm sick of
people trying to control our bodies. I'm so sorry this happened to you.'

'No matter what we do, no matter who we are inside, people
look at you in the street and just see a woman in a scarf,' Fahima
said. 'All they see is the hijab, and they make their assumptions
about who I am. That's the way it is for us as Muslim women who
wear the hijab. We are constantly judged. Look at you, Sumaya . . .
this wouldn't have happened to you.'

Sumaya felt an uneasy pang of guilt. Her sister-in-law was right;
she didn't know what it felt like to walk in Fahima's shoes, to feel
like she had a target on her back because of a piece of cloth covering
her head. It had been her choice not to wear the hijab when she
was a teenager, even when other girls at school did. Her choice was
between her and Allah. Perhaps, in some way, she'd feared she'd be
treated differently, too. Perhaps it was easier to conform to Western

standards. But she'd always felt it was braver still for Fahima to make the choice to wear the hijab. And it wasn't anyone else's business.

'No, Bhabi,' Sumaya said. 'People are always going to say something. You wear the hijab or you don't wear the hijab, someone's always going to have an opinion. You wear the hijab but you style it differently – someone's always going to say you're doing it wrong. You can't let what other people think dictate your life. The way I see it is that wearing a hijab should be about you and your faith, an expression of your faith, not based on anyone else's opinions. And if it feels right to you, then that is what you should do. At the end of the day, it's our relationship with Allah that matters, and we all believe in our own ways.'

Sumaya stroked her sister-in-law's hair, imagining that with each stroke she was washing away the thoughts that plagued Fahima. 'There's no rhyme or reason to why people are so triggered by the hijab,' she said. 'In a perfect world, we'd just accept everybody as they are, and not get so worked up about other people's differences. But life is a fucking bitch.'

Suddenly, Fahima snorted with laughter, surprising Sumaya and even herself. 'It is! It is . . . a fucking bitch.'

The curse words felt abnormal coming out of her sister-in-law's mouth. Fahima was not one to use bad language, but from the meek smile on her face now, Sumaya could tell it must've felt good, must have been cathartic to channel even some of her anger into something subversive – to go against the grain of the rules that governed her.

'I'm sorry,' Sumaya said. 'About what happened, about the baby . . . you don't deserve it. Please know that.'

'Sometimes I have nightmares about it . . . that man, his hand in my face, pulling at my hijab. And sometimes I even dream that I see him again, but this time I'm ready. That I might be able to defend myself. That I'm behind the wheel of a car and he is in front of me and I just . . .' Fahima motioned with her hands as if at the steering wheel, bumping into something.

'Does that make you feel better?' Sumaya asked her.

'It does,' she said emphatically, a coldness in her tone that struck Sumaya as curious. 'I think I'd do it for real.'

Sumaya didn't respond, distracted by thoughts of what she might do in the same situation. Who was she to say that revenge wasn't the answer? Truth be told, she would want to mow down her attacker too if she were in Fahima's shoes.

Perhaps her sister-in-law wasn't so genteel after all, she thought. She saw a piece of herself in Fahima for the first time – something raw and indelicate, untamed – and she felt kinship in her heart for this woman she had always assumed was the opposite of her. Of course, everything that had happened – the baby, the attack – would change her. How could it not? She had always assumed her sister-in-law was docile, that a bad thought never ran through her mind. How foolish she had been to confine her to a box. She admired this spirit she was now seeing in Fahima. Dare she say she was even impressed? Perhaps they weren't so dissimilar after all.

Fahima's change in attitude was ironic. Sumaya had always felt her brother thought of her as inferior to her sister-in-law, admonishing her for her Western clothes at Baba's funeral, for following Western traditions, for abandoning her family. How the tables had turned. A Pandora's box had opened in Fahima, and Sumaya was almost amused at the thought of Imran trying to shut it, to revert his wife to the way she was. After all, wasn't that what he wanted? Why he'd called her? In a twisted way, she couldn't help but think that Fahima's misfortune and heartbreak might be the jolt she and Imran needed in their relationship to upend their traditional dynamic. That was if her brother ever re-emerged from wherever the fuck he was.

Just as she considered this, she heard the sound of keys in the lock downstairs, the door opening and shutting.

It was almost as if she had summoned Imran back from the ether.

Chapter 10

Imran

As soon as Imran walked through the front door, Sumaya came marching down the stairs towards him, her face like thunder.

'Where the fuck have you been?' his sister shouted midway down the staircase, her booming voice reverberating in his ears.

Imran's head was groggy, his ears sensitive from the effects of his hangover. The last thing he needed was his sister screeching at him. He tried to ignore her, but Sumaya refused to relent, oblivious to his delicate state.

Imran hadn't intended to drink, but the way the golden-brown whisky numbed his mind and muted his frayed nerves had felt good. How he had ended up at The Eleanor the night before was a mystery even to himself; he'd driven down the A12, turned on to Tredegar Road, then Old Ford Road, and somehow ended up stopping in front of the pub, as if something inside were calling him in. He ought to have gone home, he ought to have been with Fahima, but he couldn't deny the urge within him – irrational and animalistic – to go inside. It had been reckless, he'd realised earlier that morning, as he clung to the toilet seat in a local café and purged his guts out, having fallen asleep in his car after last orders.

But he'd also felt a sense of control in the anarchy when everything else around him felt like it was falling apart.

The first drop of whisky to pass his lips had been harsh. It burned at his throat and made him gag. But still he persisted, another sip, and another, until the oaky flavours settled, coating his tongue and relaxing his muscles. Around him, pensioners downed their cheap pints in peaceful accord, nary a word passing between them, each in their own world. Together but alone. This suited Imran just fine. He didn't want to talk to anyone, and he remained unbothered as he finished one glass of Glenfiddich and ordered another.

Now, of course, his head throbbing, he was full of regret. He hadn't touched a drop of alcohol since he was at uni. He had tried so hard to be observant of his religion, to be faithful to Allah. And now, he had sinned. The guilt clawed at his throat just as intensely as the alcohol that had passed through him the night before. He had added to his multiple failings. He'd been looking for a way out, he told himself. Looking to forget, for a moment, the mess he'd made of things at home and at work. His self-flagellation would have to wait, however, because Sumaya was in his face, quick to remind him of his shortcomings too.

'Your wife has been worried sick!' she shouted. 'We've been trying to call and text all morning!'

At the mention of his wife, Imran felt a pang of guilt. The clock on the living room wall said 12.34 p.m. How long had Fahima been worrying about him? It should be the other way round.

'My phone died . . .' he said meekly.

Sumaya scoffed. 'Fuck that. Where have you been?' She repeated her earlier question more adamantly.

The events of last night replayed in his mind. He knew he didn't warrant any sympathy from his younger sister; and she was right to be angry. He should have been here. With his wife. He should never have gone to that pub in the first place. How could he explain that seeing his wife so fragile and afflicted with a sorrow that he could not cure had made him question his very essence as a husband, as a protector, as a man?

Sumaya sidled up close to him, her eyes filled with indignation. 'Are you having an affair?' she spat at him in a hushed tone.

Imran took a step back, eyes wide at this accusation. Was she being serious?

'Where have you been all night?' she continued, her voice muted – he presumed because Fahima was upstairs and she didn't want her to hear this accusation.

'What are you talking about?!' Imran stuttered.

Sumaya closed the gap between them again, looking him straight in the eyes, as if squaring up to him. He almost admired her bravado.

'Tell me the truth,' she hissed.

'Of course I'm not!' he hissed back indignantly.

How could Sumaya even think that? And how dare she even imply such a thing to an elder? In his own house! Again, she had shown she had no shame, and no respect for the cultural norms and values their parents had instilled in them. Suddenly, he was incensed.

'Who do you think you are?' he bristled. 'Who do you think you're talking to?'

Sumaya threw her hands in the air. 'Oh, here we go,' she said. 'Time for the big-brother routine, is it? You're about sixteen years too late. I'm not a little girl. I know you like to think you've got us all under your thumb, but that doesn't work with me anymore. I don't care if I'm pissing you off. I don't care if you think you can silence me. You don't have any power over me.'

'Yes,' Imran fired back. 'You're a New York woman now, right? Is that what they teach you in your yoga classes? "You don't have any power over me"?' He mimicked her voice. 'You sound like one of those gora women. It's pathetic. How dare you come into my house and speak such filth.'

'That's rich, coming from you,' Sumaya said. 'Don't think I don't know what alcohol smells like . . .'

All at once, Imran was conscious of the stench of whisky on his breath, his clothes, seeping from his pores.

'Yeah,' Sumaya said, noticing the recognition on her brother's face. 'You're such a hypocrite. Walking around like you're the perfect, upstanding Muslim, lording it over the rest of us, thinking you know best for me and Majid. But here you are, stumbling home like a drunk! I always knew you were full of shit.'

The animosity in the air was suffocating. Imran was still queasy from the night before, and now a rush of blood coursed through him, making the room feel stifling in its heat. He worried he might be sick or pass out. He tried to walk past Sumaya, to put an end to this, turning his back to her as he walked further into the room. He needed to hydrate and lie down. But Sumaya wasn't finished.

'Your wife is upstairs and needs your support, and you're out all night drinking? How can you be so selfish?' she said, following him into the living room. 'How can you be so insensitive? She is going through so much right now! Have you *really* tried to talk to her? She is hurting so badly. You have no idea! What is wrong with you?!'

'Don't you think I know?!' Imran snapped, turning once again to face his sister. 'I just feel like . . . I don't know what to do . . .'

'So what? Your solution is to do nothing at all?!'

'No.'

'It sure seems like it. Isn't that why you made me come all the way here? To take your problem off your hands? For me to fix things for you so you don't even have to try. So you can go out and go drinking.'

'You have no idea what we've been going through . . .'

'Oh – *we*?' Sumaya mocked him. 'It's *we*, is it? Am I supposed to feel sorry for you? How hard things must have been for *you*. All I see is your poor wife scared to even go outside the house, confining herself to her bedroom, and you barely even being at home.'

91

'Enough of this,' Imran responded tersely. 'Just leave it now, Sumaya.'

He tried to walk away, to create space between them by heading towards the kitchen, but Sumaya still had more to say.

'The truth too much for you to handle, brother? Why did you make me come all the way here then? If not to clean up your mess? Just like Amma and Baba have always done for you. You think you're the big brother. The man of the house. But you can't even take care of your own problems!'

'I said, *enough*!' Imran shouted.

Imran saw Sumaya flinch as she registered the anger on his face. She stood there stock-still, in shock, as Imran walked into the kitchen.

Imran stood at the kitchen sink, deep breaths in and out, trying to tame the volcano that threatened to erupt within him. This rage scared him, the way it had suddenly exploded to the fore.

Amma would be so disappointed. This was exactly the kind of thing she'd warned him against before she died. He had promised her he would control the fire within him. And now he had broken that promise. His anger was in command of him, not the other way round, and he didn't know how to reclaim control. He was in free fall through an endless void, able to see the light that he had strayed so far away from – the guiding light of his mother – but helpless to reach it; and the further he fell, the more the light diminished.

He wasn't sure how long he stood like that, lost in his thoughts, in his confusion, but the creak of the kitchen door opening snapped him back to reality. He looked up from the sink to find Sumaya dressed in her coat, her bag over her shoulder.

'I'm not doing this,' she said. 'You can figure it out on your own. I'm done. I'm going home.'

A sense of déjà vu came over him; he'd seen this scenario play out before – after Baba's funeral. It was typical of Sumaya to walk away, but he didn't have that privilege.

'Yeah, go. That is what you do best, isn't it? Well, bye,' he said flatly, trying not to give his sister the satisfaction of goading him.

Sumaya breathed out heavily. 'It's you who is pathetic, by the way. Earlier, you said I was pathetic? Nah, that's all on you. Always needing other people to come to your rescue. Amma, Baba, me . . . you just don't grow up, do you? All this bravado is a front. Bhabi deserves better than you. It's her I feel sorry for.'

Her words stung. Imran had tried not to be provoked, but the mention of his wife renewed the heat in his voice. 'If you want to leave, then fucking leave, yeah? Why are you hanging around?'

'You're the one that made me leave my home, leave my life, and come here . . . because *you* have no idea how to look after your own wife, because you wanted me to be some sort of magic solution. Growing up, I watched silently when Amma and Baba let you get away with murder – things I'd never have been able to get away with. Failing an exam? Not to worry, he's just a boy. Dicking around and getting caught smoking weed by the imam? It's what young boys do! You have always had someone to pick up after you, King Imran. Everyone is just here to serve you. And now your wife really needs you, you don't even know what to do.'

Imran's rage grew. 'I had it so easy, huh? Where were you then, Sumaya? While I was here, looking after Dad when he had his heart attack, where were you? I worked every day to provide for my family, for my wife, and took care of Baba, and made sure Majid was in school. What were you doing? You want to talk about selfish? Let's talk about you leaving and going to New York.'

'Here it is again, the "woe is me" act. You really have a short memory, don't you?' Sumaya spat. 'What about Amma? I did my part for this family. I put off my studies when Amma got ill. I was practically Majid's surrogate mother when she was in hospital. I cooked and I cleaned this house . . . Have you forgotten all that?'

'I was here too!'

'When you were here, you barely lifted a finger. That's the truth. All those times Baba asked you to go grocery shopping while he was at the hospital with Amma, and you conveniently forgot. Who had to do it? Me! And let's not act like you did as much as Baba and I did for Amma. You think I've forgotten these things? How you disappointed her time after time, not coming to the hospital when you said you would. You were too consumed with your own life. Don't you dare tell me that we were equals, because we were not.'

A tense silence filled the room, both siblings casting their minds back to what had been, to that point, their biggest struggle: their mother's sudden illness and the dramatic shift in their family dynamic. There was truth to what Sumaya was saying, Imran had to concede. Amma's stroke had come at a crucial time for him in his university years – and when he'd met Fahima. He hadn't been as present as he should have been. But he'd never abandoned his family like his sister had.

'I'm glad I went to New York, I'm glad I left,' Sumaya said, breaking the silence. 'At least I'm living my life how I want. At least I'm not just pretending to be something I'm not. You want to be like Amma and Baba so bad you cling to these ideals of what it means to be a good Muslim family, and you judge me for wanting something different. You act like you know best, like you're some alpha male. You're just a little boy pretending to be an adult. The first sign of trouble and you freak out. And this time there is no Amma or Baba to save you. And I'm done trying to help.

'You need to grow up. What kind of man are you? I'll tell you, it doesn't make you a man to throw your weight around. It doesn't make you a man to say, "I pay the rent, I pay the bills, what I say goes." You have always been self-absorbed, and you still are. You were blind to the sacrifices that Amma made for you, the things she did for you . . . that *I* did for you. You're blind to whatever might be going on in anyone else's life but your own. No wonder your own wife doesn't want to open up to you! She is really hurting, more than you know: about the miscarriage . . . everything . . . You wouldn't know that because you have never dared to ask her how *she* feels. As long as she makes you your dinner, keeps the house tidy and massages your ego, yeah?'

This last jab sent Imran reeling. What had Fahima told Sumaya? He hadn't known that she was still upset about losing their baby. It had been three years, after all. What else had Fahima kept from him? Of course she'd been upset at the time, but he'd thought she was over it. They had tried to get pregnant again; they were still trying, until the attack a few weeks ago. This was all news to him.

But in that moment, with his sister before him and the rage palpable between them, the animosity he felt towards Sumaya superseded everything else. He'd have to speak to Fahima later. Right now he just wanted to get Sumaya out of his house – and possibly out of his life.

'Tell me, then, what exactly is it you think you've done for me, Sumaya?' he asked, his tone dripping with sarcasm.

Sumaya remained silent, her brow furrowed in deep meditation.

He goaded her again. 'Come on, spit it out . . . Tell me! What could I possibly need *you* to do for me?'

'I . . . I . . .' Sumaya stammered. 'Look, forget it.'

'Just go back to New York, yeah. Stay out of our lives.'

'Oh, I'd be glad to,' Sumaya retorted, and because she couldn't help a final blow, she added: 'Amma should have let you ruin your life back then. Maybe you wouldn't be so unbearable now.'

'What did you say?' Imran seized on the mention of Amma. 'How was I ruining my life?'

Satisfaction crossed Sumaya's face – this last barb had done its trick; she had got firmly under his skin. 'I promised her I wouldn't say anything,' she said, knowing this added piece of mystery would only make him angrier.

'You're chatting shit,' Imran smarted. 'Amma wouldn't tell you anything she wouldn't tell me. I'm the oldest. She asked me to look after you all before she died.'

'Yeah, what a fucking great job you're doing!' Sumaya shot back. 'How is that working out for Bhabi? Let's not forget, you called me, and I came here to clean up your mess. Again.'

'Just get out!' he shouted.

'Fuck it,' she said. 'Maybe it's time you realised what a fuck-up you are – the fuck-up Amma, Baba and I have always known you to be. Do you remember my friend Sophie?'

Sudden recognition crossed Imran's face, as if he'd seen a ghost.

'My friend that you were secretly shagging. The one you told to keep quiet about it. To not tell me about the two of you. You got her pregnant, you idiot,' Sumaya screamed in her brother's face.

'She told me everything. She was shit-scared her mum would find out. I was fifteen – what the fuck did I know at the time? I had no idea what to tell her. I told Amma. She was so afraid that this would ruin your life, that Baba would find out and send you to Bangladesh. You were just about to start university. Amma took her to the hospital . . . can you imagine how she must have felt? Can you even begin to imagine how scared Sophie was? Amma made me promise to keep it a secret. She didn't want Baba to find out. She protected *you*.'

The weight of Sumaya's confession bore down so heavily on both of them that the room was rendered silent, as they were left too stunned to speak.

Until the sudden noise of the door swinging open startled them. Sumaya spotted her first, and then Imran. Fahima in the doorway, eyes wide, tears streaking her cheeks.

And Imran knew that she had heard everything.

Chapter 11

SULTANA

Sultana burned with shame. Where had she gone so wrong? It was a mother's job to teach her children right from wrong, to guide them down a righteous path. Not only had her son committed a sin, but her daughter was implicated in the whole sordid affair, too. Sumaya had been dragged into this mess, and Sultana wept for her daughter. She shouldn't have her innocence corrupted like this, because of something Imran had done. This would forever change the girl. Nothing she could do or say would erase what Sumaya knew, what she had confided in her. This was the stuff of the English television shows the children watched – how could something so unsavoury happen in her own home?

'Amma,' Sumaya had whispered, pulling her into the kitchen and closing the door behind her. 'I need to tell you something.'

The girl's tone was grave. Sultana was immediately unsettled. All manner of anxiety ran through her mind. What had Sumaya done? Had she stolen? Or had she got herself into trouble with a boy? Nothing could have prepared her for what her daughter then told her.

'I have a friend at school . . .' Sumaya struggled to get the words out. 'She . . .'

'Spit it out,' Sultana said, impatient.

Sumaya burst into tears. She could barely keep eye contact with her mother. This was unlike her daughter, Sultana thought. Her pulse began to race.

'Whatever it is,' Sultana said, taking the girl by the shoulders, 'please tell me. You're worrying me now, Sumaya.'

'It's Bhaiya,' the girl blurted out.

Sultana's face went blank. She had been certain that it was her daughter who was in trouble. She hadn't even considered that whatever news Sumaya desperately needed to share was about her son.

'He . . . my friend . . . Amma, she said she's pregnant . . .'

Sultana's face drained of all colour. She gripped the back of a kitchen chair to stop herself from falling, as her legs had become gelatinous. She clasped her hand over her mouth. Mother and daughter stood silently for what felt like an eternity. Sultana's mind went blank. It was as though she were stuck in stasis.

'Amma,' Sumaya said, shaking her mother. 'Say something . . .'

Sumaya's eyes bulged, panic written on her face. She had never seen her mother so despondent. Sumaya had turned to her, thinking she would have all the answers. The lifeless expression on Sultana's face now terrified her. Sumaya needed her to share this burden with her – to take it off her shoulders and carry it on her own. Isn't that what a mother did?

Sumaya shook her mother again. This time, she saw the cogs slowly turn in Sultana's mind, the life return to her eyes.

'Amma?' she said sheepishly.

Sultana saw the anguish in her daughter's eyes, and it seemed as if a switch flicked inside her. Her daughter needed her. Her son would need her, not that he'd know it. She wouldn't dare let him find out. She wouldn't let him jeopardise his future – because if Abdul found out, Imran's future would be over before it began. The thought of Abdul shipping her eldest child off to Bangladesh, a place he had never been, was unimaginable. So she steeled her mind. That could never happen.

'Okay,' Sultana told her daughter, suddenly springing into action. 'This is important, Sumaya. Have you told anyone?'

Sumaya saw the steel and resolve return to her mother's eyes and breathed a sigh of relief. 'No. Just you.'

'You mustn't tell anyone, Sumaya. Not your baba, not your brother, not any of your other friends . . . anyone. You mustn't tell a single soul. This must stay between us. Do I make myself clear?'

Sumaya nodded her assent.

'Who is this girl? Tell me exactly what she told you.'

Sumaya recounted the conversation she'd had at lunchtime in the school playground. Sophie had timidly asked if they could speak in private. Though Sophie was a year older than her, the girls had known each other since primary school and still hung out from time to time, when they weren't hanging out with girls in their own year. Everyone knew who Sophie was. She was one of the popular girls in school.

They'd stood out of view of the other pupils, behind one of the prefabs, which had been 'temporarily' erected while the English wing was refurbished but had now somehow become part of the landscape.

'I'm sorry,' Sophie blurted out before dissolving into a flood of tears.

Sumaya listened in disbelief, her body numb, frozen to the spot. She couldn't comprehend what she was hearing. Surely there must have been a mistake? Not her brother. It must have been someone else. But there was no mistake, Sophie told her.

Sumaya felt sorry for her friend. In her desperation Sophie had sought her out . . . a fifteen-year-old girl. What was she meant to do? Deep down, something else burned in the pit of Sumaya's stomach: her brother's betrayal. He knew that they were friends and had purposefully instructed Sophie to keep their relationship a secret from her. And now he had really messed things up. How could he do this? To her? Sophie was *her* friend. She felt a sting of betrayal from her friend, too. Part of her wanted to reach out and grab the girl by the hair. Scream at her. Call her a slag for her part in all this secrecy. For the trouble she threatened to bring to Sumaya's family's doorstep. But the hopelessness she saw in Sophie's eyes stopped her from raising a hand and causing a scene. Besides, this wasn't her fault. It was Imran's.

In an instant, she understood why Baba was so exasperated by Imran. She saw him not as her loving brother but as a careless, fickle man. Not even a man. A child. A child who had thought himself a man. But he was no more a man than the Action Man figures he had played with when they were children. Perhaps this was the moment her heart began to harden towards her brother, because for the first time she saw him not with the rose-tinted gaze of a younger sibling – as deific, preternatural. What she saw now was sheer treachery.

So Sumaya told her mother what Sophie had told her. Sophie couldn't risk her own mother finding out. Sophie's mother had had Sophie when she was young and raised her as a single parent. She'd be heartbroken to discover that her daughter had been caught in the same vicious cycle. Sophie had to get rid of the baby. The words made Sumaya's head spin as they tumbled out of Sophie's mouth. Made her stomach turn. What did she mean 'get rid of'? She had registered what Sophie was implying, but things like that were never spoken of in households like hers. A child was meant to be a blessing from Allah. What Sophie was asking her assistance with was unthinkable.

Sultana didn't move for some time after Sumaya told her about Sophie's plight. She was rooted to the spot, deep in contemplation. *Oh, what a stupid, stupid boy, Imran*, she thought. She wanted to weep – or worse, fling open the kitchen door, find the boy and give him a good slap across the face. What had he done? His dalliance with the girl was bad enough, but that she could just about over-look – he was just a boy. But it was everything else her daughter had told her that made her blood run cold.

She knew immediately what she might have to do. The moral and religious codes she might have to break.

But in her mind, there was never a question of *might*.

For her son, she would do anything.

◆ ◆ ◆

That night, Sultana tossed and turned, and grieved. She grieved the end of the age of innocence for her two older children. One had committed a sin and pulled the other one unknowingly into it, making his sister an accomplice. She grieved as well for her own part in the whole affair. She, too, had implored her daughter to conceal the truth from her father, to lock this secret away deep within, and thus made her complicit in Sultana's own shadowy machinations. *Allah, forgive me*, she prayed silently.

Next to her, Abdul snored into the night, none the wiser as to his wife and daughter's sudden immorality. Sultana feared more how her husband would react and what he might do to the boy than any sin she might commit on Imran's behalf. He couldn't and wouldn't know the truth; of this she was absolutely determined. She had always been told it was a man's job to protect and provide for his family. Now she realised through her own actions that a woman could bear all that a man could and more, because a woman needed guile as well as strength and fortitude. When pushed, when deter-mined, she was capable of being more ruthless than any man. And she could do all this without her husband knowing.

The next afternoon, Sultana met her daughter at the school gates. A thin, blonde girl in a school uniform matching Sumaya's straggled behind her. The girl didn't appear any different to the other English girls her children went to school with. Her translucent skin and grey eyes were as common as the dark hair and eyes that Sultana shared with the countless other Bangladeshi women in the area. To her eye, the girl looked positively plain. What wild ideas might she have given her son? What had she done to corrupt him? But even as she tried to cast blame on Sophie, she knew the timid girl before her was not to blame, and her glare thawed. Imran was more than capable of getting himself into trouble without anyone else's help. As his mother, she knew better than anyone how unsettled his spirit was. The girl before her was almost the same age as her own daughter, for goodness' sake. A baby still. She needed guidance. Someone she could trust. She needed her own mother, but Sumaya had told her how scared the girl was to tell her. Part of Sultana wrestled with the idea of calling Sophie's mother – she had a right to know, and she'd expect the same courtesy if it was Sumaya in Sophie's position. The other part feared that if she did call, it would complicate things even further. What if the girl ran away? It'd be her fault. The girl would be out there, all alone, with a baby in her belly and no one to turn to. After much praying, she decided to respect the girl's wishes. But if Sophie's mother couldn't find out, it was up to her to ensure this matter was taken care of. For both the girl and Imran.

'Amma, this is Sophie,' Sumaya said.

Sultana studied the white girl's pale features: her nose was slightly crooked, her teeth misaligned. Sophie's cheeks turned red as she shuffled her feet. Clearly the girl was as uncomfortable about this whole scenario as she was.

Sultana turned to her daughter and asked her to translate: 'Is it true?'

It burned her to again make her daughter complicit in her scheme – to have to rely on Sumaya to act as broker between her and Sophie – but it was the only way. Who else might Sultana ask for help, anyway? And the more people who knew, the harder this shame would be to contain. The Bangladeshi community in Bow was small. Gossiping men and women could sniff out the smallest kindling of scandal and ignite it into a bonfire. Her son would be branded one of those *gundas* that the other mothers would never want their daughters to marry. Overnight, the women in the supermarket would struggle to look her in the eye. The men would snigger behind Abdul's back at the mosque. Her family's entire reputation was at stake.

The girl said something in English to Sumaya and then nodded in her direction.

Next, Sultana asked through Sumaya, 'Are you sure you want to do this?'

Again, Sophie nodded, but this time she held her head low, not meeting Sultana's eye. *A mere child*, Sultana thought. This was all she needed to know. All that was needed to justify what came next.

Sultana had Sumaya take the girl's phone number and a few other details. In a week's time, they would be sitting on plastic chairs in a waiting room at Royal London Hospital in Whitechapel.

Sultana tried to keep her mind as blank and sterile as her surroundings; if she thought too much or too hard about why she was there, she would fall into a pit of despair. She had to stay steadfast; the girl had made her decision and, quietly, she was relieved. Once this was done, there would be no child to burden her son or hamper his prospects. He would be the first of her family and Abdul's to attend university. She reminded herself of the brighter future that she had gripped on to so tightly when she moved here all those years ago with Abdul. She wanted a better future for her children than they'd had. A child would impede his education. And he was but a child himself! He didn't know the sacrifice and selflessness it took be a parent. She had given up her own aspirations, her own individuality, for her children. She dreamed for them what was never possible for her. He would be a father one day, inshallah, but not now. The girl, too, deserved better than this; she was also a child. Her life was still ahead of her, and if and when she became a parent, it should be when she was ready. Sultana told herself whatever she needed to convince herself that this was just. Her son's future depended on it.

The wait seemed infinite, but once Sophie was seen to by the doctor, time passed at warp speed. She was given a pill, and another to take home. It all seemed so simple, this banishment of life. So impersonal. For just a moment, in a microsecond of weakened resolve, Sultana imagined the child inside the girl. Her grandchild. A flicker of grief as short as a passing thought.

The taxi dropped Sophie home first. The discomfort of her experience was evident on her face and tears streaked her cheeks. Before the girl got out, Sultana turned to Sumaya and had her relay her message to the girl.

'You were very brave today,' Sumaya repeated her mother's message. 'I'm sorry for what my son has put you through. Take care of yourself.'

Sultana tried to keep her expression neutral, but the sorrow written on the girl's face made her ache – as a mother, as a woman. Before she could comprehend what she was doing, Sultana extended her arms and enfolded the girl in a tight hug.

Sophie got out of the taxi, and mother and daughter rode the rest of the journey home. Sultana silently prayed for the girl and the child that might have been.

Chapter 12

Imran

Fahima had locked herself in the bathroom.

If Imran wasn't already spent from Sumaya's confession about Sophie and the abortion, the sheer look of betrayal on his wife's face when she entered the kitchen had zapped him of his remaining mental strength.

'Fahima,' he pleaded through the door. 'Please. Come out and talk to me. I'm sorry.'

No response but the sound of his wife's strained sobs from inside the locked room. Imran imagined how heavily the tears flowed, and thought how he had caused this and how he wished he could measure the weight of all the tears she had no doubt spilled recently and match it with gold, for his gentle, kind wife didn't deserve the burden of this cruel pain. But no amount of gold could erase what she had heard. He sat heavy-hearted in silence, his back to the bathroom door. He pictured her on the other side, her back also to the door, in perfect symmetry, and yearned to be able to communicate telepathically how sorry he was for what she had discovered.

Imran's mind raced, piecing together hazy memories of his adolescence – his life before Fahima. He'd only been seventeen, going on eighteen, when he started hooking up with Sophie. She was in Year 11 and he was in his second year of sixth form. Sumaya would have been fourteen or fifteen, in Year 10, at the time. It was nothing more than a bit of fun and experimentation, a youthful folly. He didn't even consider Sophie his girlfriend, and he certainly didn't have romantic feelings for her beyond the amorous physical need that coursed through any teenager's body.

Crude as it felt now, Sophie had been a means to an end; all his school friends were hooking up with girls, particularly the white girls, who tended to be more open to sexual experimentation than the Muslim girls. Sophie lived in a small flat near Bow Comprehensive with her mother, whom he had never met, and her grandfather. He vaguely remembered sneaking into the flat with Sophie after school while her mum was at work, carefully tiptoeing past the living room, where her grandfather was sitting in front of *Countdown*, and creeping into her bedroom. Sophie was his first. They were careful not to make too much noise or arouse her grandfather's suspicion. In that cramped little bedroom – a single bed pressed against the far wall, under the window – Imran earned his manhood.

He hadn't known what to expect when he received his first blowjob; it wasn't like the illegal porn he watched on mute in his bedroom, fearing Amma or Baba might catch him. Sophie was awkward and graceless, constantly stopping to get her blonde hair out of her face, unlike the professional porn stars who seemed to make it look so easy. It was in Sophie's bedroom that he fumbled to unhook his first bra. Where he had sex for the first time. It lasted less than two minutes – again, unlike the online films he watched. He'd expected groans of ecstasy, for Sophie to comment how big he was, but the sex was clumsy; it took him longer to fully insert himself than it did for him to finish. And when it was over, they were both coy, embarrassed by their gangly teen bodies.

They met up like this over and over again for the next few months, until suddenly Sophie stopped responding to his text messages. That was the end of the invitations to her house. He hadn't cared at the time, ambivalent to her feelings; there were plenty of other girls at school who'd love to shag him!

Now, he knew what had happened. It all started to make sense. Why Sophie had abruptly broken off their arrangement. Why Sumaya's attitude towards him had seemingly changed overnight. He'd stupidly put it down to teenage apathy at the time, but the resentment she harboured was so much more than that. *He* had caused it with his recklessness. *His* actions had turned her against him, had made his younger sister – who had once adored him – see him in a different light. It was him. It was all him.

His mind turned to Amma, and suddenly he couldn't bear the shame, willing himself to think of something else, anything else. But the image of her burned at the forefront of his brain. *Oh, Amma*, he thought. How could he have put her through such disgrace? The guilt stabbed at his heart like the point of a sharp knife. How could he have put her in such a situation? Sumaya, too?

His heart beat faster still as he contemplated the implications of Sumaya's revelation. His mother would have known he had sinned, that he'd had premarital sex, that he'd gone with a white girl. Yet she had never castigated him, and nor did her affection for him ever change, despite knowing what she knew. And then there was all that she'd had to compromise for him. Abortion was a sin. Amma had clearly bent her own beliefs on the matter to protect him. She must have been so desperate . . . He tried to blink away the tears, to not fall down the rabbit hole of what-ifs. His head was dizzy. He tried to stand up from his position in front of the bathroom, but he felt unsteady on his feet. Like the weight of it all might make him collapse into a heap on the floor. The walls were closing in on him, suffocating him.

He needed to get out of there.

He needed an escape.

◆ ◆ ◆

'Same as last time?' asked the bartender, a stout woman with translucent skin, shoulder-length brown hair and glasses. He liked that she didn't attempt to make conversation, like the chatty bartenders he saw on television. And what would he even say? What would he even have in common with this woman whose only purpose in life seemed to be to stand behind a pub counter, subservient to the needs of craven men like him, all trying to find solutions at the bottom of a glass?

Imran nodded, taking a stool at the bar and blending into the scenery, becoming just another inconspicuous shadow in the gloom of the bar.

As he looked down into the brown liquor, Imran knew he had reached rock bottom. He knew he shouldn't have left Fahima alone, sobbing in the bathroom, but it had all been too much. It had felt as if the very walls of the house were judging him, the ghostly echoes of Amma and Baba castigating him for what a mess he'd made of his life. He'd had to get out of there. He'd craved release. Some temporary solution to dull his mind.

Now, however, as he sipped the earthy whisky, it burned as it went down. He shouldn't be here. What would Fahima say if she could see him now, drowning his sorrows in a pub? He was jeopardising what little he imagined was left of his marriage by drinking his problems away. But with each sip, the edges of his shame began to soften, and though he hated himself for it, it felt good to dull the pain.

Imran felt a tap on his shoulder, jolting him as he put his glass down. He turned around, surprise clearly written all over his face.

His friend Hakeem looked back at him with what must have been an identical expression of shock.

'Imran?' Hakeem asked. 'Brother, what are you doing here?'

Imran suddenly felt alert. The effects of the whisky seemed to dissipate, overpowered by the shame he felt at being seen here. 'I . . . er . . .'

The two men looked at each other silently.

'What are *you* doing here?' Imran said eventually.

'I'm just with a couple of clients,' Hakeem said, pointing to a pair of white men in suits at a table on the other side of the bar. 'We just closed another deal. Can you believe it? Another investor, mashallah! They wanted to celebrate. I said this isn't really my scene, but they insisted. You know how it is . . . the drinking culture.'

Imran tried to steady his thoughts, but his cheeks flushed red at the sight of his old friend. He wiped his sweaty palms on his jeans.

'Brother, are you okay?' Hakeem asked, placing an arm around his shoulders. 'You don't seem too well . . .'

Imran winced. 'Look . . . just, please don't tell anyone I was here,' he said, shuffling off the barstool and past Hakeem, towards the exit.

'Wait,' Hakeem said, holding him by the arm. He looked down at the empty whisky glass on the bar. 'Brother, this isn't like you. I've never seen or heard you talk about drinking before. What's going on?'

Imran tried to maintain his composure, but at his friend's compassion, a dam within him broke. Tears streamed down his face.

'I've really fucked up, brother,' he said, his voice cracking.

Hakeem pulled Imran closer to him, wrapping his arms around him. 'It's okay . . .'

In the embrace of his friend, Imran wished he could just disappear. That he could make everything go away. The problems at work, his troubles with Fahima, and now all that had been unearthed today. He had got Sophie pregnant. His mother and sister had gone to such lengths to protect him.

'Listen, wait for me outside. I'll say goodbye to my clients, and we can chat, okay?' Hakeem said.

Imran gave Hakeem a childlike nod and followed his friend's instructions, suddenly depleted from the emotions of the day.

After a few minutes, Hakeem joined him outside and they sat on a nearby bench, watching traffic pass, people getting on and off buses, and the occasional tracksuited teenager whiz by on a bike blaring loud music.

'Brother, I want you to know, I don't judge,' Hakeem said. 'Whatever brought you here . . . you don't seem yourself. I just had to make sure you're okay.'

Imran shut his eyes, trying to deflect his friend's kindness. He didn't deserve it. He had sinned and forsaken his family. He didn't deserve sympathy. He wanted to tell Hakeem not to waste it on him. To leave him here. Alone. That's what he deserved.

'You can tell me anything you want to. It'll stay between us,' Hakeem said, resting a hand on Imran's shoulder.

Something about Hakeem's gentle demeanour compelled him to speak. To unburden his heart. 'I don't know where to start . . .' he said, taking in a deep breath and sharing the truth of his troubles. Fahima's attack, the miscarriage they had experienced before, and how he had felt powerless both times to support his wife. How he didn't feel like a man at all. Why couldn't he do or say the right things? Then he told his friend about what had happened in the past, the painful secret his mother and sister had kept, and the shame he had brought on them. All of this was taking its toll, he said. He was getting into trouble at work, and he'd even been taken off Hakeem's account.

'Bro, do you want me to do something? I can call your boss,' Hakeem offered.

'No.' Imran shook his head. 'Please. It's my problem to solve. I don't want to get you involved in all of the office politics.'

'It's always politics, though, ain't it?' Hakeem replied. 'Listen, if you need my help at all, I'm here. Just call me. I brought my business to your company because you're one of the smartest brothers I know. I trust you, bro.'

'Thanks,' Imran said sheepishly. Hakeem's stamp of approval meant a lot to him, even if he felt unworthy of it right now. 'I appreciate it, man.'

'I mean it,' Hakeem said. 'You're one of the realest people here. You've always been good to me, and here, in these parts, it's rare that people like us get to thrive. The other boys from these parts got into drugs or dodgy scams . . . but you've worked hard to make a name for yourself. And you've got a beautiful family. It's inspiring, bro.'

Imran scoffed. How could Hakeem hear all that he had unloaded and describe him as 'inspiring'? 'I don't know about that, man.'

'Look, man. I remember how happy you looked on your wedding day,' Hakeem said. 'That's real right there. That's love. Do you know how many brothers wish they had that? It isn't easy to find. I wish *I* had that. Finding someone you can just vibe with, that you can't live without . . . it's one in a million. You and Fahima have always had that. I've always been envious of you two, to be honest.'

Imran furrowed his brow, surprised by his friend's admission.

'I'm spitting facts, bro,' Hakeem said. 'You two are meant to be together. That's why I know – and trust me when I say this – that there's nothing you can't overcome. You're Imran and Fahima. You're our hope, man. Go home and show your wife you love her. That's where you should be. Not here.'

Imran felt a spark ignite within him. He had never seen his marriage through others' eyes before, but Hakeem was right. He and Fahima were meant to be. Their love had felt fated from the day he met her, and no matter what happened, she'd be the only one in his heart. Even if she rejected him.

Imran suddenly felt the need to go home, to return to his wife and fight for his marriage. He hastily thanked Hakeem and said his goodbyes before rushing in the direction of home, half walking and half running.

On the way, he spotted the Co-op. Still running on adrenaline, he dashed inside and picked up the first bunch of flowers by the entrance. It was a meagre gesture by any estimation, he realised, but it was the best he could do given the lack of shops on the route home.

He envisaged returning home with the bouquet of flowers and pleading with Fahima to hear him out. He wouldn't take no for an answer, even if he had to stay up all night, talking through the bathroom door. He would beg on his knees for her forgiveness, concede that he had been a useless husband, and convince her with every fibre within him that he would change. Sumaya was right: he had tried to magic away his problems, and had called on his sister to fix what was his to mend. *No more*, he told himself. *From this day on, I will be better.*

He expected there to be tears. His own as well as Fahima's. Imran didn't cry easily. He'd grown up believing it wasn't masculine to cry. Tears were unmanly, a sign of weakness. But life had brought him to his lowest ebb already, and now, confronted with the choice between facing up to the consequences of his actions or losing his wife, he realised that there was no more truth in that macho bull-shit than there was in a fad diet. What use was a man who couldn't give his wife what she needed, emotionally as well as physically? Fahima needed the emotional comfort that only her husband could provide. Why had he closed himself off for so long? Why couldn't he allow himself to be more vulnerable with the one person who showed him kindness unconditionally?

Imran thought of Amma and Baba. The gut-aching pain of losing his parents. And then his unborn child. It had been better to block the pain than truly feel it. At first, it had been a coping mechanism to get through the trauma, but somewhere along the way, he realised, it became no longer a temporary solution but a dependency. He moved through the world with ice in his veins, unable to reciprocate even his wife's empathy. What had he done? He was determined to make it right.

Imran arrived home and threw open the door. He rushed inside to find his wife.

But it was too late.

I can't do this anymore, the note on the kitchen table read. She was gone.

The shock took a few minutes to register. Imran bounded from room to room, up the stairs and down again, expecting to find Fahima curled up in their bed, or where he had left her in the bathroom. He willed the note to be fake. But it was unmistakably his wife's handwriting. In their bedroom, he noticed a drawer in the white chest was half-open, items of clothing missing, underwear and socks. She must have hastily packed her things and left. The realisation came as a cold shock to his nervous system.

She had left him.

Chapter 13

Sumaya

Sumaya had spent the last hour tossing and turning, trying to make herself comfortable, but to no avail. Lying on the single box-spring, with its thin mattress and pointy, sharp coils, was not how she had imagined spending a night in her thirties. She could have stayed in a hotel, but Majid had insisted she take his roommate's bed while Andrew was with his parents in Aberdeen for reading week. Andrew's scratchy bed had seemed the best of the potential sleeping arrangements in Majid's student flat – the alternative was to sleep in her little brother's room, on a mattress on the floor.

'It's better for your back,' he had said when she asked why he didn't have a bed. 'Anyway, I'm on a student budget, innit. Who needs a bed when you can buy booze?'

Grime and dirt caked the skirting boards in Majid and Andrew's flat, dishes had been left abandoned in the sink, and she was initially too squeamish to even use the toilet, fearing she'd step into a puddle of Majid or Andrew's piss – or even worse, a combination of both. The toilet, however, was surprisingly clean – perhaps cleaner than the kitchen – the bowl pristine and white, and the toilet seat unscathed by urine. Still, she refused to touch the seat without a piece of toilet tissue acting as a barrier between her fingertips and the porcelain. There was a time when she'd regretted missing out on the student flatshare experience in her own university days – she had lived at home to take care of Amma – but now she was glad she hadn't had to live in a poorly insulated flat with peeling wallpaper and a perennially leaky tap in the bathroom.

It wasn't just the bed that prevented Sumaya from falling asleep. She also kept picturing Fahima's face earlier, at the house – the combination of confusion, hurt and betrayal when she'd walked in on her and Imran arguing in the kitchen. The last thing she'd wanted was to add to her sister-in-law's pain, to cause her more grief and sadness. She had been impulsive. How could she have been so foolish as to drop the bomb about Imran's past after all this time – after she had promised Amma that she would never say anything? And especially at that particular moment, with Fahima in earshot. She couldn't have known Fahima was just outside the kitchen door listening in, but she shouldn't have been so reckless. In one fell swoop she had betrayed Amma and hurt Fahima, and now she was paying penance, wracked by her own guilt. But standing there in her brother's smug presence, going back and forth as they had, had unleashed the entirety of the contempt that had built up for him over the years. And if she were truly honest with herself, she'd felt some perverse satisfaction in finally revealing the truth and watching the colour drain from Imran's face. So why didn't she feel more victorious?

Haunted by the vision of her sister-in-law, Sumaya gave up on trying to sleep, pulled on a hoodie that she assumed belonged to Andrew, and walked out of her room into the living area. It was only midnight. She spotted a glare of light from the small balcony and made out her brother's figure. As she reached for the door and opened it, she caught Majid in a panic, trying to hide something – and then she caught the unmistakable whiff of weed in the air.

'Relax,' she said, stepping on to the wooden slats of the balcony, barely enough space for them both to stand. 'I'm not here to arrest you.'

'Don't tell Bhaiya, yeah?' Majid pleaded. 'It just calms me down . . .'

'You don't need to explain yourself to me, Maj,' Sumaya replied. 'You're an adult, you can do what you want. It's only weed.'

'Try telling that to Bhaiya. If he found out he'd freak the fuck out. As if I'd farted in mosque or something.'

Sumaya let out a laugh. 'Let me tell you, Maj, our brother isn't so squeaky-clean himself. I wouldn't worry about it.'

Sumaya motioned to her younger brother to pass her the spliff. Majid's eyes grew wide in surprise.

'Okay, sis, I see you,' he said, passing the joint. 'I didn't have you down as a pothead.'

'There's a lot you don't know, Maj,' Sumaya said, before taking a deep inhale. Her head was suddenly cloudy, all thoughts of Fahima and Imran pushed out, just a haze of nothingness. She exhaled the smoke, coughing a little as it passed from her lips.

'Ah, lightweight,' Majid teased her.

'Please!' Sumaya retorted. 'Back in the day I would've smoked you under the table,' she said, passing the blunt back to Majid.

'Damn, sis, who knew you were so cool?'

'Hey, listen,' Sumaya shifted to face Majid, her tone more serious. 'I'm really sorry I haven't been around for you these last few years, Maj. I don't blame you if you feel like I abandoned you.'

'Look at me.' Majid jokingly puffed his chest out. 'Do I look abandoned? Nah, it's cool, sis. You had to do what you had to do. We only have one life, innit.'

Yes, Sumaya thought, that was exactly how she felt about her move to New York – *we do only have one life*. To hear it put so succinctly by her younger brother caught her by surprise. She inspected him more closely; he had the same eyes and jawline as Imran, the same hair texture – though Majid's was unkempt and longer – and the same nose. Majid was the spitting image of Imran when he was that age, and yet her two brothers couldn't be less alike in personality. If anyone should have felt abandoned by her swift departure after Amma died, it was Majid; he was just a kid when she left and had been so reliant on her in Amma's absence. She had taken him to school, helped him with his homework, and given him money out of her own pocket to go to the cinema with his friends so he could feel like all the other kids his age – not just the boy whose mother got sick when he was seven and couldn't look after him. And yet, Majid didn't begrudge her decision at all, unlike her older brother.

'I wish Bhai saw it that way,' she confided.

'Man,' Majid said, exhaling smoke into the night air. 'He's the one that could *really* use a zoot. Man is so uptight, always on my case about my studies, about whether I'm getting good grades in my modules and shit.'

'It's because he cares.' The words poured out of Sumaya's mouth instinctively, without thought. How strange it felt to come to her brother's defence after all that had passed between them, not least today. But her younger brother needn't be dragged into their feud, and so she was glad that her reflexes had filtered her personal disdain for Imran.

'He wants you to be successful,' she continued. 'I get it. Amma and Baba aren't here and he feels responsible for your future. I'm not saying I agree with him being overbearing, but he just wants the best for you.'

The words felt unusual in Sumaya's mouth, like gargling a mouthful of marbles. This afternoon she and Imran had hurled insults at each other, tried to hurt each other, and now she was talking him up.

Sumaya was light-headed. Perhaps it was the weed, but she suddenly felt like she was having an out-of-body experience. Nothing about this trip to London was going as she expected – Imran, Neha, and even now, looking at Majid, seven years older than when she'd left, physically a man, if not totally matured mentally. Returning home was like stepping out of a time machine – confronted by all the faces of her past – only to realise she'd ended up in an alternative timeline.

She tried to shrug off the feeling. 'It's getting cold. Let's go inside.'

◆ ◆ ◆

'Now, I know there's gotta be some booze in here somewhere,' Sumaya said to her brother with a smirk and a raised eyebrow as they stepped back into the flat.

Majid feigned shock. 'Who do you think I am?' And then, assuming a stereotypical Asian accent, he added: 'I am a good Muslim boy, sister.'

Sumaya playfully hit him on the arm.

'Okay, fine . . . I've got some gin in my room. I have to keep it away from Andrew because once he gets started . . .' Majid conceded, walking towards his bedroom. 'Get some glasses. Tonic's in the fridge.'

Sumaya walked over to the kitchen, trying not to look at the pile of unwashed dishes in the sink for fear that something might be moving among them. She opened various cupboards looking for glasses until she reached the right one, taking out two highballs. As she tried to close it again, the doorknob came off in her hand . . .

'Er, Majid,' she called. He re-emerged with a bottle of Bombay Sapphire. She showed him the doorknob resting in the centre of her palm.

'Oh, yeah,' he said nonchalantly. 'Been meaning to get that fixed.'

'For how long?' she teased him.

'Oh, let's see . . . it's nearly the end of my third year, so . . . the beginning of second year?'

Sumaya cackled, not only at the absurdity of her younger brother's living conditions, but also at his quick-witted humour. She'd had no idea Majid was so funny. Watching him grow up, grow into his own, was one of the things she'd had to give up to pursue her own dreams. She hadn't realised just how much she'd missed in her time away. She'd barely spent any time at all with Majid when she was last here, for Baba's funeral – she had cut her trip short after that fraught encounter with Imran. But she felt at ease in Majid's presence, and enjoyed his company.

'Do you think I could stick around for a few days?' she asked him. 'I was going to go back to New York . . . but I've already got the time off. I thought maybe we could hang out?'

'Yeah, calm, sis,' Majid replied. 'Just maybe not tomorrow night, yeah? One of my peng tings is coming to link up, you know what I'm saying?'

Again, she laughed uproariously. 'Oh, and how many of those have you got then?'

'I got a few links . . . what can I say? The Majid magic is irresistible.'

'Oh my . . . oh my god. I hope you don't actually say that to women,' Sumaya teased him as she poured the gin into the highball glasses, measuring the quantity by eye. She knew there was no point asking Majid if he had a jigger.

They walked over to the sofa, which Sumaya assumed had once been cream-coloured but had become discoloured and brownish over time.

'You know what . . . I'll just sit on the floor,' she said, sliding into the space between the sofa and the brown coffee table.

Majid joined her, and they sat side by side, resting their backs against the edge of the sofa.

'How's New York, anyway?' Majid asked. 'I see you been meeting bare celebrities!'

'I love it,' Sumaya said. 'I have a good job, friends, Jonathan . . . I've made a life there, you know?'

'Are you happy?' Majid asked.

Sumaya was taken aback. The question consisted of three simple words and yet it felt so deeply personal – and so perceptive of her younger brother to ask. Had he read something in her answer that made him think she wasn't happy? Or was it something she gave away with her facial expressions or body language? She was unexpectedly self-conscious about what her brother may have intuited. Her mind turned back to the way she'd left things in New York – Jonathan's proposal. Why had it felt more like an ultimatum? It was as though suddenly she had blinked and five years had passed, and while she was wondering where the time had gone, he had experienced the same time at half the speed. How else could she explain why they were on such different pages?

She returned to reality, in Majid's living room. 'Yeah, I am happy . . .' she said, and then, sensing that Majid might be able to see through her hesitation, she added: 'I think I'm just surprised by how quickly time has gone. There's something about my life there . . . it's so fast-paced, there's always something to do, someone to see, and I guess I still feel like the same girl who just landed in New York. And now, coming here, I'm realising that it's all gone by so quickly.'

'I feel you, sis,' Majid replied. 'It's like uni, innit? You're stuck in this perpetual student life – and then, bam, you're out of it and it's like, what happened? That's how I feel, anyway. It's gonna be hard when I graduate.'

Sumaya was again surprised by her younger brother's perceptiveness – that *was* what it felt like. Like the last eight years in New York had been one long university experience that she'd never had, and now she felt like she'd been thrust back into reality.

'Jonathan wants to marry me,' she blurted out, taking a long sip of gin and tonic.

'That's great!' Majid said. 'You can make some mixed brown-and-white babies!'

'You don't think I should be with someone Bengali, then?' she added, stopping short of adding what she was thinking: *like Imran.*

'Nah,' he said. 'Who cares? It's the twenty-first century! Everyone is in mixed-race relationships now. It isn't like it used to be.'

'Yeah, you're right. I guess I'm not so much worried about that, but more about if I even *want* to get married right now,' she confessed. 'I feel like I went to New York to be free of all that – the weddings, the biodata, the arranged shit.'

'Don't even get me started, bro!' Majid said animatedly. 'Your boy Imran is already on my case about getting married . . .'

'Don't call him Imran. That's disrespectful. He's your bhaiya,' Sumaya said, for the second time tonight coming to her older brother's defence by instinct. 'And that sounds about right. If he can't marry me off, he'll have turned to you . . .'

'Innit, though. Take one for the team, sis – give him his wedding,' Majid joked. 'But seriously, I'm only twenty-one. I'm just about to finish university . . . it's too soon. There's so much I wanna do, so much I wanna see before I get married and settle down and pop out kids. You get what I'm saying?'

And Sumaya *did* get it, because she felt similarly. There was more for her to explore and experience in life before committing to marriage and children. But she was also self-conscious about sharing her brother's wavelength – after all, she was ten years older than him, and while seeing the world and sowing your oats might be acceptable at twenty-one, she worried that, at thirty-one, this was the time she *should* be looking to settle down. So why was she so adamant on running the other way? She couldn't help but feel that she was anomalous compared to other women her age. Especially ones from her cultural and religious background. Was there something wrong with her?

'Besides,' Majid interrupted her train of thought, 'I'm not ready to commit right now. I'm still discovering what I like . . . Why limit yourself when you don't have to? I want to experience as much as I can . . . as many *people* as I can . . .'

Sumaya felt the hairs on the back of her neck prick up. The conversation had taken a turn, but she wasn't sure if she was understanding the implication of Majid's words properly.

'Are you saying you like girls . . . and boys . . . ?' Sumaya hesitated, fearing that her own secret, the one that Amma had made her so fearful of sharing with her family, might itself be exposed.

'Yeah,' Majid said nonchalantly. 'Well, I don't know, actually. I'm just fluid, innit? It's more about the person and the vibe than their gender.'

Sumaya took a swift sip of gin and tonic, contemplating what her brother had just told her. It had seemed so easy out of his mouth. He made it sound so simple: he did whatever his heart told him. Perhaps it was a generational thing? People Majid's age were much more open and free in expressing their sexuality. She had always known she was attracted to men and women, but her generation was different. There'd been more stigma around being gay or bisexual while she was growing up, especially in their close-knit Muslim community. Amma had frightened her into keeping her sexuality a secret, and said that people in their community wouldn't understand. She felt envious of Majid.

Conscious that she hadn't said anything for a while, Sumaya cleared her throat. 'Maj, that's great,' she said. 'You should be with whoever you want to be with.'

'Thanks, sis,' her brother replied. 'It's the twenty-first century, innit? It shouldn't be such a big deal anymore.'

Sumaya simply nodded, but her guilt spread through her. Majid was so open about his fluidity, and the more she stayed silent about her own sexual orientation, the more she felt like she was lying to her brother.

'Majid,' she said hesitantly. 'I understand . . . what it's like to be different too . . .'

The words felt strange leaving her lips. The secret she'd kept hidden from her family for years. She glanced uncertainly at Majid, wondering how her own revelation would land.

'What do you mean?' he said.

Sumaya looked down into her glass, all of a sudden unable to look him in the eye as she said the words. 'I'm bi, Maj,' she said, without looking up. A strange relief came over her, but so too did a feeling of dread. She had spoken it out loud. She had broken her promise to Amma.

Sumaya felt an arm around her shoulders. Majid squeezed her tightly.

'It's cool, sis,' he said. 'Like I said, it shouldn't be a big deal anymore. You don't have to hide it with me.'

Sumaya flushed with relief. She looked up at her brother at last. The warmth in his eyes told her she didn't have to be afraid.

She flung her arms around her little brother and held him tight.

'I . . . I never told anyone, except . . . Amma,' she said softly. 'She thought Baba and Bhaiya wouldn't understand, that they'd . . .

I don't know, disown me or something. I know she was just trying to look out for me, but . . .'

'Shit,' Majid said, sensing the heavy burden Sumaya's secret had been to carry. 'I'm sorry, sis. That's some bullshit. I guess she was scared? It was a different time; there weren't many people like us, out and proud. Look, I'm not saying we live in some utopia, that everything is amazing now, but there are more and more people who, like us, who are visibly out, there are more communities for brown queer people to be themselves. You don't have to think you're alone anymore, sis.'

Majid hugged his sister again. And then he said: 'Don't just take my word for it, sis. I think you should meet my friends.'

Chapter 14

Imran

Imran was already on edge when he arrived at work the next day. He had barely slept the night before, worrying about Fahima, and there was still radio silence from his wife this morning.

Amma had told him once, when he was a young boy, that there was a moment and a time for everything. She had meant it to be reassuring, a balm to soothe the ache of him not being picked for the school football team. But now, as Imran thought about what wisdom she might offer him, and as he pored over his memories for some comfort, the words felt hollow. *What now, Amma?* he asked himself derisively. Last night had been the time. He had finally come to his senses. He had come home humbled. He had been ready to profess his love for Fahima and throw himself at her feet, to beg for mercy. But he had missed his moment.

The previous night, Imran had sat for a long time on the bottom step of the stairs, his eyes locked on the front door, willing it to open. For Fahima to return to him. But deep down, he knew that he wouldn't be so lucky. He had tried to call her but all his calls went to voicemail. She must have turned her phone off – or worse, blocked his number. Perhaps he was reaping what he had sowed, he had thought, his head leaning against the white banister, the paint peeling off to reveal flecks of brown wood. He had pushed away everyone who loved him: Sumaya couldn't stand to spend even two days in his company; Majid avoided his calls, and when he begrudgingly took them he seemed antsy and eager to get off the phone as quickly as possible; and now, Fahima, too, he had driven away. The last good thing remaining in his life.

Before resigning himself to bed, weary from the high emotions of the day, he had made one last attempt to call his wife. He had prayed silently that she'd pick up this time. If he could just hear her voice and know that she was okay . . .

'The number you are trying to reach . . .' the voicemail had begun. Imran had clicked off the call.

Now it was a new day, and Fahima had still made no attempt to call or text him back. He'd tried to ring her again when he woke up but got the same response as last night – an automated voicemail message.

Imran entered the office already jittery, but when he saw the rigid expression on Shelly's face, his stomach turned. Shelly nodded to the kitchenette, and so Imran hastily put his bag and coat down at his desk, avoiding eye contact with Joe and Martin – who smirked at him gleefully, like cats toying with a mouse. The atmosphere in the office told him that things were not going to be any easier today.

'Shit, Imran,' Shelly said, shutting the kitchenette door behind them. 'Where were you yesterday? Giles is going spare . . .'

It only then dawned on Imran that he'd missed work the previous day, so wrapped up was he in everything around him crumbling. Shit, he thought. Of course Giles would blow a gasket. His boss was already pissed off with him about the Dagenham and Barking account, and he'd only made things worse by storming out of the office the day before yesterday.

'He blew his top when you didn't turn up,' Shelly confided. 'Listen, I'm only telling you this because you're my mate. He was banging on about firing you. Call me selfish, but I don't wanna lose my only mate here and get stuck with Tweedledum and Tweedledee out there,' she said, pointing towards the office. 'I know this place can be shit, especially for you, but you've got to try to smooth things over with Giles. Today. Just tell him what he wants to hear, you know? I said to him, "Maybe he's just sick," and he wasn't having it.'

Imran could feel the urgency in his friend's voice. Shelly didn't mince her words. And though she wasn't part of the boys' club in the Celeritas office either, the other men in the office didn't dare try to treat to her the way they treated him. Her family was old East End, and Imran had heard there was some familial connection to the Kray brothers. Like him, she'd come from working-class roots and had to work hard to get out from the shadow of her past. Unlike him, however, she wasn't brown and therefore foreign to Giles, Martin and Joe. The possible affiliation to East London's criminal underground didn't hurt either.

'Shit,' was all Imran could say.

'Mate, I know it's shit,' Shelly said. 'But we've got to pay the bills, right? You've just got to suck it up till we get out of here.'

Shelly was right. Though he was still smarting from losing the Greenr account and wanted to tell his boss exactly what he thought, the last thing he needed right now was to lose his job on top of everything at home. He couldn't afford to either, because then he'd have no income whatsoever. And that was worse than losing the extra commission. He'd have to swallow his pride and apologise to Giles.

'Thanks, Shelly,' he said. 'I appreciate you looking out for me.'

'We've got to look out for each other,' Shelly said, giving him a gentle tap on the shoulder. 'Or we'll be overrun by those numpties.'

When Giles came into the office, Imran tried his best to put on his finest show of contrition, to apologise for storming out of the office the day before last and for not coming in yesterday. 'I'm sorry for the way I left,' he told his boss. 'It wasn't right or professional. I have no excuses,' he said, holding his hands up.

'That's a warning, son,' Giles said, his eyes narrowed. 'Any more stunts like that and that's it.'

Imran gritted his teeth and accepted Giles's admonishment. It wouldn't serve him well to rock the boat now. 'I'm sorry,' he said, head bowed, though it pained him to kowtow to Giles. Joe and Martin had called in sick with hangovers and had never had so much as a slap on the wrist.

Besides, he had more important things to think about.

After work, Imran drove straight to Maida Vale, to Fahima's parents' home. That was where she must be, he'd deduced. Imran's relationship with his in-laws was strained at best. But as Hakeem had said the night before, he and Fahima were meant for each other, and if that meant withstanding her parents for a few minutes, so be it.

Fahima loved Shah Rukh Khan's movies. She had grown up fawning over the Bollywood heartthrob, and so had insisted that 'Bole Chudiyan' – from her favourite Shah Rukh movie, *Kabhi Khushi Kabhie Gham* – was played at their wedding. She loved how Shah Rukh made bold declarations of love, spilling the entire contents of his heart to his love interest. Imran would do the same. He'd turn up at Fahima's parents' house and insist she hear him out; he'd tell her everything that was in his heart. He'd beg for her forgiveness until she returned to him.

On the way to Maida Vale, he picked up new flowers from Marks and Spencer. Fahima was worth more than the Co-op, he determined. She deserved the best.

Imran psyched himself up as he drove. He couldn't afford to fuck this up; he had to win her back. *Tell her you're sorry*, he told himself. *Beg on your knees, if you have to.*

Imran rang the doorbell, tail tucked between his legs, hoping that Fahima would answer, but it wasn't his wife who unlocked the door, it was his mother-in-law, disapproval written all over her face.

'Imran,' Bisha said sternly.

Imran panicked at his mother-in-law's terse greeting; what had Fahima told her? What did she know about his past transgressions?

'Amma, are you okay?' he said sheepishly. 'I've come to see Fahima,' he added, not letting his mother-in-law know that he was simply acting on a hunch. That he didn't actually know if she was here.

'Yes,' Bisha said, still taciturn. 'She said you'd be coming.'

Imran wasn't sure if Fahima's mother was just trying to save him from his own embarrassment, if this was some small act of mercy to a man already on his knees – which felt unlikely – or if Fahima really had assumed he would turn up at some point. He wished for the latter, because that meant all was not lost.

'Is she upstairs?' he asked, shuffling past his mother-in-law and into the home his wife had grown up in. 'Thank you for letting her stay last night. I had to work,' he said, lying both to himself and to Bisha. 'We'll get going now.'

The shame of his lies felt as obvious as the crevices on his moth-er-in-law's elderly face, but still he kept up the facade.

Imran raced up the stairs to what had once been Fahima's bed-room; the only time he'd stayed here with her was the week after they were married, when they had visited her parents for a few days as per traditional Bengali custom. Even then, fresh from the

129

wedding, Bisha and Junan had struggled with his presence. Imran knew he wasn't the son-in-law they had expected, nor what they had wished for their daughter. They had been perfectly pleasant, of course, welcoming him with nightly feasts of slow-cooked curries, and fresh langoustines grilled over low heat with lemon and chilli. But Imran had felt the frostiness in their welcome – the way they dismissed his stories about his work with a disinterested flick of the head. He didn't fit their world and he never would, they told him implicitly. After that, Imran had preferred to let Fahima go to stay with her parents by herself, convincing her that he wanted her to enjoy her family time without him. If only he'd been more honest, he thought – more open about how he felt about her parents, and everything else besides – there wouldn't be such an emotional chasm between them.

But he was determined to fix that now. Fahima's door was closed. He knocked gently.

'Fahima, it's me,' he said.

He tried to twist the doorknob but the door was locked.

'Fahima, can you let me in, jaan?' he asked.

Imran could hear the rustle of footsteps on the other side of the door, but Fahima made no attempt to unlock the door.

'I just want to talk . . .' he said. 'Please, jaan.'

Even to his own ears, his pleading tone sounded childlike, desperate, but he didn't care.

The creak of a floorboard on the stairs. Of course Bisha was eavesdropping, he thought.

'Fahima,' he said again through the keyhole, quieter, conscious of his mother-in-law's lurking presence in the stairwell. 'I got you some flowers.'

Suddenly, he felt the lock click and the door spring open. Fahima stood before him in a purple dressing gown; even with no make-up, and the sallow complexion her face had taken on since the attack, he was awed by his wife's beauty.

He timidly held out the flowers to her. His wife's eyes darted from him to the bouquet in his hand, and back again. A moment of relief washed over him, and a smile began to form on his face. Perhaps this would work, he thought. But, wait. No. Fahima took the flowers out of his hand and threw them on the floor before him.

'Seriously? Flowers? You think I want flowers?' she huffed, slamming the door shut in his face.

The barely formed crescent of a smile did a 180; suddenly, he was like a child whose ice cream cone has fallen out of their hand. He stood there shocked, speechless, looking down at the expensive bouquet, errant petals strewn over Bisha and Junan's cream-coloured carpet.

He slumped on the spot, his back against the bedroom door, much as he had the night before at home when Fahima had locked herself in the bathroom. The discarded bouquet was beside him. A pathetic sight by any measure, he thought. What now? All he had wanted to do was to speak to her, to pour his heart out, like he'd seen so many times in the Shah Rukh movies they watched together.

Imran bolted upright, reaching into the pocket of his jeans for his phone. An idea had suddenly struck him.

He took out the phone and opened Spotify. If his mere presence couldn't capture Fahima's attention, maybe this would.

Imran played 'Bole Chudiyan' on loudspeaker, sliding his phone into Fahima's bedroom through the sliver of space at the bottom of the door. Sure, his mother-in-law was probably listening in and thought he was insane, but he didn't care now. He just wanted to get through to his wife.

He rested his head against the door, the muffled sounds of their wedding song playing through the gap, hoping it would stir Fahima, make her open the door and hear him.

The opening chords transported him back to that day. Their family and friends united all around them, the way he'd been unable to suppress his smile, feeling as if he'd won the lottery. If it could take him back to that moment, surely it would take her back, too.

'Fahima,' he said gently through the keyhole. 'It's our song . . .'

Again there was rustling on the other side and then the door unlocked. Imran quickly jumped to his feet, again filled with hope that perhaps he'd finally got through to her. Fahima opened the door with his phone in her hand.

She thrust it into his chest. 'Leave me alone and go home, Imran,' she said sternly, before shutting the door and locking it again.

Imran stood motionless in front of his wife's locked door, the tinny sound of 'Bole Chudiyan' reverberating from his phone.

This wasn't how things were supposed to go. This wasn't how it happened in the movies.

What would Shah Rukh do?

Chapter 15

SUMAYA

Sumaya woke the next day feeling lighter. She had slept soundly for the first time since landing in London, and that was no easy feat in Andrew's scratchy bedsheets. Opening up to Majid the previous night had felt natural, and the burden she had carried alone for so long had begun to lift, if only a little.

Sumaya checked her phone to find a message from Neha responding to her Instagram DM. *Hey, sorry for not getting back to you sooner. I'd love to see you, too. What are you doing tonight?*

Sumaya's heart began to race, and the small grin she'd woken up with widened. She was going to see Neha! So far, her visit had been so consumed by Imran and Fahima that she had put her own feelings aside the last few days. Though her family didn't know it, this was also why she had come back to London. For answers. If she could just see Neha one more time, get closure, she'd be able to say yes to Jonathan. Why hadn't Neha come with her to New York? Why had she broken her heart? But even though she had tough questions for her first love, she still ached to see her.

The day couldn't go by fast enough for Sumaya. She had agreed to meet Neha at seven o'clock at a bar in Tottenham Court Road. All day, she paced around the flat, looking at the time on her phone, willing the hours to pass quicker. She agonised over what to wear, flinging clothes out of her suitcase as she tried to find the right outfit, and took extra care applying her make-up in Majid's bathroom. As she got dressed, she tried to tell herself that she was just catching up with an old friend, that she shouldn't make this a bigger deal than it was. But, still, she hated everything she tried on, and finally, after multiple changes, settled on the flared mustard jumpsuit that Rachel had insisted made her 'look like a goddess'. No matter how many times she tried to steel herself, butterflies took root in her stomach and refused to abate.

In the bar, Sumaya sat at a corner table, nervously peering over at the door every time it opened. When Neha at last walked through the entrance, Sumaya was taken aback. She was wearing a hijab, which made punters turn their heads in her direction, and was dressed conservatively in a loose-fitting black shirt-dress and jeans. The Neha she'd known hadn't worn a hijab, and so it took Sumaya a moment to recognise her.

Neha spotted her and waved. As she got closer, Sumaya smiled at her, but within she felt uneasy. Had she judged this wrong? Seeing Neha dressed like this made her feel insecure about her own appearance in a way she'd not worried about in years. Did she appear 'too Western'? And in this setting, with other people in various states of inebriation, she felt uneasy for Neha, sticking out as she did.

Whatever her own insecurities, Neha appeared unfazed by the roving eyes, flashing Sumaya a smile that instantly took her back to a time when everything had been different. Neha's lips still curled upwards in that delicate way that used to arouse Sumaya so, and her teeth still gleamed pure, blinding white. Much had changed, and yet Neha's smile felt familiar, warm. Like returning to a creature comfort from which she'd been long deprived.

'Neha,' she simply said, at a loss for words. Neha still beguiled her with her beauty.

'Sumaya,' Neha answered, taking a seat on the stool opposite her, the small round table the only thing between them.

'Can I . . .' Sumaya stumbled. 'Can I get you a drink?'

Neha shook her head. 'I don't drink anymore.'

'Oh.' Sumaya was taken aback, and more than a little embarrassed. 'You should have said . . . we could have gone somewhere else . . .'

'No, no,' Neha insisted. 'I don't care. I wanted to see you! Just a Coke is fine.'

Sumaya nodded and went to the bar, bringing back a pint of Coke for Neha and a small rosé for herself. She'd wanted to go for a large, but thought better of it as Neha wasn't partaking too.

'So,' Neha said when Sumaya sat down, a smile welcoming her back. 'It's been so long, Sumaya. Tell me everything. How are you? How is life? How is your family? Are you in love? Are you happy?'

The questions were rapid-fire, but nothing in Neha's tone or her friendly smile indicated anything other than warmth. Neha was genuinely interested in her life – and her happiness. Her last question was not lost on Sumaya, for all that it contained as well as all that went unsaid. *Are you happy?* After all these years, after leaving her behind in London, Neha still cared for her happiness. Sumaya's cheeks flushed.

'I'm good,' she said confidently, telling Neha about her job and her friends in New York, a flourish of pride in her voice as she spoke about all that she had achieved. All that she wished Neha could have been there to see.

'Wow, Sumaya . . . you did it,' Neha said, smiling broadly. 'You always said you wanted to get out of this place, do something big, be someone – and you have. I'm so happy for you.'

Sumaya closed her eyes, savouring her recognition, and felt a tingle in her stomach. It hadn't dawned on her until now what

135

those words meant to her – to have her individuality and her ambition celebrated by those who knew her before. Amma and Baba were gone, and though she hoped they'd be proud of her, she'd never know. Imran seemed uninterested in her achievements at best. Sumaya hadn't been sure she was doing the right thing when she left London all those years ago, sacrificing her relationship with Neha, but here was her first love confirming to her that those sacrifices had been worth it.

It had been Neha in whom she had confided her hopes and dreams for a world beyond the one she knew; with whom she had shared her pain over Amma. Neha had understood her predicament that day seven years ago when she'd said she had to leave. After Amma died, she knew it was time to uphold her promise to her mother. She'd begged Neha to come with her. They'd sat in a bar just like this one, and Sumaya had begged. But Neha had broken her heart.

A tear fell from her eye and pooled on the tabletop. 'I . . . you don't know how much that means to me, Neha,' she said.

'I never had any doubt you'd succeed,' Neha added, beaming that indelible smile again.

'I wish you'd been there with me,' Sumaya said in a hushed tone, dabbing a tear from her eye.

'Oh, Sumaya—'

'I mean it,' Sumaya interrupted. 'Why didn't you come with me? Why not . . . ? I've never really understood . . .'

The words flew out of her mouth, half-formed thoughts. All the things she'd always wanted to ask but had never dared. Tears continued to roll down her cheeks.

'Sumaya,' Neha said, reaching across the table and taking her hands in hers. 'We were just kids. You had this big dream, you wanted to get away and live in New York . . . but that wasn't my dream.'

'You could have been happy, too . . . You could've found your own dream,' Sumaya pleaded.

Neha shook her head. 'That wouldn't have been fair. On me or on you. My life is here, Sumaya. And would you really have wanted me to move across the world and be miserable, while you were out building a new life for yourself?'

'But I – I needed you,' Sumaya said.

Neha squeezed Sumaya's hands. 'But you didn't really, Sumaya. Look at you. You've done everything you said you were going to do.'

Sumaya's tears stung her eyes. Though she had dreamed about this moment, the outpouring of emotion was overwhelming.

'I need a minute,' she said, separating her hands from Neha's, standing up and walking to the bathroom.

She stood in front of the bathroom mirror, a stretch of toilet roll in hand, dabbing at her eyes and willing herself to be strong. It hurt her to admit it, but Neha was right: New York was her dream, not Neha's. And yet . . . she still felt the rejection so deeply.

After she'd composed herself, she returned to the bar. Neha was fiddling with her straw, and even from across the room she looked as beautiful as she always had. They were no longer the girls they had been, but fully grown women in their thirties. Yet Neha was as youthful and glistening as the day Sumaya had left her.

'So . . . you didn't answer the crucial part. Is there anyone special in your life?' Neha inquired as Sumaya sat back in her seat.

Sumaya shifted uncomfortably. She pictured Jonathan in her mind's eye. Now that it came to it, she realised she hadn't really given Jonathan much thought since touching down on British soil. They had texted several times, but she had stopped short of calling him. She ought to feel guilty, so why didn't she? Thinking about him, to bring him up now, felt like a betrayal of what she'd had with Neha. This was their time.

'I am with someone,' Sumaya said coyly. ' . . . a man.'

A flicker of surprise crossed Neha's face. 'Really?'

'His name is Jonathan. We've been together five years . . .'

'I have to say, that surprises me,' said Neha. 'When you left—'

'I know,' Sumaya interrupted her. She had left London to be free from the heterosexual norms imposed on her, and then had ended up in a heterosexual relationship anyway. 'But what can I say, I fell in love . . .' she said in a tone that didn't entirely convince herself. She wondered if Neha had picked up on it too. A part of her wished for Neha to probe her further, to make her own up to what she felt inside.

'As long as you're happy, Sumaya . . .' Neha said.

Sumaya took another sip of her wine and returned the line of questioning. 'What about you? Are you with someone?'

And for the first time, Sumaya noticed the gold ring adorning the fourth digit of Neha's left hand.

Neha spotted the direction of her glance. 'Yep . . .' she said, half laughing. 'Six years now. Two kids.'

'Wow, kids?' Sumaya said, sounding surprised. She had only been able to guess at what Neha's life was like – her Instagram account wasn't particularly helpful – but a wife and kids seemed so mature, so grounded, compared to her own situation with Jonathan.

'What's her name? What are their names?' Sumaya asked.

'Oh . . . you misunderstand,' Neha said. 'I have a husband . . .'

Now it was Sumaya's turn to look puzzled, raising an eyebrow quizzically. And because she couldn't think of what else to say, she blurted out: 'But why?'

Neha simply laughed. 'I could ask you the same! You know what it's like here, Sumaya . . .'

'But . . .' Sumaya began to protest then quickly swallowed her words. She didn't want to offend Neha, nor presume to know what her life had been like in her absence. But just as Neha had assumed she would end up with a woman in New York, she had pictured the same for Neha. Though, of course, Neha came from the same background as her; their lives were governed by cultural norms and religion, and the community was small and quick to gossip. She wouldn't have been able to be herself. And that is exactly why Sumaya had fled, had she not?

Sumaya considered what to say next. 'I guess we've surprised each other tonight,' she said, sounding as diplomatic as possible. 'And are *you* happy?' she added.

Neha smiled, and this time it seemed to Sumaya that there was something more affected in this smile. 'I am fortunate,' Neha said. 'I have my children – Sabir and Elena – and they are my joy.'

'And your husband . . . you love him?' Sumaya asked hesitantly. She didn't want to appear as if she was prying . . . but she was. She burned to know whether Neha felt the same way she did. Perhaps there might be something there still . . .

Sumaya read the contemplation on Neha's face as she paused for thought before replying.

'I am content, Sumaya,' she said softly. 'He is a good man, he has a steady job, and our children are loved. I can't ask for more.'

Sumaya wanted to blurt out that she *should* ask for more! That if she wasn't completely, 100 per cent, totally in love with her husband, was that a marriage worth staying in? But fearing the Pandora's box she might open if she said what was really on her mind, she restrained herself.

'I'd love to see pictures of your kids!' she said instead, prompting Neha to whip her phone out of her clutch and open up her camera roll.

The remainder of the evening whizzed by as they cooed over little Sabir and Elena, and caught up on each other's lives – Sumaya's job with Rachel, her life with Jonathan, Neha's arranged marriage to Bilal, and her baby-knitwear Etsy store – and before they knew it, the landlord was calling for last orders.

Sumaya found herself wishing for a little more time. A few hours wasn't enough to make up for seven long years without Neha.

And, truth be told, she still didn't have the clarity she was looking for about her heart's desires.

The two women hugged goodbye outside the bar, and because Sumaya couldn't help herself, she asked: 'Can I see you again while I'm here?'

Neha took a moment to consider this, before replying: 'Yes.'

On the way home, Sumaya's mind raced with regrets and what-ifs. She had only now come to realise the consequences of her promise to Amma – on her and her family, and on Neha, too. After Sumaya left, Neha had allowed her parents to find her a suitable match, and though she said she was content, to Sumaya that did not seem equal to love and was nowhere near equal to what they'd had. What might have been different if she hadn't left London? Might she and Neha be together now, even if it meant being shunned by their families? Might Sabir and Elena be *their* children? In Elena's face she saw some of the youthful exuberance that she had seen in Neha all those years ago, and it made her all the more nostalgic about the past – and the future that might have been.

Her phone pinged as the train pulled into the platform at Angel. A message from Jonathan. *How's it going?*

And this too added to her pensive state. How could she blame Neha for settling, when Jonathan messaging her left her . . . There was no better word for it than 'placid'. She didn't feel the butterflies in her stomach opening his message as she had with Neha's earlier. Theirs had been a love – blazing and audacious.

Walking back to Majid's, Sumaya was consumed by the questions she so often pushed aside. Hadn't she settled, too? She had gone to New York to be free, to love whomever she wanted, and had settled into a relationship that she wasn't truly satisfied with.

And then the thought crystallised, the clarity she had been seeking tonight: she wasn't happy in her relationship at all.

It was Neha, not Jonathan, she wanted.

Chapter 16

Sultana

The plane hummed and vibrated as it prepared for take-off. Inside, Sultana felt sick, her stomach fluttering so much that she thought the meagre breakfast she had eaten before setting off at dawn – a dry cake rusk and a lukewarm cup of tea – might come back up. She had never seen a plane up close before, let alone been on one. She worried how she might react when the plane finally began its ascent. She willed herself not to scream or cause a scene, but her fears overpowered her thoughts. What if the plane fell out of the sky and crashed? What if it was so turbulent she was impossibly sick? Her fears were further compounded by the fact that sitting next to her was her new husband, Abdul, who was no more than a stranger to her. She didn't want to embarrass him. She knew she had to make a good impression on him. Ammu had told her to stay calm and pray to Allah that their journey would be safe. But her stomach churned and her knuckles turned white from the force with which she gripped the armrest.

Yesterday, when Abdul had taken Sultana to her childhood home to say goodbye to Ammu and Abbu and her sisters, Sultana had clung to her mother and wailed so hard that she thought her heart might burst out of her chest. She and Abdul had been married three months, and now the visas were settled, they were going to London to begin their new lives as husband and wife. Sultana had known the day would come, and though she'd dreaded it, the reality of not seeing her mother again had finally sunk in. She didn't know when she would be able to return to Bangladesh – how many years might pass until her mother held her again. She belonged to another family now, another man, and no more could Ammu shroud her in her comfort and wipe away her tears.

'Sshhh,' Ammu had said, holding Sultana and letting her tears seep into the fabric of her sari, expanding into dark pools of grey against the white cotton. 'You can cry now, but then that is it. Promise me. You mustn't let your husband see you so melancholy. You have to show him you are happy. Understand?'

Sultana nodded through sobs.

And though she was now a married woman, Ammu had spoken to Sultana like the child she still felt she was, instructing her in her duties as a wife and, in future, a mother. Sultana was only eighteen, but it seemed her short life up until that point had been leading to this. She had been groomed for this moment. The sum total of a life for a young girl in Bangladesh was to eventually become a wife and mother.

'Remember, don't talk back to your husband, don't let him see you angry,' Ammu had said. 'You must hold your tongue. I know it'll be hard. You have always been a vexatious young girl, but do this, for my peace of mind. I need to know you will be safe.'

Ammu knew all too well how precocious her middle daughter was. The girl had no filter. If she was short-changed at the shop when Ammu sent her to buy paan, for example, Sultana would kick up a fuss with the man behind the counter. 'You think I can't count because I'm a girl?' The man would come to the house and complain to Abbu that his daughter had been rude to him.

This fiery trait in her daughter had been there from a young age. When she was just a girl, tasked with looking after her younger brother and sister, Sultana would barter with the boy next door to keep an eye on Munir and Shyla while she cavorted in the paddy fields with her friends. But now she was a wife, and she had to behave like one. The time for games had passed.

'I will . . . I will,' Sultana cried.

'Don't try to be smart,' Ammu continued. 'You have to listen to him, even if it doesn't seem right – a man needs to feel like he is right, even when he's not. Massage his ego and he will be generous. Don't, and there will be trouble. This is what we must do as women.'

'Ammu—' Sultana began to fidget.

'No, listen to me, Sultana,' her mother cut her off. 'Ammu won't be there with you anymore. It's important you understand these things. You must be obedient and kind, and meet his needs . . . remember what we talked about?'

How could Sultana forget the excruciating talk her mother and aunts had given her the night before she wed. It was the first and only time in her eighteen years that Ammu had spoken to her about sex. The conversation had been as uncomfortable for mother as it was for daughter, both women turning beet-red. Ammu rushed through what to expect – 'It will hurt but you must endure, pretend it's enjoyable' – without pausing for breath, and both were flushed with relief when she had finally dispensed all her wisdom. In the background, her eldest aunt, Nazma khala, laughed boisterously at both her sister and her niece. These words were not spoken in polite society. Nazma had been through this herself with her own daughters, and she understood the discomfort that came with such a conversation. But in a life of hardship and little joy, a woman must embrace humour and laugh when the rare opportunity arose, and so she had cackled, her puerile mirth still echoing in Sultana's ears long after she rushed out of the room. And when she grew older, she would still hear her Nazma khala's laughter, and eventually she'd laugh, too, because now she understood. Humour was a commodity which women expressed infrequently. It was a luxury in a life built around others. *So, laugh*, she'd tell herself. *Laugh when you can. As often as you can.*

When Abdul said it was time to leave, Sultana had looked at her mother in despair. She'd howled so fiercely, held on to her mother so tightly, that both Abdul and Abbu had to prise them apart.

'Be strong,' Ammu had whispered in her ear.

That had been less than eighteen hours ago. And now the pain of that final moment with Ammu surged through her again as the plane took off and she looked down at the familiar sights of home for the last time. On that plane, her adolescence ended and her womanhood began.

The journey was long, and Sultana excused herself to go to the bathroom numerous times, the turbulence causing her to heave what little she had eaten. Abdul said little on the flight. Perhaps, she wondered, he was as disquieted as she was by this radical twist of fate that Allah had bestowed on them, but she dared not ask. She'd speak only if he spoke to her first.

It seemed impossible to Sultana that all of her future was pinned on the man who sat next to her – a man she barely knew, and had never known until just a few months ago. She had met Abdul but once before the wedding, on the day of their sinifan five months ago – the small engagement party held at her parents' house. Ammu had instructed her not to look too closely at her future husband, and instead to look down and act demure, but when she knew that there were no eyes on her, Sultana caught glimpses of him. He was much taller than her . . . would their height difference make them appear mismatched? Black hair that was slicked back with pomade, a healthy beard, and an oval-ish face. Sultana couldn't say she was immediately overawed by her suitor – he looked like most of the men she knew. 'Marriage takes time. You will find things in common. It isn't immediate,' Ammu had told her.

Now, five months later, here she was sitting next to Abdul on a plane taking them to begin their new lives, and her insides felt queasy from the uncertainty of it all. She was being asked to place all her implicit trust in this man. They would have to sleep side by side every night as husband and wife, and Sultana would have to make herself smaller – not just to appease her husband, but to fit into a new world where she'd be in the minority.

This was the culmination of her parents' struggle. The culmination of all that she had been prepared for since she was a little girl. To be someone's wife. To be a mother. Little remained of the idealistic girl who'd dreamed of shooting into space. Those were fantasies to be had by girls far more privileged and whiter than her.

Life had moulded her to accept her lot.

The first thing that immediately struck Sultana about her new home was its paleness. Men and women so alabaster that she could see the thin lines of veins through their translucent skin. She had never seen so many white people before, and though she had known to expect this, it still came as a shock.

As she acclimatised to her new surroundings, Sultana tried her best not to gawp at the natives in sheer astonishment, though the same could not be said in return. For the first time in her life, she wasn't able to merge into a crowd, and stood out everywhere she went. Women and small children followed her with their eyes as she walked down the street, fascinated by her stride, her headscarf, her ethnic clothing. In Bangladesh, she was considered a mundane girl – she wasn't as fair as her younger sister, Shyla, nor as tall and graceful as Polly next door – but here, she seemed to inspire awe, for better or for worse.

The other thing that Sultana noticed was the abundance of dogs. Everyone seemed to have a dog, and Abdul had warned her that sometimes they were used to chase and scare the migrants. 'Stay away from them,' he said. It all seemed preposterous to her, for she had grown up with livestock from chickens to goats and cows. How harmful could a dog be? The dogs she encountered looked overfed, barely able to toddle along the street without huffing and puffing, and then there were the ones that the white women cradled as if holding a child. What nonsense! Yet she took heed of Abdul's earnest tone, not wanting to upset the delicate balance in their fledgling marriage over something so trivial.

The first home Sultana knew in London was a shabby council flat in Aldgate East that she and Abdul shared with another couple, Sayeedul and his wife, Rukshana. Abdul and Sayeedul were from the same village – which, here, made them the closest thing to relatives that they had. The flat was on the fourth floor, the walls so thin that Sultana could hear the neighbours' conversations and babies crying through the night. The two couples shared all the common areas – the kitchen, the bathroom and living room – and Rukshana and Sayeedul claimed the bigger bedroom. Abdul and Sultana made do with a box room large enough for a bed and little else. The first few months, they lived out of their suitcases. Compared to the open space around her parents' basha in Nabiganj, her new surroundings were suffocating, and on more than one occasion, Sultana locked herself in the bathroom long after everyone had gone to bed, silently weeping for all that she had given up through marriage.

Soon after they arrived, Abdul quickly took up work; Sayeedul had introduced him to the owner of an Indian restaurant on Brick Lane where Sayeedul, too, had worked when he arrived in London years earlier, before going into tailoring. He mostly worked nights, clearing plates and washing dishes for pitiful sums of money paid in cash every Friday. He soon realised that this wouldn't be enough to sustain both him and Sultana, or to get them into a flat of their own, and so he took up day shifts on a fish stall in Whitechapel market. Sultana, already homesick, suddenly felt adrift – abandoned by her husband for more than eighteen hours a day. Her night-time bathroom routine extended from twice a week to every other night, and then every night. Each morning, after she'd made Abdul his tea and toast and sent him off to work, she returned to bed and lay wide awake, unable to muster the energy to feed herself or bathe. She wished she could make herself so small as to disappear. That her tears might create a tide and carry her all the way home.

Rukshana had taken pity on the newcomer, selflessly cooking for all of them. Each night, she shared credit for the meal with Sultana when the husbands would ask who prepared what, a small mercy that Sultana gratefully appreciated – and yet she couldn't find it in herself to suspend her melancholy and actually help.

One morning, Sultana skulked into the kitchen in her nightgown, her hair unkempt, while Rukshana padded around the stove. She was making a fish curry for their evening meal, gently stirring the delicate pieces of boal, a Bangladeshi catfish, with the back of her spoon. The scent of the fish and spices sizzling in hot oil made her long for home. Food here didn't taste as good; the fish was frozen and imported from Bangladesh, rather than fresh from the sea. The vegetables they kept in the fridge tasted more like plastic compared to the fresh coriander Ammu would pick from the garden.

As Sultana helped herself to a glass of water, Rukshana turned to her.

'Sister, you need to start helping me,' she said, not unkindly. 'Your husband will begin asking questions. And my back is starting to ache. I am with child.'

Sultana looked at Rukshana with a mix of happiness and anguish. If Rukshana and Sayeedul were to have a child, surely they'd need more space. How would she and Abdul be able to afford their own flat? And though she was often feeling too low to make conversation, Sultana was comforted by the sounds of the other woman pottering around the flat – at least she knew someone in this godforsaken country other than her husband. At least someone other than Abdul would care what became of her.

'Mashallah,' Sultana said, giving Rukshana a weak hug.

'I'm going to need your help,' Rukshana reiterated. 'Come, sister, this wallowing will do you no good. You must make your life here. I've been in your shoes. I have missed home, my family, my friends, too. But that doesn't mean you can't make a good life for yourself.'

Rukshana put a hand tenderly on her stomach. Her smile radiated a warmth that was unmistakably genuine happiness. If Rukshana could overcome the same blues she was experiencing now and find her personal joy, then couldn't the same be true for Sultana?

Sultana silently took a knife and chopped fresh green chillies, passing them to Rukshana to stir into the curry.

'This will pass,' Rukshana assured her.

Sultana took over more and more of the cooking as Rukshana progressed in her pregnancy. The other woman guided her around Whitechapel market, showing her the best stalls for fresh herbs and vegetables and introducing her to the best butcher for meat and chicken. The familiarity of the market, and the company of the Bengali stall-owners and shoppers, all speaking in their mother tongue, eased her homesickness. Haggling over prices made her feel more like the girl she had once been, and striking a bargain on a pound of oori – lablab beans – was positively thrilling. For the first time since arriving in London, she felt she belonged there.

The two women quickly fell into a rhythm, sharing the household responsibilities and also relying on each other for company. If her husband was at work, Rukshana would ask Sultana to accompany her to prenatal appointments, and when Rukshana experienced pre-eclampsia in the later stages of her pregnancy and was put on bedrest, Sultana sat by her side and they whiled away the afternoon swapping stories about their lives back home. Rukshana's father had been a judge in Bangladesh, her family much more affluent than Sultana's own. She had married Sayeedul for love. Sultana imagined the gated house she must have lived in; the maids, the cooks, the drivers. And now here they were sharing a small two-bedroom flat in an austere building with flickering lights in the hallways and lifts that rarely worked. Rukshana had had to give up more than she had. What a culture shock she must have experienced moving here! But the way Rukshana carried herself – never complaining; innately satisfied with her life – made Sultana admire her friend's courage and character more than she could have imagined when she first moved in. Rukshana reminded of her of her older sisters, and Sultana soon thought of the bond between them as being as good as that between blood relations.

When Rukshana went into labour, they were too late to make it to the hospital. Rukshana's contractions were so close together that she began pushing right there on the living room floor, tightly gripping hold of Sayeedul while Sultana helped deliver the baby. She had seen the cows have their calves in the village, but the intimacy of watching her friend give birth – and being there to receive the baby, covered in blood and other matter – was both exhilarating and terrifying. Sultana wrapped Sahidur in a blue bath towel and handed him over to the new mother. Only after the baby was safely delivered did the adrenaline wear off and she was able to fathom what she had been part of. A miracle from Allah.

Sultana continued to support Rukshana with Sahidur in the months that followed, rocking him to sleep and feeding him his bottle, allowing Rukshana to get some much-needed, precious rest. She would watch the young baby while Rukshana bathed, taking in his diminutive features as she cradled him in her arms. Sahidur's eyes were bright and alert, his eyebrows silken wisps of fine hair. How precious a child was. She began to contemplate what her own child might look like. She and Abdul were coming up to one year in London. Perhaps it was time.

'You will make an excellent mother,' Rukshana told her once, catching a glimpse of Sultana doting on baby Sahidur.

The scent of chicken biryani and mutton curry filled the air. Children zigzagged through the crowd playing tag, their infectious giggles pleasant to the ear. In the background, someone had set up a sound system in the doorway of a corner shop, playing a cassette of old Bengali songs that captured the mood of the crowd.

It was a warm Sunday afternoon, and locals from the neighbouring tower blocks around Brick Lane had gathered to celebrate the Pohela Boishakh, the first day of the Bengali New Year.

The sun cast its glow over Sultana, coating her in its warmth. It was mid-April, and the new season had begun to take effect, and though she'd experienced spring in London last year, this time Sultana allowed herself to embrace the seasonal change – from cold to warm, from short days to long. Now into her second year, this place was finally starting to feel like home.

The four of them had set off for the street party just after lunch-time. It was Abdul and Sayeedul's idea that they attend – both had a rare day off. Sultana had been surprised by the proposition, for both men usually spent Sundays sleeping the day away, exhausted from their six-day work week. Most nights, Abdul didn't return home until past one o'clock, after the restaurant closed, and he had just a few hours to sleep before waking up to work the market stall. This rarity seemed too good to be true, but neither Sultana nor Rukshana were willing to tempt fate by questioning their husbands' generosity, in case they changed their minds.

Rukshana had bundled six-month-old Sahidur into a tight sling across her chest using a ketha, a light hand-woven blanket, that her mother had given her before she moved to London, not knowing when she might – if ever – meet her future grandchildren. The material was made from colourful old saris and other thin pieces of fabric, delicately stitched together. Her mother must have spent hours on this parting gift, and Rukshana hadn't dared remove it from the cloth sack it had been presented in until the time was ripe to use it. The ketha covered Sahidur's tiny little limbs at night in his basket, and Rukshana would swaddle him in it before placing him in his pram to run errands. The scent of home had, over time, commingled with the smell of her new son, a convergence of all that she held dear in life. And when Sultana saw Rukshana beaming down at Sahidur wrapped in the blanket made so lovingly by his grandmother's own hands, she knew that her friend had found fulfilment in this new life. And one day, she would too.

Sultana walked beside Rukshana, and the women smiled at each other as they arrived at the street party. Sultana had not seen anything like this since she left Bangladesh – men in their panjabis, women in bright red saris, children with their arms decorated with henna tattoos. Food-lined plastic trestle tables as far as she could see – fresh pani puri, chaat, and sweet mishti of varying neon colours. The music, too, brought back memories of home – of her sisters fanning the hems of their long salwar kameez and dancing to the beat of the music on the radio. This was how she chose to remember her sisters – the carefree joys of their shared childhood, rather than the women, wives and mothers they had all been raised to be.

She and Rukshana sat on plastic garden chairs while the men sought refreshments, and it took Sultana some time to ground herself in the moment – so overwhelmed were her senses by the sights, sounds and smells.

'I've never seen so many people who look like us in one place!' she confided to her friend. 'I never thought London could be like this . . .'

'Not just London. Lots of us are settling across the country – places like Bradford, and my cousin is going to move to Leicester with her husband. It's a new world, Sultana,' Rukshana said. And then, looking down at the sweet black-haired baby asleep against her bosom: 'Allah has blessed us – our children will be the generation that really benefit from the new world we are creating here. They won't have to struggle like we have. Inshallah.'

Since Sahidur's birth, Rukshana spoke more and more of the future with near-certain prescience; of the bright fortunes her children and future generations would have. And while Sultana still often felt sorrow for the hopeful future her younger self never achieved, she allowed Rukshana's certainty of golden days to come to soothe her, and eventually began believing it to be true.

Both Sultana and Abdul doted on Sahidur as if he were their own, and when she looked into his alert brown eyes and fed him his bottle, she wanted nothing more than to believe his future would be all that his mother was foretelling. In his plump face and dimpled cheeks was pure, unbridled innocence, and she hoped this sweet young child would never have his future mapped out for him. With all her being, she wanted it to be filled with hope, love and opportunity – so much so that sometimes it felt all consuming. Was it natural to feel this deep love for a child that wasn't your own?

Sahidur, she realised, was slowly recalibrating her own desires, her own sense of self. If she could love him so much, what might it feel like to love her own child? It would be a bottomless well. There would be no cloud or boulder that she wouldn't move for her child, and there would be no extreme that she wouldn't go to. Her child, or children, would never be without her as their compass. For this love, this rarefied air of transcendence, Sultana had begun to yearn, though she had no child in which to channel her devotion. At least not yet.

Sultana placed a hand on Sahidur's head, and the sleeping child cooed, comforted by both mother and aunt. For all the excitement of the mela and the joy of the months since the boy's arrival, a nugget of anxiety still pressed into her heart.

'Afa,' Sultana said reluctantly to Rukshana. 'I . . . I will understand if you want us to leave . . .'

The other woman turned to her, confusion on her face. 'What? I don't know what you're talking about.'

'You are a family now. You and Bhaisab will need your space,' Sultana clumsily explained. 'We don't want to impose on you any longer than we have to. If you want us to leave the flat . . .'

Rukshana took in the measure of Sultana's face – the worry that crept over her visage, her eyes pooling with the first teardrops, her mouth slightly aquiver – and smiled at her companion.

'This is what worries you, sister?' Rukshana said, her tone silken and soothing. 'What nonsense!'

Now it was Sultana who was confused. It wasn't nonsense to her. She had spent months with her stomach in knots at the thought of being unceremoniously kicked out of the small flat. Where would she and Abdul go? She had only just begun to feel at home in London. Allowed herself to embrace this new life. Allowed herself to exhale. She wasn't ready to lose what amity and companionship she had found here in the woman she called sister.

'Sultana, you worry too much,' the other woman said with a laugh. 'Of course we're not going to kick you out! What on earth made you think that? You are Sahidur's uncle and aunt. We'd never do that. You are our family.'

To hear Rukshana say the words – lending credence to her own feelings – brought an instant calm over Sultana. They were family. The other woman thought it too. She wasn't just idealising the friendship they'd created in this strange and distant country. And then she felt silly for allowing herself to run away with the anxiety of her doubts. Her concerns had been unfounded. But when you had so little, even the most minor worry could feel like a boulder.

'Thank you, afa,' Sultana replied with gratitude in her heart. This life wasn't opulent or steeped in riches, but it was rich with love.

Sultana closed her eyes and said a silent prayer to Allah.

◆ ◆ ◆

Bellies full and ears ringing with the sound of home, Sultana and Abdul fell into bed that night exhausted and satisfied. The taste of paan and betel nut lingered on her tongue; the tanginess of the white soon still prickled the inside of her mouth. As she lay in bed, Sultana's heart pounded, both with adrenaline and the rush from the paan. This day had felt the closest to her life at home that she'd recalled in the last year, and even as Abdul had pulled her away, ready to call it a night, she could have stayed longer – eaten a little more gulabjam, listened to one more song. But Abdul was tired and had to wake up early for work the next day. She couldn't begrudge her husband, for she understood how hard he worked, but how she wished that the evening could have lasted just that little bit longer. That she could forget this was a foreign land. That she could finally accept these English streets as home.

It had seemed so impossible a year ago, but now she was willing to allow her mind, her and soul to feel contentment; to lay down her arms and cease fighting against it. How exhausted she was, yearning for a plane to take her back home. How weary her bones were with homesickness. She had wasted so much time and motion resisting her surroundings, but today she truly accepted that Rukshana might have been right. This could be a home, if she let it.

She made up her mind then and there that she would let this strange country become her home. Perhaps it wasn't the adventure she had imagined as a little girl longing to conquer the moon, but this was in itself a new frontier, no? A land Ammu and Abbu could only dream of. That so many of her countrymen would never see. She was blazing a trail, after all, and she hadn't even realised it.

This realisation wasn't the only thing that surprised her. It took Sultana a moment to snap out of her thoughts and feel the weight of Abdul's hand holding hers; he had turned to her in the bed and had been watching her intently, softly, as she raced through the day's events in her mind. Now, she turned to her side so they were eye-to-eye, and she stroked the back of the hand that encased hers with her thumb. In their brief marriage to date, Sultana couldn't say she had felt any great amorous affection for her husband, for he still felt like a stranger to her. They had been intimate, of course, but she thought of it as a duty, as Ammu had told her, not an impassioned physical act of love. But now, between them, something felt different. In this light, in this breath's distance between them, her husband looked at her with tender affection such as she'd never seen, and suddenly it felt natural.

'I know this hasn't been easy for you,' Abdul whispered into the darkness.

She didn't need to play coy or ask for elaboration, for it was clear what her husband meant. She had assumed he was busy, struggling to make enough money to tide them both over, that he had been ignorant to her melancholy. But he hadn't. He had seen her. Truly seen her.

'I'm sorry,' he whispered breathily.

Sultana felt a pang in her chest. A rush of remorse. Ammu had told her that it was her job to attend to her husband, and that had been what she assumed her husband expected of her. To be a silent partner. To do her duty. It seemed wrong of him to apologise to *her*. She felt like apologising back, begging him not to worry himself over her well-being, for she was just a foolish young girl, a nuisance. But something stopped her from fawning in apology. That rebellious spirit she had tried to quell could not be wholly silenced. So, she kept quiet and waited for her husband to fill the silence. What else might he reveal to her that she had not foreseen?

'I'm sorry I'm always at work,' Abdul said softly. 'I'm sorry there aren't more days like today. I wish there could be. I know it's not fair to you. It isn't easy for me, either. I wish I could come home earlier, like the other men who get to have dinner with their wives and families. I wish I didn't have to work two jobs, all hours of the day. This isn't the life I imagined, either.'

It dawned on Sultana that in her own apathy, she hadn't taken a moment to consider that Abdul might feel the same. Ammu had instructed her not to question her husband, and she had taken that to mean in the totality of his being. To question a man was to emasculate him – at least, that was what she had been raised to believe. And so she hadn't deigned to imagine that he, too, might miss home; that leaving all he knew was as difficult for her husband as it had been for her. It hit her in a sudden wave. A tightness in her stomach. Shame. Shame that she had been so selfish. Looking into her husband's eyes, she saw that there, too, was a fragility. It was like his eyes mirrored her own. How had she not seen it before? Now she *really* wanted to apologise, but the words felt insubstantial compared to the guilt that suddenly pained her. Instead, she shuffled closer to him and put her free hand to his face, caressing his cheek, her supple hand contrasting with the coarseness of his stubble.

'I promise it won't always be like this,' Abdul said. 'It just has to be like this now, so we can build a life. I want to give you a good life, Sultana. I want *us* to have a good life. If I have to work every hour that Allah gives, then so be it. It's a temporary sacrifice for the rest of our lives. I want us to have a house with a garden where our children can run around. Near good schools. Good, honest neighbours. A home that we can call our own. It may be a while away, but that is my promise to you.'

There was purity in his voice, a guilelessness in his words that stirred something within Sultana. Ammu hadn't taught her how to navigate the emotions of a man. Sultana's husband had been a stranger in her bed, a man to whom she was betrothed, but now she suddenly saw him not as another patriarchal figure to obey, but as a three-dimensional person, an equal.

It was a flashlight in the darkness. A spring of water in a drought. In that moment, Sultana came to realise what marriage truly meant: it was all that she had been taught by Ammu, yes, but all that she hadn't been taught, too. It was faith in another, even in uncertainty. It was compassion. It was this, here and now, between her and her husband.

One hand clasped in Abdul's, the other caressing the side of his face, Sultana closed her eyes and made a silent vow. Just as she'd given herself over to this foreign land, she would give herself completely to her husband. Allow her love to grow.

As she opened her eyes, Sultana did something uncharacteristic. She initiated intimacy for the first time in their marriage. Not out of a sense of duty, but as an act of love.

A few months later, Sultana learned she was pregnant with their first child.

Chapter 17

Sumaya

'Don't you think it'd be better if you came home?' Jonathan said down the phone. 'You've done what you can.'

Sumaya was squatting on the pavement, a finger in her ear to hear Jonathan over the reverberation of the music from the club and the chatter of people in the smoking area. She was wearing a shiny blue spaghetti-strapped top that was ill-equipped to keep her warm from the London weather. Her body flinched with each gust of wind. She couldn't wait to get back inside the club, the thrumming hive of activity, and leach the warmth from the revellers. Or at least that's what she told herself.

'I know. It's just . . . I haven't seen Majid in years. We're connecting,' she said.

She realised she sounded curter than she had intended, but she told herself it was just because she was cold. Deep down, though, she knew it was about him and what she was now beginning to realise she felt about their relationship. This was the first time she'd picked up his call since arriving in London, and somehow his American drawl felt like an imposition to her here. Since seeing Neha, something instinctively made her turn away from her relationship, to respect the ocean's distance between them. Jonathan hadn't done anything wrong, she conceded. But how could she tell him that she much preferred the company of her twenty-one-year-old brother and his uni mates in a dive bar than talking to him on the phone?

'Have you thought any more about what we talked about?' Jonathan asked.

Sumaya winced. This was her cue to end the call.

'Listen, I really have to go,' she said, her tone clipped. 'I'll call you soon.'

A couple of days had passed since Sumaya had ended up at Majid's flat and they had both opened up about their sexuality. Neither she nor Majid had heard from their elder brother, and as far as Sumaya was concerned, that was fine by her. Despite the creaking back pain from sleeping on Andrew's uncomfortable box spring, Sumaya was surprised by how much she was enjoying her younger brother's company. She had even taken him to Wilko and bought him matching crockery. 'I literally cannot eat off another chipped plate, Maj,' she had protested.

Majid had invited her out with his friends, just as they'd discussed. They were all a decade younger than her, and the student haunt they found themselves in had sticky floors and fluorescent-coloured £2 shots. 'It'll be good for you to meet other queer people,' Majid had primed her before they left the flat. 'You don't have to be afraid to be yourself, sis.'

'Oh my god, you don't look thirty at all! You're so hot!' his friend Seema, an Indian girl with long black hair that reached just above her bottom, had said when they arrived at the club. Truth be told, Sumaya had been apprehensive about her appearance and fitting in with her brother's peers, but his friends had immediately made her feel welcome, and her self-esteem rose further after one or two questionable green shots.

Now, as she walked back into the club, carefully darting her way through the horny young couples who were stuck to each other and the walls, Sumaya felt a certain relief. Tonight she didn't need to think about Jonathan or Imran, or even Neha. Tonight she could redress her misspent youth, even if, inexplicably, it was with her younger brother. What would Amma and Baba say? She laughed as she imagined them watching her and Majid from high above, dancing among the throngs of sweaty partygoers to DJ Khaled and Drake.

Sumaya re-joined her brother and his friends at a rounded booth. The sofa, seemingly once nicely upholstered leather, was missing patches so that the foam poked through. She imagined bringing Rachel and the girls here – they'd scream and run away!

'Got you another shot, sis,' Majid said, thrusting a purple-coloured drink in her direction.

'Actually, I got it!' said Simon, Majid's ginger friend with a Mancunian twang. At first she'd struggled to understand what he was saying, but now that they were several shots deep, it didn't even matter.

'Yeah, yeah,' Majid said to his friend. 'Fine, Simon got the shots. Happy now?'

'To your sister!' said Seema, holding up her shot glass. 'To Sumaya!'

Sumaya clinked her plastic shot glass against those of Majid and his friends before downing the dubious liquid. She thought she could taste tequila, but also, surprisingly, juniper berries? It was better not to think about it.

'Sumaya, I was wondering if you might be able to help us,' Seema asked while Sumaya was still distracted by the aftertaste in her mouth. 'Majid said you're a hotshot television producer? As it happens, me and Haroon,' she said, pointing to the young Bangladeshi man canoodling with Simon, 'are making a short documentary. About being queer and Asian. It's silly really. It's just for a uni short film competition. You can say no, of course . . . it's probably beneath you . . .'

'No, that sounds cool,' Sumaya said without hesitating. 'I'd love to help.'

'Oh my god, thank you!' Seema jumped on the spot. 'You're amazing *and* beautiful.'

'Oh shit, this song is a banger,' said Haroon, taking Simon by the hand and leading him towards the dance floor. 'Let's dance!'

Majid and Seema also made for the dance floor, and Sumaya dutifully followed as the sound of Calvin Harris's 'Rollin'' played throughout the club. Majid, Simon and Haroon jumped up and down boisterously as the girls swivelled their hips to the beat. Was this how the new generation lived? she wondered. When she was their age, she had been scared that her sexuality would be a scarlet letter, but Majid and his friends all seemed to live freely and fully.

Under the bright lights of the club, perspiration slowly pooling on her forehead, Sumaya suddenly felt more alive than she had in a long time. What an unexpected turn of events this trip had been, and what unexpected joy she had found in her younger brother. She smiled as he bobbed jubilantly to the music. He was so full of life and joy. Pure joy. Not a trace of his expression gave away his difficult upbringing. How had he turned out so well adjusted while she and Imran were so . . . there was no other word for it than 'fucked-up'.

She couldn't fathom how Majid had come out of their upbringing unscathed. She was glad of it, but she considered the invisible scars she'd had to bear, the family she'd had to leave behind and now felt so estranged from. She had always told herself it was her choice to go to New York. That Jonathan, her job, Rachel and her other friends were all part of the life she had chosen. The life she had wanted to lead. But it suddenly felt like a pretence. How else could she explain the fact that she could barely get through a conversation with Jonathan without shutting down? That she was glad they were oceans apart? No normal person in a loving relationship did that. And Neha. She hadn't stopped thinking about her since they'd met up, but their lives were so different, so complicated. And then there was Imran . . . Their relationship was beyond dysfunctional. What kind of siblings tore strips out of each other for pleasure? She had weaponised his past with Sophie to hurt him – and she had got a perverted thrill out of it. What brother and sister behaved this way and then acted like everything was okay?

She had been blind to the reality of the last eight years, thinking she was in the driver's seat. But she had become a passenger in her own life. She had done and said things she wasn't proud of, let emotions fester that should have been addressed . . . and now she was thirty-one in a room full of young people with their lives ahead of them. She couldn't turn back the clock and undo her mistakes.

As quickly as the room had come alive with music and body heat, it turned suffocating. The music became distorted. The lights began to flash in her eyes. Sumaya felt like she was gasping for breath. Her head felt dizzy, and then she saw nothing.

'Woah, easy, sis,' Majid said, guiding her by the arm and placing on her the weathered leather sofa they had sat on earlier. 'Hold on. Let me get you some water.'

Sumaya sat there, dazed. She couldn't make head nor tail of what had just happened. One moment she'd been dancing, enjoying herself, and the next, she'd felt light-headed and like she was about to faint. Thank god Majid had caught hold of her and moved her away from the crowd before she'd collapsed. She didn't think she could bear the utter humiliation of passing out at a student night. And she did not want any inch of her skin to come into contact with that sticky floor.

'Here,' Majid said, passing her a plastic cup filled with ice-cool water. He sat beside her as she drank it down. She must have been parched. 'At least you didn't stack it in front of the whole club.'

A small smile crept over Sumaya's face. 'I'm sorry, Maj. I just don't know what happened . . .'

'Just sit for a moment. Catch yourself.'

'I'm sorry. You don't need me here cramping your style . . . go back and hang out with your friends.'

'Nah, don't worry about it, sis. Anyway, Simon and Haroon are probably all over each other, and Seema already has a couple of hotties circling her. They won't even miss me.'

Sumaya took a deep breath and surveyed her surroundings. All around her were young people – kids, really – caught up in the revelry of a bog-standard student night. These kids didn't need to worry about the responsibilities of adult life yet, they needn't grow up before their time, they needn't worry that one bad choice could alter their entire lives. They were too young and carefree to under-stand yet that adulthood was a sacrifice. There was no such thing as simple pleasure without some consequence. Her life felt tethered to the actions of others. Who was she really?

'What am I doing here, Maj?'

Majid looked at his sister, confused. 'I mean, we were danc-ing and having a good time before you decided to pull a Sleeping Beauty . . .'

'No, not *here* here . . . I just . . . never mind,' Sumaya responded. Whatever she was feeling was too difficult to put into words, not least because she didn't want to engage in a philosophical discussion with her younger brother.

'Nah, go on . . . tell me,' he prodded her.

'I just . . . I've missed all of this . . .' she tried to explain. 'I missed out on *living*. I can't explain it . . . Like, one day I woke up in the body of a thirty-something-year-old and I'm standing at the edge of a cliff.'

'Mate, it sounds like you're having a crisis,' Majid said bluntly.

Is that what this feeling is? Sumaya questioned herself. Was she in crisis? It seemed implausible, because she lived her life so meticulously: everything she said and every action carefully composed. Crises were for people who didn't have their shit together.

Then it hit her. She didn't have her shit together at all. Not if she was brutally honest with herself.

'Life hasn't really turned out how I expected,' she blurted out. 'I thought all this time I was in control of my own destiny. That everything I did was because I wanted to. But I don't feel fulfilled.'

Majid's expression was blank. She'd expected to read judgement on his face, something that told her she was being self-indulgent, feeling sorry for herself. She had expected him to react like Imran. But he didn't.

'Me and Imran, we're cut from the same cloth, I think. We push and push ourselves to do the right thing. To do what Amma and Baba would have wanted. But I don't feel like I'm truly living. I've gotten so used to trying to please others and fulfil their needs. And then I see you, and I see your mates. And I feel so envious . . .'

Sumaya broke into tears.

'I wish Mum hadn't got ill and died. I wish I hadn't had to take care of her. It's selfish, I know. I wish I hadn't had to fight with my brother over who would do what around the house. I was just a kid. Just a kid, Maj. I was forced to grow up, to be a carer to Mum, a substitute mum to you . . . I never asked for this.'

Sumaya wept into the palms of her hands, the years of hurt pouring out of her. Majid placed his hand on her back, consoling his sister in what little way he could as she let out the tears and pain.

'You did the best you could, sis,' he said quietly.

'It's never enough.' Sumaya's response was muffled through her hands. 'Imran, Jonathan . . . everyone wants to put me in a certain box. They all want to mould me in their image. It's never enough that I did the best I could.'

'Well, it was enough for me.'

At this, Sumaya took her hands away from her face and looked intently at her younger brother. She saw flashes of the boy he had been and the relationship they'd had. Walking home from school hand in hand. Preparing his fish fingers while helping him with his homework. More tears fell from her eyes and landed on her jeans.

'Really? Do you mean that?'

'I do,' Majid said earnestly. 'I may have been just a snotty kid, but I could see how hard it was for you, for Dad, even Imran. You sacrificed a lot for me, to make sure my life wasn't disrupted. You stepped up, sis. You should be proud of yourself for that. You did your part and I don't care what anyone else says or thinks, you've paid your debt to our family. You deserve to be happy.'

Sumaya sobbed even harder, a snot bubble forming around her left nostril. She wrapped her arms around her brother, pulling him in close. 'Thank you,' she whispered.

'You've sacrificed enough in one lifetime,' Majid said, holding his sister. 'You don't have to do anything or be anything you don't want to be, sis. Life doesn't end at thirty. It's not too late to reclaim your life, to live how you want to live.'

Sumaya pulled away from her brother and looked at him in wonder. How had he grown to be so wise and compassionate?

'How did you end up so well adjusted, and not fucked up like us?' she snorted.

'What can I say, I'm one of a kind,' he laughed. 'Nah, for real, I'm just out here going with the flow. Going through what we went through – losing Mum and Dad at such a young age . . . it just,

I don't know, put life into perspective for me. I just want to live each day to the max and be happy. I've never felt the pressure that you guys did. Even when Imran tries to put pressure on me to be a certain way, I'm like, "You're good, bro." This is my one life. I just want to laugh. I want to be happy. I want to make people laugh and be happy! What's the point in trying to be someone I'm not? Allah made me uniquely me.'

Sumaya gazed at her younger brother, enchanted, and in that moment she had never felt more proud of him. She rested her head against him and praised Allah that at least one good thing had come out of the tumult of their upbringing. That Majid hadn't been traumatised or had his light dimmed by losing their parents. That he had come out relatively unscathed. That he was full of vim and vigour.

What was the point in trying to be someone you're not? she thought.

She wanted to be more like her younger brother.

Chapter 18

IMRAN

Days later, Imran was still feeling the sting of Fahima's rejection, but he was determined not to give up. He had come so close to losing everything he loved, and he realised he didn't want to be this person anymore. He had to do everything he could to win Fahima back. He'd been foolish to think she'd simply open the door and talk to him. He had to show he was a man of actions, not just words. Why would Fahima believe him, after everything that she had learned about his past, and all the hurt that he had put her through? He had to show how much he loved her.

That evening after work, he resolved to try again, but to pull off his elaborate declaration of love, first he needed to stop by the local Card Factory, where he picked up a multipack of one hundred tea lights and asked the customer service assistant to blow up various foil helium balloons – love hearts in red, purple and blue, and stars in pink, copper and silver. Then he made his way back to Maida Vale, the balloons bobbing at confused passers-by in the back seat at every red light.

He looked at the clock. It was nearly 7.30 p.m. He knew that her mother and father would be out – they went to the same Indian restaurant every Monday, sat in the same booth, and ordered the same meal. After all these years, it was the one tradition they had kept up from their early days of marriage, before they had had children. Now, recalling Junan and Bisha's routine, he was reminded how wistfully Fahima had spoken about her parents' date nights. Their standing weekly appointment with no kids, no distractions. It dawned on him, finally, that perhaps Fahima's nostalgic recollections of her parents' weekly date had been a hint. One that he had failed to pick up on. *How stupid have I been?* he thought as he drove to West London. He told himself that if this worked, if he could bring her home, he'd make sure they had a weekly date night of their own. But first, he had to execute his plan.

His father-in-law's car wasn't in the driveway when Imran pulled on to their street, although he could see the yellow glow of the lights upstairs. Fahima must be home, he told himself. She had to be. He was off to a good start. He tried to push down the nerves and wipe his sweaty palms on his trousers. He had to get this right.

Imran took hold of all the items he'd bought earlier and walked round to the back of the house, letting himself into the garden through the gate. Fahima's room overlooked the garden and it was here that he'd stage his gesture to win her back. Fahima's parents grew their own Bangladeshi lemons, kodu – bottle gourd – and spinach, and in one corner of the garden was Bisha's prized collection of roses.

Imran tried not to make too much noise as he got to work, lighting up the garden with the tea lights, little fireflies perfectly illuminating the dark. In the centre of the garden, taking care not to trample Junan and Bisha's fresh coriander, he set down the balloons, each tied to equally colourful weights so they wouldn't float away. Proudly, he looked around at the scene he'd set. This was much more like Shah Rukh, he thought. This was how he always got the girl in the movies, with romantic displays of affection.

Satisfied, he picked up pebbles from the ground and gently launched them, one by one, at Fahima's window, hoping and praying that he'd catch her attention. The first pebble hit the window-sill, the second the concrete wall beside it. He picked up a larger stone still and launched it at the window. This time, the stone connected. *Come on, Fahima*, he thought. He picked up another stone, similar in size and, pulling his arm back slightly, volleyed it at the window. The stone hurtled into the glass and Imran heard a crack. *Shit*, he thought. The stone had left a crack in the corner of the window. His eyes flashed in terror as he watched a silhouetted figure shuffle towards the window. Fahima. She pulled back the curtain and looked at the window in confusion. Then she looked below into the garden and caught his eye. Fahima's confusion turned to anger. *No, no,* he panicked. This wasn't how it was supposed to go.

Suddenly, she disappeared from view. In an instant Imran's mind went blank and he stood frozen to the spot. Should he run? But she had already seen him. Should he try to ring the doorbell? Explain?

Light illuminated the kitchen and then he heard the sound of the garden door being unlocked. Fahima now stood before him, her brow furrowed. He was fully panicked now.

'Imran. What are you doing?' she spat. 'You just broke the window!'

Still gripped with fear, he found he couldn't even form words.

'What are you doing here?' Fahima continued to admonish him. 'What is all this? Really? You're breaking into my parents' garden now?'

'I . . .' Imran stumbled for words. 'I . . . I'm sorry . . .'

Imran stumbled backwards, tripping over one of the balloon weights. Then, he heard Fahima gasp.

'IMRAN!' Fahima shouted, pointing at something on the ground.

As he tried to regain his balance, he looked down, following the direction of her finger, realising all of a sudden that she wasn't pointing at the ground – she was pointing at him! At his leg!

One of the tea lights had set the bottom of his right trouser leg on fire!

'Oh shit!' Imran yelped, hopping up and down on the spot and trying to fan the flames away. 'Oh my god!'

Fahima ran out of the house with a large mixing bowl in her hands. She doused his legs with the water, putting out the small fire. Some of the tea lights in his immediate vicinity also sizzled out.

There they stood – Fahima, an empty mixing bowl in her hands, and him with a charred brown stain on his trousers.

'What on earth do you think you're doing?' Fahima suddenly flew into a rage.

Imran felt his stomach drop. This couldn't have gone any worse.

'First, you break into our garden. Then you break the window. And now you're setting yourself on fire!'

The words coming out of his wife's mouth seemed absurd, comical, but she spoke the absolute truth. He had made a fool of himself.

'And all this,' she said, gesturing her hands around the garden, at the tea lights and the balloons. 'Do you really think this is what I want from you? Some bloody children's party balloons and a few candles? Do you think this is some . . . movie?'

Imran's face fell. If the earth could swallow him up, he wished it would. Right now. He'd made a mess of things. Again. He'd thought she'd be impressed by his gesture, that they might sit in the garden, warm cups of tea in hand, in the glow of the candles, and she might hear him out. It had all gone so horribly wrong.

'I'm . . . I'm sorry,' was all he could muster. A feeble apology.

'I'm going back inside,' Fahima said sharply. 'I suggest you clear all this up before my parents get back. Go home, Imran. I mean it.

I need time to think. And I don't want to see your face until you can show me some real change.'

'But . . .'

Imran could barely get a word out before Fahima turned on her heel and stormed back into the house, shutting the garden door behind her and turning out the kitchen lights.

For the second time in a row, Imran found himself standing alone with a door slammed in his face. *But I am changing*, he wanted to say. Wasn't this proof that he was trying to change?

How could he have messed things up even more?

More than a little bruised by the previous night's humiliation, Imran made his way towards the Celeritas office wearing his embarrassment like a shroud, eyes sullen and mouth downturned. As he opened the door, he was met by an ominous silence; Martin and Joe were huddled together, whispering. Shelly was at her desk and even she looked sheepish, offering him a weak smile instead of the big grin she usually greeted him with each morning. Somehow, Imran realised, his day was about to get a lot worse. He already felt lousy. What else could go wrong? Depleted of energy as he was, he knew that he had no fight left in him. All he could do was brace himself for the impact of whatever was to come. But it was as if the air had been completely sucked from the room, leaving him gasping for breath.

'Ooh, you've done it now, big boy,' Joe said with a sly smirk, breaking off from his hushed conversation with Martin.

Imran looked at the two men, but Martin quickly avoided his eyes.

All he'd wanted to do today was get through the next eight hours, then go home, curl up in a ball and lick his wounds. But getting through the next eight hours suddenly felt more like an obstacle course than a breezy walk.

'With me,' Giles said tersely, sauntering into the office, the heels of his brogues clicking against the parquet floor. The sound of impending doom.

Imran hadn't even had a chance to take off his coat or put his messenger bag down at his desk, but he dutifully followed his boss into the kitchenette, his stomach somersaulting. As he walked past Shelly's desk, she reached out and stealthily squeezed his hand in solidarity. At least there was one person in the world he hadn't alienated.

Giles held the door open for Imran to walk in first, which he reluctantly did, feeling the heat emanating from his boss's face as he passed him.

Giles walked in behind him and shut the door, before turning to him.

'What the fuck is this?' Giles suddenly raged, holding out his phone for Imran to see.

Imran was instantly taken aback. He blinked, as if to test that what he was seeing was real. His boss was slimy in that vindictive, behind-your-back way that he had known his colleagues to be, but the scorn was rarely as overt as it was now.

He looked more closely at the phone screen; it was a banking app. A charge for £142. Imran's confusion was written all over his face. He continued to scan the screen. A charge for £142 at Card Factory the day before. Shit, he thought. He must've accidentally used the wrong card at the shop. He'd been so caught up, dizzied by the excitement of what he now realised was his futile stunt, that he must've pulled out his company card at the checkout instead of his personal card.

'Oh! I can explain—' Imran began before Giles cut him off.

'No, I don't want to hear it. You're already on thin ice, *boy*,' Giles sputtered, emphasising the final word. The force of his boss's tone nearly knocked Imran off his feet. His eyes stung with indignation. This was what it came down to – it always did. With a single word, it was as if Giles had ripped away all his qualifications, all his achievements, and stripped him down to his basic corporeal form – the way he truly saw him: a worthless brown body. He saw him not as a colleague or a sales executive. Imran saw himself through Giles's eyes now. He may as well have been a chaiwala, a servant, and Giles his liege.

'Giles, it's honestly . . . can I just explain—' Imran tried to speak again, only to be cut off.

'I'm curious what exactly warrants spending £142 in a *card shop*?' Giles seethed. 'Having a jolly on the company account, were you?'

'Giles . . . there's been a mistake . . . Listen—' Imran tried to plead with his boss, but the indignation in Giles's eyes didn't change. It didn't matter what he said, Imran realised. Giles had been looking for something – anything – to pin on him. He wouldn't care that he'd made a mistake.

'I've had enough of your insubordination. You know, there are a million men out there who'd love to have your job. And now, using company finances on . . . I don't even know what!' Giles shouted at him.

The glass window that looked out on to the office seemed to reverberate with Giles's fury. Imran could see Joe and Martin watching on in astonishment. Even Shelly was reluctantly watching the commotion. He wondered if they could hear what was being said, but their faces told him that the sheer theatricality of his admonishment was clear with or without sound.

'Frankly, I'm at my wits' end. I'm suspending you. Without pay.' Giles delivered the fatal blow.

Imran's eyes widened. 'What?!'

Giles ignored him and continued coldly. 'You are to leave the premises immediately. I have spoken to regional HR, and we will arrange for a letter to be sent to your address. There will be an investigation, of course.'

'But, Giles, you can't be serious. It's an honest mistake—'

'Frankly, I'd have had you fired, so consider yourself lucky you even still have a job,' Giles said as he turned his back and walked out of the kitchenette.

There was no opportunity for Imran to explain himself. Giles hadn't intended there to be one. This had been a display of authority; Giles had wanted to exert his domination over his subordinate, both professionally and personally. *Boy.* The word rang in Imran's ears. There was no mistaking the intent behind Giles's choice of words. He had meant to denigrate him, to re-establish their hierarchy in work and in life. This felt all too familiar. It's what white people did when they wanted to remind people like him of their place. To redress the natural order of things as they saw it.

Imran reeled with shock as he left the kitchenette and then the office, not daring to exchange glances with or speak to his colleagues. He could see Shelly's lips moving; she was trying to talk to him, but the words sounded muffled to his ears. His cheeks flushed with anger and humiliation. In that moment he was too shellshocked to call out the implicit racism he had just experienced.

It wouldn't be till later, at home, that he'd realise what he'd allowed to go unchallenged. And he'd burn with regret, as well as anger and bitter embarrassment. He'd wish he'd called it out. He'd wish he wasn't just another in a long line of minorities to accept the abuse and march on.

But that didn't occur to him now. Instead, as he walked out to his car, he was struck by something else Giles had said. 'Consider yourself lucky you even still have a job.'

Luck. Gratitude. Why were brown people always expected to be so grateful? It was never 'you deserve this' or 'you earned it'. It was good fortune. It was never hard work and being suitably qualified for a job, but some stroke of sheer luck. This, too, Imran had dealt with his whole life. His years of education and experience negated because of the colour of his skin. His livelihood not earned, but graciously bestowed upon him by the white man, and just as easily taken away.

Imran smarted. He'd never heard Giles even remotely raise his voice to Joe or Martin. He'd always been cognisant of the precarious nature of his employment: he'd get pulled up over his performance where Joe and Martin would not. He was kept on a tight leash, his work monitored and surveyed, while theirs was rubber-stamped without a second look. Then there were the things they got away with. Offences far worse than his own. He recalled the Christmas party two years ago when Martin, so drunk from the free booze and possibly a line or two deep in sniff, had groped a waitress's ass. Giles had witnessed it all and laughed with the younger man. Martin should have been fired – or worse. But Giles didn't even consider Martin's behaviour unacceptable. If it had been Imran, it would have been a completely different story. He'd have been paraded out in handcuffs and splashed on the front pages as a 'predator'.

Time and time again, he was reminded what it meant to be a minority.

Chapter 19

SUMAYA

Sumaya awoke groggy, her bedsheets soaked through with sweat. She noticed she was still in last night's clothes, her blue top crumpled. She recalled bits and pieces of the night before: stumbling home with an arm around Majid; her younger brother pulling off her boots and putting her into bed. What irony. It had been her who used to tuck him into bed and read him a bedtime story when Amma was ill and in hospital.

As she lifted her neck, a searing pain shot through her head and forced her to stop mid-motion. She remembered the dubious shots from the night before. She hadn't felt this hung over since . . . well, ever. She could kill Majid for insisting she down so many.

But despite the heavy head and full-body shakes, mentally she felt pleased, too. She had crossed a messy student night, like the ones she had never been able to have when she was a student herself, off her bucket list. She smiled as she thought about her conversation with Majid the night before – it was unlike any she'd ever had with Imran. Their conversations, when they went beyond the surface level, always descended into perceived slights and recriminations. How refreshing it was to be able to open up about her emotions with her younger sibling; only the three of them would ever know each other's hurt and trauma from their mother's illness, but she and Imran had not once truly sat down and commiserated about the scars they each carried, consoled each other, shown each other the love and compassion she expected siblings to have. After last night, the guilt of leaving Majid for New York had dulled. He had turned into a young man she could truly be proud of.

'Morning,' Majid said, walking into the room at that precise moment with a mug of coffee in hand. He placed it on the bedside table.

'Why are you so chirpy?' Sumaya said. Her voice was hoarse and raspy. 'I'm dying here.'

'I don't know what to tell you, sis. Old age, innit?'

Sumaya chuckled and threw one of her pillows at her brother. 'And *you're* not too old for me to slap you!'

'By the way, I gave Seema your email address. She said she was sending over some clips from the documentary she's making with Haroon. I'm going to a lecture. I'll catch you later,' Majid said. 'And your phone is in the kitchen. It was buzzing all night. I think your boy Jonathan is missing you.'

Sumaya's stomach felt funny at the mention of Jonathan. Or was it the copious alcohol she had ingested? She couldn't quite tell. Talking to her brother in the club last night, she had felt such clarity – no doubt emboldened by booze – about what she wanted for her life. And it wasn't being Jonathan's wife. There was no way she would allow herself to be trapped in a life she didn't want. Now, however, in the cold light of day, the confidence the booze had given her had worn off and she was conflicted. Could she really go through with it? Tell Jonathan no? Admit that her love still lay with Neha?

Nothing seemed as clear-cut as it had the night before.

Sumaya hit the bed with the full force of her closed fists and let out a scream before forcing herself to get up.

In the living room, she turned on her laptop and opened up Seema's email. She had sent her a private YouTube link. *What we've got so far! xx*, the email said.

Sumaya clicked the link while she took a sip of coffee. The video played instantly. It was Seema sitting at a kitchen table across from an older Indian woman. Her mother, Sumaya deduced.

'So, Mum, how did you feel when I first told you I was bi?' Seema said in the video.

Sumaya's ears pricked and she turned the volume up.

'I guess . . . I was scared,' Seema's mother said. 'A parent's job is to protect their child. Don't get me wrong, I knew you'd be fine, but I think I was frightened how the world would treat you. What would people say? You hear about gay people being attacked . . .'

'So, it wasn't my sexuality that concerned you, but how society would treat me?'

'Yes,' Seema's mum said. 'To me, it doesn't change anything. You are my child. As a mother, you want your child to be able to go out safely into the world. As a girl, a brown girl, I have always worried about how you'd be treated. And with your sexuality – it makes you even more of a minority. I think that's what I worried about most.'

'And now? You see me going to uni and living my life. Are you still scared?' Seema asked her mother.

'Less now,' her mother said. 'I think you are teaching me a lot about the world today, just as I taught you about the world when you were younger. I see you're happy, you have good friends who take care of you, that you're safe. I think I'll always worry, but I don't want you to ever be unhappy.'

Sumaya paused the clip and felt her eyes water. Suddenly she felt consumed by tears. The tender way Seema and her mother spoke about Seema's sexuality, the way Seema's mother was so accepting of her, struck a chord.

What if Amma hadn't made her keep her sexuality a secret? What if she hadn't had to live her life in half-truths? Sumaya thought as she sobbed. It felt like so much of her life had been preordained – governed by what society thought. Amma had done her best, and it wasn't her mother Sumaya blamed, but the social constructs that meant she'd had to hide who she was all those years ago. Amma had feared what the men in the community would think – Imran and Baba included – and what the wives would say behind their backs. She had projected her fears on to her daughter and made her afraid to be free.

But it didn't have to be that way. Seema and her mother were proof.

This is so beautiful, Sumaya wrote in her email back. *This really hit home for me, and I think it will for a lot of other people, too. Let's get Haroon to do a similar interview with his parents?*

The two women held each other's forearms for fear of falling. Neither was particularly skilled at ice skating, so their choice to go to a skating rink now seemed questionable. Perhaps it was to relive their youth. But they hadn't been any more graceful on the ice then either.

Sumaya moved her hands away from Neha, trying to balance herself on her thin blades. 'I think I've got it,' she said.

'Wait! I'm going to fall!' Neha said, before duly collapsing on to her bottom on the cold ice.

Sumaya burst out laughing. Then Neha did too. Sumaya helped the other woman up and gingerly, in sync, they moved towards the outside of the rink and held on to the barrier.

Sumaya, now in front of Neha, gripped the boards as they moved around the circumference of the rink. Neha followed her lead.

'I'm glad you called,' Sumaya said.

In truth, Sumaya had been elated when Neha called her that afternoon and had leapt at the opportunity to meet up. She desperately wanted to see her again, and now that she was beginning to make her mind up about Jonathan, she was teetering on the brink of hope that Neha might still hold even a flicker of feeling for her. It was only a few days since they'd last seen each other, but Sumaya's hunger for Neha wasn't remotely satiated.

'I'm glad you were free! I needed to get out of the house. I can't tell you the last time I did something without my husband or kids,' Neha said.

'You sounded a bit . . . off. Is something the matter?' Sumaya asked.

Neha had sounded agitated on the phone, and Sumaya had immediately wondered if something had happened with her husband. She didn't voice this, of course, though she secretly hoped that Neha was as unhappy as she was. What she imagined would happen, she didn't know, but Neha had reached out to her, of all people. That had to mean something?

'Oh, it's not that big a deal,' Neha said, looking down at her feet. Trying to talk and stay upright at the same time was proving to be a challenge. 'Just the usual mum stuff. Who is going to pick up and drop off the kids? And Sabir has already torn his school blazer. Do you know how bloody expensive school uniforms are these days? Sorry . . . I'm rambling . . .'

'No, it's okay,' Sumaya replied.

'I'm sorry,' Neha said. 'It's just my mind is always on the kids and what's for dinner, bills . . . Me and Bilal, we had a bit of tension over the electricity bill this morning. If he had it his way, we'd never turn on the heating! But I keep telling him the flat is too cold. The insulation is terrible . . . Sorry, I'm going off on one again. I just needed some time away.'

Though Sumaya knew she was at risk of prying, she couldn't help but ask anyway: 'Do you . . . argue a lot?'

'I mean, no more than any other couple, I guess. It just feels like arguing with a brick wall, though. You know how it is. These men are raised by their mothers to think they are perfect and can do no wrong . . . they are put on a pedestal from childhood and expect you to bow to them.'

Sumaya's thoughts immediately turned to Imran. She knew exactly what Neha was talking about, for Amma had treated Imran like he was the heir to some proverbial throne. He had been coddled and given chance after chance, never told no or that he was wrong. And now look where that had got him. He was an egotistical manchild who still needed others to carry him to water.

'I'm sorry to hear it,' Sumaya said. 'If you want to talk about it, how about I buy us a coffee?'

'Bloody hell, yeah. Get me off this ice!'

◆ ◆ ◆

They huddled in the corner of a quiet Starbucks, Sumaya sipping a black Americano and Neha a mocha – just like old times in the days when their futures hadn't yet been mapped out for them and everything had seemed possible.

Sumaya remembered how they'd sit in the corner of coffee shops with their university coursework sprawled out in front of them, sharing a set of earbuds and listening to an eclectic mix of songs on Neha's iPod – Arctic Monkeys into Rihanna into Kasabian. Neha's close proximity felt good, the smell of her perfume – white gardenia, jasmine and patchouli – transporting Sumaya back to a life when she had been so full of optimism.

Sumaya held her head in her hands, her elbows perched on the table. 'When I saw you the other day, I asked you if you were happy. With Bilal, I mean. When you talk about him . . . you sound so . . . I don't know. Sad?'

Neha tried to bat the question away with her hand. 'No, not at all,' she began. 'Is any marriage perfect? If there is one out there, I've never seen it.'

Sumaya thought of Amma and Baba. Their relationship had been as close to perfect as any she could recall, but even so it had had its faults. Amma had been so scared of Baba finding out about her and Neha, about Imran and Sophie's pregnancy, that there must have been so much unsaid in their marriage. Amma and Baba had loved each other, of course, but Amma wouldn't have asked Sumaya to hold her secrets if she hadn't feared Baba, too. If she hadn't been worried about how he'd react to his children's transgressions. They'd kept secrets from each other. So, no, she didn't believe in a perfect relationship either.

'We have ups and downs like anyone else,' Neha continued. 'I wouldn't say I'm any different to the millions of other women out there. Besides, it's different when you have kids. They just take over your life.'

'But you're still your own person . . .' Sumaya blurted out.

Neha laughed. 'Try telling them that! To them I was born "Mum".'

'Does Bilal help with the kids?' Sumaya probed. It felt intrusive to ask, but she couldn't help it.

'When he can,' Neha said. 'He's a good father, don't get me wrong. But he's always at work, so all the house stuff falls on little old me.'

'Have you tried to ask him for more help?'

Neha scoffed. 'I've tried. It's always "one day". "When we're more financially secure I can work less . . ." But I don't know if that day will ever come. Amma says a man needs his work to feel important, that I shouldn't push him too much. "Even when a man is wrong, he is always right . . ." – all the stuff they told us growing up.'

'That's bullshit,' Sumaya blurted out without thinking, her face suddenly hot with anger. 'Sorry, I didn't mean . . .'

Neha laughed again. 'It's okay. I'd think it was bullshit, too, if it weren't my life. But this is how it is here, in this bubble. When we were young, we were idealistic. We thought we could change the world. Be supermodels or astrophysicists – both at the same time even! But the reality is, change doesn't happen so quickly. It will take generations of us women to change the way things have always been. That's why I'm proud of you, Sumaya. You escaped the rat race. You realised what life would be here and you did something about it. Yes, it hurt to lose you, but . . .'

Neha suddenly turned her face away. Sumaya could hear her stifling her sobs with the palm of her hand. She placed a hand on her knee.

'You deserve to be happy, Neha,' she said earnestly. 'You were always the best of us. You still are.'

Neha turned her face back and Sumaya could see the tears that had formed in her eyes. How she wished she could wipe them away with her own two hands, but she daren't. It would be too intimate. She didn't know what she should do next. She was standing at the edge of a lake, dipping her toe in the water, telling herself not to dive in. No matter how warm and inviting the water seemed.

'Do you mind if I ask . . .' Neha said sheepishly. 'When you moved to New York, did you date any other women?'

Now Sumaya was the sheepish one. 'I . . .' she started, and then stopped, wondering how to articulate herself. 'I mean . . . I tried. It just never happened, I guess? I met some girls, but nothing . . .'

She stopped short of saying what was on her tongue. *Nothing like what I had with you* . . . She found herself distracted by Neha's bold, brown eyes and the fullness of her upper lip. She shook herself free from temptation; this couldn't happen.

'Um, I guess I just met Jonathan and the rest is history,' she said, speaking at what felt like double speed.

Both women could tell it wasn't quite so straightforward, but neither wanted to put what they were thinking into words: that Sumaya had settled.

'So, do you think you'll get married?' Neha asked, prompting Sumaya to nearly choke on her Americano.

Neha had no idea that the subject of marriage was what was plaguing her about her relationship at this very moment. That her head and heart were in a battle over what she thought she *should* do and what she *wanted* to do.

'One day . . . ?' Sumaya said non-committally.

Neha cocked her head and stared at her. It was as if she were penetrating her with her eyes, and Sumaya suddenly felt flustered.

'Shall I tell you what I think?' Neha said playfully.

'Go on . . .'

'I get the feeling that you're not entirely happy with this man, Sumaya,' she said slowly, deliberating over each word, as if unsure whether to voice her concern. 'The Sumaya I know – or *knew* – always knew what she wanted and went for it. She didn't say "one day" or things like "the rest is history". She felt everything deeply . . . vividly. She dreamed in colour when the rest of us dreamed in black and white. I think there's a piece missing, Sumaya. A piece of the magic that was you.'

Sumaya's eyes blazed as she tried to simultaneously hold back tears and keep Neha's gaze. She willed her eyes not to betray any sign of emotion. She didn't want to admit that Neha was right. She always was. Neha always saw through her like no one else, even when she thought she was being impenetrable.

The two women were locked in a game of who'd blink first, and Sumaya was desperate not to lose.

Neha delicately put a hand on Sumaya's arm. 'You deserve to be happy, too,' she said simply, in that sweet, earnest voice that told Sumaya that this was not a game. Neha wasn't trying to read her mind to get one up on her. She was, as always, speaking from a place of love.

That was it. A dam inside Sumaya broke. She quickly leaned in and planted her lips on Neha's. It all happened so fast that she didn't even have time to process what she was doing.

But just as quickly as their lips collided, Neha pulled away and turned her head.

'Oh fuck . . . I'm sorry . . . I didn't mean to . . .' Sumaya felt her face flame.

Neha looked around the shop to see if anyone had caught them in this illicit moment.

Then she turned back to her and, with a glint in her eye, she said: 'No . . . just not here . . .'

What happened next, Sumaya convinced herself, was a mirage. It could surely not have been real?

When she replayed the events in her mind later, they came to her in flashes. She remembered her and Neha quickly gathering their things and heading out of the coffee shop. She texted Majid on the way home to confirm he was out with his friends.

She recalled the moment she and Neha burst through the door, and the look of longing that passed between them, which had felt like it lasted minutes but was in reality mere seconds. Then they came together as one, their lips uniting like lock and key. After so many years apart, Sumaya was thrilled to find that their cadence was still there. That they still fit each other. They moved together passionately, lips entwined the whole time, to the sofa, and not once did Sumaya care about its questionable state. She was in a state of delirium. Their lips wrote a symphony, moving up and down from top to bottom, and the rush of dopamine was unlike anything she had experienced in years. Her body and libido came alive under Neha's spell.

Another flash of memory. They had moved into the bedroom, Neha atop her on Andrew's bed. The box spring that had been the bane of her existence the last few days suddenly felt like a cloud on Mount Olympus itself.

Clothes came off.

Hair, limbs and moans flew in every direction . . .

When it was over, Sumaya lay next to Neha, panting.

This was the life she should have lived this whole time.

Chapter 20

IMRAN

Imran straightened his back and held his head high as he walked into the Celeritas office. He was still suspended and hadn't called ahead of his visit, but he'd imagined the look on Giles's face when he sauntered in and knew it would be priceless. He couldn't wait to wipe the smarmy grin from his boss's face.

Giles was at his desk, huddled over his laptop. He sat at the front of the office, positioned like a teacher, facing out over his employees. Joe, Martin and Shelly were at their desks, too, when Imran opened the door. Collectively, all four looked up. This was it. This was the moment he had been dreaming of.

Imran immediately made eye contact with his boss. Giles's sour expression told him everything he was thinking: how dare Imran turn up when he was under strict instructions not to step on to the premises? But Imran simply grinned. He was done playing by Giles's rules.

'What are you doing here?' Giles said coldly. 'You aren't sup-posed to be here—'

Imran cut him off with a wave of a hand. 'Hi, Giles,' he said coolly. 'I just thought I'd come and tell you this to your face. I won't be long.'

'Tell me what?'

Imran flashed his boss a disarming smile and reached into the back pocket of his trousers, pulling out an envelope with Giles's name on it. He threw it down on his boss's desk.

'I quit. That's my notice,' Imran said, maintaining his satisfied grin. 'I'm done with this place.'

Giles looked down at the envelope and then up at Imran with narrowed eyes. If Imran didn't know better, he might have thought he was almost impressed.

'Well,' Giles said slowly, folding his hands on his desk. 'This is quite the turn of events, Imran. But I must say, I think this might be the wisest course of action for all involved. I have been speaking to HR about your suspension, and I think it's fair to say that your performance has been . . . concerning. I was going to make the recommendation that we make your suspension more permanent. But it seems we won't have to get into a messy affair, after all.'

Giles's smug expression was too much to bear, and Imran couldn't help but be goaded.

'My performance was just fine,' he said. 'I did everything that was asked of me, and tried to go above and beyond, but the fact is you've had it in for me for years. I should have been promoted years ago and you constantly held me back. And don't give me that bullshit about the Dagenham and Barking account. I don't see Joe or Martin here responsible for the sales of an entire borough? So why was I? Could it have anything to do with the fact that there are so many black and brown people there? "We'll put the brown guy on it." Was that it?'

'Now, I don't know what you're insinuating here—' Giles said.

'Don't worry, Giles. Being brown isn't contagious. You won't catch it if you dare to walk through Dagenham, mate.'

'How dare you! Hang on a second . . .' Giles huffed.

'And that's just the start of it. I have a laundry list of the racist shit I've put up with and turned a blind eye to. But I'm not doing that anymore. If you had spent less time micromanaging and undermining me because I don't look like you, maybe you'd have noticed that pillock over there' – he pointed at Martin – 'has been sticking his fingers in the petty cash for pints. And pillock two over there' – he pointed now at Joe – 'has his face in charlie half the time he's at work.'

Giles shot out of his chair and stood eye-to-eye with Imran. 'If you're quite done with your spectacle . . . you can leave,' he said. 'Your sort is always causing trouble. Good luck finding anyone else to employ you. I will personally see to it that every other dealership knows what a liability you are.'

'It's funny you should say that, actually, Giles,' Imran said, his tone calm. 'There's one more thing I need to tell you. I'm starting my own business. And, actually, just this morning, I had a meeting with Greenr and told them all about the kind of operation you run and the shit I've had to deal with. They weren't impressed. In fact, they've agreed a five-year contract to work exclusively with my company as their licensed car supplier.'

Martin gasped. Giles's eyes bulged and his face turned red. This was the final blow Imran had been waiting to deliver, and he took every satisfaction in doing so.

Imran and Hakeem had spent the morning ironing out the details. It had been Hakeem that Imran had turned to after his suspension. 'Bro, that's just not right,' his friend told him, offering to call Giles and threaten to pull his business away from Celeritas.

In fact, it had been Hakeem's idea that he strike out on his own. 'Like I said, you're one of the smartest brothers I know. You and me, we know what it's like to work for everything we have, to come from nothing. We're cut from the same cloth. We know what it means to work, and work hard,' Hakeem had said.

Then he'd given him a whole pep talk to shore up his confidence. 'What if you went out on your own?' he'd asked. 'Clearly, those fools don't value you. They are the kind of snakes that will take your money but turn their back on you the first chance they get. But I know you've got the drive, bro. You can do big things.'

Not only had Hakeem planted the seed in Imran's mind that he start his own car supply business, but he'd also vowed to bring his business over to the new firm. 'I'll do you one better,' he promised. 'I'll give you my business, and introduce you to some of my investor friends too.'

'Nah, I can't ask that of you,' Imran had protested, but his friend had waved off his concerns.

'That's what we do for each other, brother. We have to look out for each other.'

Hakeem had put his trust in him; Imran had been nothing if not sincere throughout their years growing up in East London, and that kind of loyalty was hard to come by. Not only did Hakeem see the potential in his friend where his employer hadn't, he understood that they were of the same ilk. Both men's parents had moved here from their home countries to give their offspring a better life. They were migrants who, knowing no one else, had entrusted each other to look out for one another – Bangladeshis, Pakistanis and Somalians alike. They were each other's families all these thousands of miles away from home. Imran and Hakeem may not have been bonded by blood, but like so many other migrants, they were bonded by trust.

'Take care, Giles,' Imran said now, saluting his boss and leaving the Celeritas office for good.

◆ ◆ ◆

On the other side of London, Fahima reluctantly trailed her younger sister, Shahina, and her nephew, Kabir, at London Zoo.

Not including the Uber journey to her parents' home in West London nearly a week ago, this was the first time she had been out in public since the attack. All around her, men, women and children jockeyed for a vantage point to see the penguins and tigers. Strangers brushed past each other. It was enough to make Fahima feel claustrophobic, although the zoo spanned some thirty-six acres. She tried to grit her teeth and bear it – the alternative was another inquisition from her mother: Why was she so sullen? What had happened with Imran?

Fahima hadn't told her family about the attack, nor her troubles with Imran, though Bisha had deduced there was trouble between them after the episode outside Fahima's bedroom door last week. The shame she felt because of what had happened to her was hers to bear alone. Her parents would only worry, and blame her husband for not doing a better job of looking after her. Anything they could hold over him, they would weaponise.

Ammi had cried and thrashed her arms against Fahima's chest when she'd first told her about Imran. He was everything she didn't want for her daughter – the son of a glorified fishmonger and a housewife, a man without a penny to his name, nor an inheritance. Ammi and Abba were from a more aristocratic class, and their status and wealth set them apart from the Bangladeshi community that Fahima had grown to think of as her own in East London. Her parents ate at nice restaurants, not street food from Whitechapel market, and shopped in Harrods, not Green Street. They had wanted her to marry Rish, the son of her father's business associate. He had studied at Oxford and was expected to move to America to do a postgraduate degree at Harvard. They would have preferred their daughter to be thousands of miles away in Massachusetts with Rish than an hour's commute away in Bow with Imran. So, no, she didn't dare tell her parents what had caused her to suddenly turn up

191

on their doorstep, because, just like Imran, she knew they would hear her but they wouldn't truly listen.

That morning, Ammi had called Shahina to take her sister out, to try to get to the bottom of her melancholy. Shahina, five years her junior, was the perfect daughter that Ammi and Abba doted on, for she had done things the right way. She had married a consultant doctor and had a home in Kent. Shahina and Akhtar had given Ammi and Abba their first grandchild, Kabir, within a year of marriage.

Fahima had always wondered, if she were to have a child, would her parents' venom towards her husband lessen? Would a child mend the bridges between her two families? But there was no child for her to bring home to her parents. And when she saw how easily Shahina had got pregnant, giving her parents the most beautiful grandson, Fahima couldn't help but feel resentment towards her younger sister, though she knew it was wrong.

'Auntie, look!' Kabir said, wrapping his chubby hand around her index finger with one hand and pointing up at the monkey enclosure with his free hand.

'Yes, I can see them!' she said in a singsong tone, attempting to brighten her mood for the sake of the child.

Inside, Fahima felt overwhelmed by the number of people around her. And every time she saw a white man, she seemed to freeze on the spot. Though she couldn't remember her attacker's face, he was everywhere and nowhere all at the same time.

'I'm going to sit over here for a moment,' she told her nephew, pointing to a bench in a secluded area.

Fahima took deep breaths in and out and counted to ten, just as the doctor had told her to. From the corner of her eye she could see the little boy staring at her inquisitively.

'Auntie, you're weird. Why are you talking to yourself?' Kabir asked.

'It helps Auntie relax,' she said.

'Oh, okay. I'll do it, too . . . one . . . two . . . three . . .' her nephew roared.

Fahima let out a hearty laugh. Instantly, she felt lighter. Not because of the counting exercise, but because of the company of the precocious young boy. What a blessing a child was, with their unbridled way of seeing the world.

'Do you want to get an ice cream?' she asked him, and then looked to his mother for approval. Shahina nodded.

Fahima held the boy's hand as they walked to the ice cream van, letting him regale her with all that he had seen in the zoo. A sense of calm came over her. This was what she had always wanted.

And then she thought of Imran and the sting of betrayal she'd felt standing in the doorway of the kitchen when he was arguing with Sumaya. She wasn't stupid. She'd known her husband wasn't perfect, that he must have been with other women before her. But the betrayal she felt was far more complicated than that. She felt betrayed not only by him, but by her own body. She had wanted a child so desperately. It pained her to think that, without even trying and perhaps without his knowledge, he could so easily have had a child with another woman had she not had an abortion. It seemed so unfair!

'Fahima! Fahima!'

The commotion around her brought her back to reality. Her sister was calling her name from a short distance away. She followed Shahina's gaze to find the boy on the floor. What had happened? They had just been holding hands. Kabir must have slipped from her grasp. He was holding his grazed knee and wailing.

'What happened?' she asked.

'Some idiot rushed past and knocked him over!'

'Who?!' Fahima said instinctively.

'Over there . . . that white guy in the blue cap . . .' her sister said, pointing in the direction of a middle-aged man with his two children in the line for the aquarium.

Fahima felt a sudden surge of adrenaline as she marched up to the man. Her cheeks were hot with rage. Her eyes bulged with fury.

'You,' she said, poking the man in the back.

'Can I help you?' he said, turning to her.

'Are you blind, or did you not just see that you knocked over a little boy?' Fahima said, pointing back in Kabir's direction.

The man was flustered. 'Oh . . . I didn't see . . .'

'You didn't see that you knocked over a little boy?' Fahima cried out incredulously.

People around them stopped in their tracks to watch the brewing commotion.

'Look, I'm sorry, okay?'

Fahima scoffed. 'You think that makes it okay? Some half-hearted apology? What kind of example is that to your kids?' she scolded him, pointing vigorously at the sheepish blond boy and girl by his side.

'I'm really sorry,' he appealed again. 'I'm just having a manic time trying to keep up with these two . . .'

Fahima looked at the boy and girl, ice cream smeared on their faces, backpacks dragging along the floor. She looked back at the man, the redness of his eyes, the bags that had seemed to form under them, and she could sense he felt as exhausted as she was.

'Daddy!' The little boy tugged on his father's hand. 'What's going on?'

The boy was looking at her wide-eyed. Frightened. She imagined how she must look to him. Red-faced and angry. No better than the man who had attacked her. She instantly felt the heat leave her body. She wasn't this person; she wasn't angry and full of rage. She had felt so much pent-up anger lately – because of the attack, because of Imran – and she risked letting it consume her. The frightened look on the boy's face said it all. If she went down this path, she wouldn't know how to turn back.

'It's okay,' she said to the little boy with a sympathetic smile, and then turned back to the father. 'Thank you for apologising. And in future, please watch where you're going.'

Fahima turned on her heel, returning to Shahina and Kabir. Her sister was helping the little boy to his feet and wiping the tears from his eyes.

'What was that? I've never seen you like that,' Shahina said, startled by her sister's sudden frenzy. 'I kind of like it.'

Fahima replayed the moment in her mind; the rage she had nearly expressed scared her. She had done well not to let the anger get the better of her, to remain calm. But she had also done something she might not have done in the past: used her voice and stood up for her nephew. She had been helpless against her attacker, but this time she wasn't helpless. She didn't politely accept what came her way or run away and hide.

Fahima realised that something in her had shifted of late. She was done being silent, and she was done being afraid.

Chapter 21

SUMAYA

Sumaya, Majid, Seema and Haroon huddled around Sumaya's laptop in Majid's kitchen, watching the latest cut of their documentary short. Seema and Haroon waited with bated breath for Sumaya to deliver her verdict.

'I think it's brilliant,' she said eventually. 'It's open and honest and raw, you know? The conversations with your parents, how different generations have different attitudes to being queer.'

Seema let out a little exclamation of joy. Haroon, who had filmed a conversation with his uncle because his parents didn't want to take part, was a little more reserved. Majid put his hand on Haroon's shoulder and squeezed it.

'You did brilliant, mate,' he reassured his friend.

'You really did,' Sumaya chimed in. 'I'm sorry your mum and dad didn't want to be in it. But, for the film, it is a pretty nice contrast between your story and Seema's. I think people will really relate to it. It isn't always so easy – not everybody is so accepting.'

'Thanks,' Haroon said meekly.

Haroon's parents didn't approve of his relationship with Simon. They thought being gay was incompatible with their Muslim faith. But Sumaya was moved by the frank way he'd opened up about his parents' lack of acceptance to his uncle, and how his uncle had reassured him that there was nothing wrong with him. 'It doesn't mean they don't love you,' Haroon's uncle said on camera. 'It just means that they don't understand, at least not yet. Our generation, that wasn't the done thing; you married someone of the opposite sex, settled down and had kids. There weren't many openly queer people when we were growing up. We didn't have the representation you have now, or even the bravery to be different.'

Sumaya watched, captivated but also uneasy. Haroon's uncle could have been describing Amma and Baba. They hadn't understood a world beyond the heteronormative binary, and it had been Amma's fear of how she'd be treated that had led her to tell Sumaya to lock part of herself away. But since returning to London, and since she began working on this documentary with Haroon and Seema, the shame of who she was – who she loved – had started to fall away.

'I wonder . . .' she thought out loud. 'If we need a third act. We have you both talking to the older generation, but what about if you interviewed someone from the generation in between? A queer millennial who would have straddled the two eras, and maybe experienced things differently to you both. It would be interesting to chart the progress of how things have changed.'

'That's a great idea!' Seema said.

'Yeah, but, we don't know anyone old . . .' Haroon quickly doused the idea with cold water.

'Excuse me! Being a millennial isn't *that* old,' Sumaya interjected. 'And . . . I was thinking . . . maybe I could do it?'

'Really?' Seema was shocked. 'Are you sure?'

'I think you're both really inspiring,' Sumaya said. 'I trust you.'

'Go on, sis!' Majid encouraged his sister.

'Let's do it now, before I change my mind,' Sumaya said.

With that, the group was spurred into action, setting up Haroon's camera on a tripod facing Majid's sofa. Sumaya sat in the middle, Seema and Haroon on either side of her. Majid was put in charge of pressing record.

'Sumaya, what was it like growing up queer for you?' Seema asked. 'Do you think things have got any easier?'

'I think so,' Sumaya said. 'I see young people today who are not afraid to express themselves, who are encouraged – on television, in magazines, on the internet – to be themselves. You just have to look at all the Pride campaigns that come out each year – everyone from the NHS to KFC has ad campaigns about being out and proud. It's something we didn't really have ten, fifteen years ago. It seems there's a lot more acceptance and openness.'

'How did your parents react to you coming out?' Haroon asked.

Sumaya suddenly felt self-conscious, looking from the camera to Majid. Only Majid and Neha knew the secret of her promise to Amma, and now she was about to share it with the world.

'I . . .' she began. 'The first person I ever loved was a girl. I had always known I had an attraction to men and women, but it wasn't until I met this person that I think I really understood how difficult it would be to be in a same-sex relationship as a brown and Muslim person. My mum . . . she was the first person I told . . .'

Sumaya's eyes watered as she recalled the night she'd opened up to Amma. 'I felt a lot of guilt . . . She was scared for me, and for herself too, I guess. It wasn't an easy thing to accept. I've never really told anyone this before,' she said, turning away from the camera.

'It's okay,' Seema said. 'We can stop—'

'No,' Sumaya replied. 'No, I want to keep going . . .'

Sumaya could feel the tears streaming down her cheeks, but she persisted. 'My mum said she didn't think the rest of my family would understand, because they are obviously quite traditional and

Muslim. And so I kept the truth buried for a long, long time . . . I moved away from home, I left my family behind, and I sort of lived a double life. It's exhausting. To hide who you are. To feel so alone in the world. I think I lost sense of who I was . . . by trying to hide who I am. But I think I'm ready to come home. To be me.

'For so long, I was scared. For so long, I hid from the truth. I feared what others would say. My amma, I guess, projected her fears on to me. But that's no way to live. I don't want to waste any more time being someone I'm not.

'I'm Sumaya, I'm thirty-one, I'm Muslim, and I'm bisexual.'

◆ ◆ ◆

This must be what it felt like to be a man, Sumaya thought to herself. To act selfishly without impunity. To do as your heart desired and never be questioned. This was what Imran must feel like. And the power that came with this freedom was intoxicating.

Sumaya and Neha lay in the cramped single bed for the third time that week. Sumaya curled around her lover's back as Neha dozed serenely in her arms, satisfied and exhausted. Since they had consummated their reunion just days ago, every moment apart felt like a state of limbo, their bodies aching for each other. It was more than the rush of any synthetic high when they finally met each day in the cramped quarters of Andrew's bedroom. The exhilaration of exploring each other's bodies was unlike anything Sumaya had experienced with Jonathan. And Neha's moans of ecstasy echoed in her ears long after the deed was done.

This was what it meant to be free. Free at last.

Sumaya stroked Neha's supple torso as she slept, her fingers gently caressing the marks along her abdomen left by childbearing. The lines that had not been there when they were younger repre-sented a different life, a life lived without her. It was a curious thing to imagine her lover with child. For when they were in bed together Sumaya was transported to the young women – girls, really – they had once been. But the marks on Neha's skin only added to their story. The years lost. The sweetness of their reunion. They told the story of what they had each had to bear in the absence of the other. These lines were as precious as the woman they marked.

Now that Neha was back in her arms, Sumaya would never let her go again. Now that Neha was hers again, she would rectify past mistakes. It didn't matter to her that Neha belonged to another, at least legally. Every time she thought of her lover's husband, a coldness came over her. She could be as callous as any man. She could take what she wanted without remorse. She had lived her life governed by what men deemed acceptable. It felt good to pierce that fragile masculinity. To beat a man at his own game.

Sumaya gingerly removed her arm from where it lay across Neha's stomach, trying not to wake her. Watching the other woman sleep beside her so blissfully, her mind had begun to race with possibility. There was much to do and arrangements to make so she and Neha could be together. Gripped with fervour, she sprang into action.

As she slipped from under the sheets and sidled out of the bed, her lover stirred, murmuring as the last of her sleep faded.

'Stay with me just a bit longer,' Neha said groggily.

'I just want to check something on my computer . . .' Sumaya said as she opened up her MacBook.

'What could you possibly need to do right now? Come back here,' Neha teased her.

'I just need to check flights back to New York,' Sumaya said.

This made Neha sit bolt upright in bed. 'What do you mean?' she asked tentatively.

'I've decided,' Sumaya said determinedly. 'I need to go back and end things with Jonathan. I need to get things in order there so I can move home . . .'

'You decided all that just now?' Neha questioned.

Sumaya tapped away at the keyboard as she answered. 'I think I've known for a while that things wouldn't work out with Jonathan. But I owe him the courtesy of doing it in person. And then I want to come home. We've missed out on so much time, Neha. I don't want to miss any more.'

Confusion swept across Neha's face. 'What about your job? Your life there?'

'I can work from anywhere. I'm not worried about that.' Sumaya dismissed her concerns. 'And as for my life there – what life, really? Slowly suffocating with Jonathan? I just need to go back and tell him in person, get my things . . . and then I can be back here in a week, two tops.'

'And then what?' Neha sounded reticent about Sumaya's sudden determination.

'And then . . . us,' Sumaya said, turning from her keyboard to Neha, optimism written on her face. 'We can finally be together. I want to be with you, and only you. What I had in the entire city of New York doesn't compare to what we've had in this tiny room.'

'I'm confused,' Neha said. 'What are you talking about?'

Sumaya wheeled the desk chair closer to the bed and put out her hands. Neha reached out, too, placing her hands in her lover's.

'For the first time in ages, I finally feel like I know what I'm meant to do,' Sumaya said. 'I finally know what I want in life. You, Neha. I'm going to move home so we can be together. I shouldn't have let you go all those years ago. I shouldn't have gone to New York and left you . . . Now we have another chance, and I'm not letting it slip away this time.'

'Slow down,' Neha said, locking eyes with Sumaya. 'This isn't . . . I'm . . .'

Neha was suddenly lost for words.

'I love you, Neha,' Sumaya said, breaking the silence between them. She leaned in to kiss the other woman, but Neha turned her head away.

'What's wrong?' Sumaya said.

'I . . .' Neha struggled for the right words. 'This is crazy.'

Sumaya frowned, her optimism suddenly dissipating. 'What do you mean?'

'Sumaya, take a minute to think about this,' Neha reasoned with her. 'Yes, this has been . . . so beautiful. But I can't see how we can sustain it.'

'We can, we can,' Sumaya pleaded. 'I'll go back to New York and end things with Jonathan. I'll be on the first flight home after. We can find a place together – a home for *us*. We can have what we always wanted, Neha.'

'What about *me*? My husband? My children?' Neha cried out.

Sumaya looked at her blankly.

'I can't just walk away from my life, Sumaya,' Neha said softly.

'But you're not happy,' Sumaya said. 'Tell me I'm wrong. Tell me that you love him . . .'

Neha scoffed. 'Sumaya, life isn't a fantasy. You know that better than anyone. Happiness and love . . . those are privileges that I don't always have. I can't just risk my entire life to run away and be with you. Besides, I took vows. I have already sinned by being with you – I can't . . . please don't ask me for more . . .'

'So you just want to be miserable?' Sumaya raised her voice.

'I never said I was miserable, Sumaya,' Neha replied defensively.

'But if you don't love him, why don't you leave? He doesn't deserve you, Neha . . . Are you scared to leave him?'

'You don't know anything about my life, Sumaya!' Neha replied, exasperated. 'I'm not some desperate, abused housewife that you need to save!'

Sumaya's face turned red. She realised what she'd done, what she'd inadvertently assumed about her old friend, and now she felt ashamed. White people always assumed that Muslim women were subjugated by their husbands. That they were afraid, that they were beaten. It was a horrific stereotype, she knew, because Amma had never been like that. And yet . . . she had unwittingly cast Neha in the same light.

'I'm sorry . . . I didn't mean—'

'It's much more complicated than that,' Neha interrupted her. 'Look. It's great that you left all of this, Sumaya. It really is. I'm proud of you. I'm proud of you for making a life of your own and finding your independence. But . . . I'm not you. I'm not brave like you. This world that you left? This is still my world. I don't know anything else, and I can't . . . I can't give it up. I have so much more at stake. Sabir and Elena. I can't upend their lives. I won't.'

Sumaya looked away from Neha. A tear rolled down her cheek.

'I have a good life, Sumaya,' Neha continued. 'Really, I do. Allah has blessed me with two children who are the light of my life. Maybe I can't have everything I want, but that's okay. It isn't a bad life. I can't leave everything and start over. I have responsibilities – my husband, my children, my family, my husband's family . . . it may not be much to you, Sumaya. It may seem small. But that is my life. And I'm content with it.'

'Then why . . .' Sumaya couldn't bring herself to complete the sentence.

Neha seemed to understand where Sumaya's mind was drifting. 'Why did I sleep with you? I'm not perfect, Sumaya. I haven't seen you in years, and all these feelings came back and it was overwhelming . . . I still care about you, Sumaya. I can't help it. I do. Is it possible to hold two people in your heart at the same time? Because that is how I feel. But . . . you have to understand that that isn't enough to leave everything. You have started over before, and you can again. But I—'

'Please? For me?' Sumaya pleaded, her voice breaking.

'I can't,' Neha said more firmly now. 'I can't do that to my children. You know what it's like here – people will talk. I can't bear that shame, Sumaya. My family would probably never speak to me again. I wouldn't be able to handle it. And, besides, I haven't worked since before Sabir was born! Without Abdul, I wouldn't have a penny to my name. I can't ask you to take care of me, of my children . . . I won't. And then there's the sin I have committed . . . I am a married woman. This isn't who I am. My faith is important to me. I have been foolish . . . Don't you see, Sumaya? This can't be. I'm sorry. I'm sorry for leading you on. I got lost in the romance of seeing you again. Being with you again. But I can't do this.'

Sumaya stared blankly, silently, at a spot in the corner of the room, unable to meet Neha's eyes. Of course, what Neha said made sense, but she couldn't deny how it stung.

Beyond the intensity of the rejection, she understood Neha's plight. Sumaya had left the small-town mindset of Bow. She had forgotten what it felt like to live your life enclosed within the same postcode. She had lost what it meant for something so small and mundane as the local mela to rally an entire community together. To know your neighbours and greet the local butcher. It was a small life, but to ask Neha to give it up wouldn't be fair.

'You are a beautiful person, Sumaya,' Neha said. 'You are braver and shine brighter than anyone I know. And I will always, always care about you. But I can't give you what you need. This isn't our story. It's *yours*. I know that you will be okay. Maybe not now, but eventually. And you'll find the person you're meant to be with. You'll live the life you want to live. I have no doubt about it.'

Sumaya let out a deep breath and turned to Neha. She reached forward and kissed her on the forehead and then took in the sight of her lover one last time.

Slowly, she stood up and moved towards the door. She couldn't bear to say goodbye, to put words to this moment of finality between them. Instead, she retreated to the bathroom and locked herself in. She sat on the toilet seat, silently crying.

Neha had broken her heart yet again. How could this happen twice in one lifetime? Her head felt heavy and her eyes burned with tears, but she sat silently. Grieving what could have been.

Sumaya heard the shuffling of footsteps out in the living room, and then the front door open and close. Neha had left.

The tears fell harder now. Both for what she had briefly had over the last few days, and for what she had lost just as quickly.

After some time, her legs numb, her eyes puffy, Sumaya ceased crying. She was bone-dry of any more tears.

There would never be another like her, but perhaps Neha was right, Sumaya thought as she dabbed her eyes with toilet paper.

Perhaps Neha wasn't her happy ending, but the jolt she needed to write a new story altogether.

Chapter 22

Sumaya hastily took a black scarf out of her handbag and wrapped it loosely around her head before linking her arm through Majid's.

'I feel bad I haven't been here yet,' she told her younger brother as they walked through the Eternal Gardens cemetery.

The last time she had visited Sultana's grave was seven years ago, before she left for New York. Even when she had returned three years ago for Baba's funeral, the visit had been so fraught and fleeting that she hadn't had time to visit her mother. The symmetry wasn't lost on her as she walked solemnly among the tombstones. Once again, she was about to fly to New York, unsure when she'd return. Her time in London was coming to an end, and without Neha, there wasn't much keeping her here now.

It had been a tumultuous return; first, all that had happened with Fahima and Imran, and then seeing Neha. She had resigned herself to the fact that there'd be little resolution of her and Imran's argument. But at least she had got answers from Neha, and she knew what she had to do when she returned to New York: she had to end things with Jonathan. But not for someone else. For her.

'Do you come here often?' Sumaya asked Majid.

'Once in a while,' he replied. 'Sometimes when I feel like I need advice, before an exam or something.'

Sumaya squeezed Majid's arm. They were getting closer to Amma's grave, and then they would pay their respects to Baba, too.

'Are you going to be okay?' Sumaya continued her questioning. 'I promise I'll visit soon.'

'Sis, I've managed without you here the last seven years. I think I'll be fine,' he replied. 'Don't worry about me.'

Sumaya hadn't worked out what she'd say to Jonathan yet. She figured she'd prepare her spiel on the plane. What she did know was that the few times she had been with Neha were the most alive she'd felt romantically in years. Their relationship had run its course and she couldn't give him the marriage or children he wanted. She was done living in half-truths. This trip may not have been fully satisfactory, but she had learned more about herself during it than she had in New York. Who she was and what she truly wanted.

At Amma's grave, the two siblings stood silently side by side and prayed for their mother. Sumaya expressed her regret that she hadn't been to visit in so long and asked her mother for strength to face the tough conversations ahead. *I know you just wanted the best for me*, she said in her head. *It took me a while to realise what that was.*

At Baba's grave, Sumaya broke down in tears. This was the first time she had seen her father's final resting place. She thought back to the funeral and how she and Imran had torn into each other. She had stormed off and returned to the solace of New York. She had willed New York to feel like home, so much so that she had forgotten what home truly meant. This place had felt like somewhere she couldn't return to, because Amma had told her Baba wouldn't understand her sexuality. Now, with her youngest brother by her side, she knew there'd always be a place for her here. She promised Baba that she'd visit him again. She wouldn't stay away so long this time.

'Come on,' Majid said, tugging her arm after they had both finished praying. 'Let's get something to eat.'

They walked the length of the cemetery back towards the main entrance, their hearts weary and their eyes watery. Every so often they passed other mourners and nodded at them, for they knew what their fellow visitors must be feeling. The individual pain over the loss of a loved one was so unique, but grief was a shared human experience that touched everyone.

Majid suddenly stopped in his tracks, halting Sumaya in hers, too.

'Majid! I nearly fell over!' she said.

'Look, there . . . is that . . . Bhaiya?' Majid pointed a few metres away, to a figure dressed in a black trench coat.

'Is it?' Sumaya said.

Before Sumaya could look closer, Majid called out to the man: 'Bhaiya!'

The man turned. It was unmistakably Imran.

◆ ◆ ◆

'What are you doing here?' Majid asked his brother as they got closer to him.

'The same thing you are, I imagine,' Imran responded. 'Have you been to see Amma and Baba already?'

Majid nodded, but Sumaya remained silent. She clung tighter to Majid, as if he were a shield. What she was so afraid of, she couldn't quite say. Or perhaps it was the guilt of Fahima finding out about Sophie the way that she had.

'That's good, Maj,' Imran said. He turned to Sumaya and said: 'I didn't realise you were still in town.'

Sumaya replied sheepishly: 'I'm leaving in a couple of days.'

The three siblings stood in the spring breeze in interminable silence. Sumaya looked at Majid, gesturing with her eyes that she wanted to leave. Imran looked around the cemetery as if looking for any way out of this conversation.

'God,' Majid said, breaking the silence. 'You two are like talking to the dead . . . No pun intended.'

Sumaya laughed and hit her younger brother on the arm. 'Majid!'

'Come on, sis. You're going back to New York. How about you two make up so we can play happy families?' Majid teased his sister.

In her head, Sumaya relived the roller coaster of her trip; so much had happened in her short visit. She had come here at Imran's behest, and although she had expected there to be tension, she couldn't have predicted what the last two weeks would bring. She had been on a journey of self-discovery, and despite her ego being bruised by Neha, she almost felt something akin to gratitude to her brother for making her cross the Atlantic.

'Look.' Sumaya offered an olive branch. 'I just want to say I'm sorry about what I said that night. I never meant for Bhabi to get caught in between us. I hate that I did that, I hate that I hurt her more when she's already hurting . . . I was wrong to use what happened with Sophie as ammunition. I just . . . saw red. You were pushing me and pushing me . . . I don't like who we are to each other, Bhaiya. I can't do it anymore. I can't act like everything's okay when it's not. You get to walk through life without any repercussions for your actions. Amma protected you so much. I protected you. And then you turn around and act like you're so morally superior to me and Majid. I'm done pretending that you can walk on water. But I'm equally done fighting with you. There, I've said it.' Tears began to form in the corners of Sumaya's eyes, and she turned away from her brothers to stifle the sobs.

'Sumaya—' Imran began.

'No,' Sumaya cut him off. 'I know what you're going to say. You're the big "I am" and we should follow everything you say. I've heard it all before! I'm done, okay? Maybe we're just too dysfunctional together to be a happy family. Maybe it's for the best if we don't have a relationship anymore.'

Imran shook his head. 'That's not what I was going to say, Sumaya.'

Sumaya looked up at her older brother in surprise.

'I was actually going to say I'm sorry, too,' Imran continued. 'The stuff with Sophie . . . I was immature and irresponsible. I should've known better than to get involved with your friend. I'm sorry you had to go through that, Sumaya. I get it now. I understand why you were so angry with me all the time. I didn't back then. I understand why you hate me. I never wanted for us to be like this. You're my little sister . . .'

Imran's voice quivered at this last part.

'It wasn't fair of Amma to put you in that position, but I guess she thought she was doing the right thing. All I can say is I'm sorry. I own up to it all. I wasn't the best son; I'm sorry I was so selfish when Amma was in hospital. I wasn't the best brother to you, because a good brother wouldn't have let you carry that secret alone for so long. I shouldn't have put you in that position at all. Thank you for doing that for me.'

Regret clawed within Imran as he imagined the burden that such a secret had placed on his sister when she was just a child herself. She'd been all of fifteen. And then the added burden of looking after Amma and Majid when she got sick, while he selfishly pursued his own life. He had taken for granted that she'd help, because she was the daughter of the family. But there would be a heavy toll for his actions. The repercussions of his fuck-ups had cascaded through his family, hitting his sister especially hard; it was no wonder she harboured such resentment towards him.

'And you were right about your bhabi, too,' he said. 'I've let her down and I haven't always been a good husband. And that's something that I will have to live with and regret for the rest of my life. It took you coming here to give me that wake-up call.'

Sumaya raised an eyebrow. Was her brother actually paying her a compliment? After years of conflict between them, the words coming out of Imran's mouth were strange.

'Why did you give me such a hard time for moving away?' she asked, still unconvinced by her brother's earnestness. 'You gave me so much shit for not being here when Baba died . . .' she continued.

A new wave of tears came over her as images of Baba when he was ill flashed through her mind; she, too, would have to live with regret for the rest of her life that she had missed his final months. But it hadn't been her fault. Baba hadn't wanted to bother her in her new life. It was only her brother who begrudged her her choices, who was so venomous about her absence.

'I . . . I guess I was scared . . .' Imran said quietly. 'I didn't know what to do. With Amma, you were always there. I think I was just scared to go through it alone. When he died . . . that moment will haunt me. I took out my sadness on you, and it wasn't right.'

'All you had to do was call me, Bhaiya. You should have told me this at the time. I'd have come home!' Sumaya responded. 'If I could have been here, I would have.'

'I know . . .' Imran said. 'I'm sorry for how I treated you. It wasn't you; it was my own anger and grief.'

'I wanted to be here . . .' Sumaya broke down.

Majid put his arm around his sister as she sobbed into his Superdry parka. Imran noticed that Majid's eyes were watery too, and this bruised him even more. The three siblings' pain seemed to pour out of them and blanket the air in a thick smog. None of them could bear the reopening of these old wounds.

'Majid, I know I've always been hard on you. I've been hard on you both,' Imran eventually said. 'I know I sound like a hypocrite considering what I did when I was younger. I realise I held the reins too tightly . . . Your bhabi always told me to cut you both some slack, and I just didn't listen. I just want you both to be okay, for Amma and Baba. When Amma died . . . she made me promise to look after you guys. It was her dying wish that I always looked out for you. That's why I was so hard on you. I know I fucked it up, and I know I've let her down. But . . . that's why. She wanted me to keep this family together, and I failed.'

'You haven't failed, bro,' Majid said. 'Look, we're all standing here, aren't we?'

'Wait . . .' Sumaya interjected hastily. 'Amma made you promise that?'

'Yeah,' Imran said. 'I guess it all makes sense now. She said she was worried about me, that I had a fire inside me, and if I didn't control it, it might consume me. To focus on my family . . .'

'Was she referring to Sophie and the baby?' Sumaya said, piecing together the inference of the cryptic promise that their mother had sworn Imran to.

'I think so,' Imran said. 'She was warning me not to fuck up again. I haven't done a very good job, clearly . . .'

'She made me make a promise, too,' Sumaya said.

The brothers turned to their sister in surprise, simultaneously thinking the same thing. What other secrets was this family keeping?

'I . . . The reason I left after Amma died,' Sumaya stuttered, trying to find the right words. 'Before she died, I told Amma something. It was her idea for me to go . . . she was scared that you and Baba wouldn't accept me.'

'Oh,' Majid said. Now it was the youngest sibling piecing together the clues. 'You mean about . . .'

Sumaya nodded.

'About what?' Imran said. 'Can someone tell me what is going on?'

'Just before Amma died . . .' Sumaya said, looking away from her brother for fear of rejection. 'I told her I was seeing someone. That I was in love . . . with a girl . . .'

But for the rustle of the wind, there was silence after Sumaya dropped this bombshell on her elder brother.

'I didn't know what to do,' Sumaya continued. 'I . . . have always had these feelings, but I never really acted on them until then. And then one night, it all came out when I was talking to Amma. And she was scared about what you would say, what Baba would say, what the community would say. She said I couldn't be free here . . .'

Imran's face was scrunched up in contemplation, as he tried to digest what he had just been told. After a moment he said: 'And that's why you went to New York?'

Sumaya nodded.

'And you knew about this?' Imran said to Majid.

Majid shrugged, and Imran stood silently as he processed this new information about his sister and mother. He understood on some level why Amma would be afraid; being gay or lesbian or anything outside the heteronormative was still not readily accepted in their world. He imagined people at the mosque and their neighbours gossiping about Sumaya. But when he thought about his own feelings . . . Amma had been right, to some degree, anyway, that this would take him some time to wrap his head around. But he had to try. He couldn't risk losing her again.

'You're still our sister, Sumaya,' Imran said finally.

Sumaya was surprised by her brother's reaction. 'Really?'

'I'd be an even bigger hypocrite if I judged you, given what you know about me,' Imran said, reassuring his sister. 'I can't say I know what it's like to be in your shoes. I can't lie and say that I completely understand. But I want you to be happy. I'll be here for you. We've laid into each other enough already, don't you think?'

Sumaya tried to keep the relief and shock she felt from showing on her face. She hadn't expected Imran to react this way. At least, not the old Imran. It felt as though the tectonic plates of their family were shifting. That there might still be a family left to salvage.

'Well done, guys,' Majid said, wrapping an arm around each sibling. 'We've done some good work here. Now, how about we get some tea? I'm bloody freezing.'

Imran and Sumaya laughed in unison, and the three siblings walked together towards the exit.

'Hold up,' Sumaya said as they neared the gate. 'Amma made us make promises before she died. Maj, did she make you promise anything?'

'She just said she wanted me to be happy,' Majid replied. 'I reckon I am pretty happy.'

◆ ◆ ◆

'You did what?!' Sumaya asked incredulously, setting her mug down.

The three of them had found warmth in a local coffee shop and were now huddled around a small table. Imran was opening up about what had happened with Fahima, how she had left him the same night that she had heard him and Sumaya arguing in the kitchen. 'I'm sorry,' Sumaya said, feeling guilty all over again for her part in hurting her sister-in-law. Imran reassured her it wasn't her fault. 'It's mine,' he said. 'If anyone should feel responsible, it's me.'

Now, as he told them about the ways in which he had tried to win back Fahima, to profess his love for her, his siblings were slack-jawed.

'My trousers caught on fire,' he said as he sheepishly recounted the events. The tea lights. The balloons. The cracked window.

Sumaya and Majid burst out laughing at the thought of their brother pathetically stumbling into a miniature candle, setting himself alight.

'Wow, that's smooth, bro,' Majid teased.

'She won't even speak to me,' Imran said solemnly. 'I don't know what to do. I thought if I could just show her how much I loved her . . .'

'By setting yourself on fire?' Majid couldn't help himself.

It was strange for Sumaya to see her brother so lovelorn. Was this the same man who always thought he knew best for her and Majid? But as he told them about the flowers, the song, the balloons, and, yes, the candles, she couldn't help but shake her head.

'Seriously, Bhaiya, that is the most juvenile thing I've ever heard,' she said eventually. 'Do you know anything about women?'

Imran looked at her blankly.

Sumaya sighed. 'Some cheap flowers and a few candles isn't going to do it after everything she's been through,' she said. 'She needs to know that she can depend on you. You can't just expect her to run back and be like, "All is forgiven," because you bought her some flowers. She is hurting. I mean, seriously hurting. And she feels alone. You're meant to be a team. That's what a marriage is. She needs to know that you understand what she's feeling. That you care about how she feels.'

'But I do care . . .' Imran whimpered.

'Then *that's* what you need to show her. Not how flashy and cheesy you can be. Honestly' – she sighed again – 'I can't believe you thought playing a soppy song would have her weak at the knees.'

'So, what do I do, Sumaya? I . . . I need your help,' he said with a gulp.

How pathetic, he thought, turning to his sister for relationship advice. But nothing he'd done had worked. He was desperate. And he knew now how wrong he was about Sumaya, that he'd been wrong to think she was impetuous and selfish. Now he knew the truth of what she'd done for him, with Sophie and Amma, he knew that it could only have come from a place of love. Fierce love. This time, he wasn't looking to dump his problems on her. He was genuinely seeking her advice, a brother to a sister. This was how it should always have been.

'You need to hear *her* out,' Sumaya said. 'Listen, and I mean truly listen, to what she needs. And not just one time, but all the time. You need to treat her more like she's your equal, and not just like you know what's best for both of you. She wants to feel valued, Bhaiya. She wants to feel heard.'

Imran nodded, mentally taking notes. Sumaya looked at him with a renewed sense of sympathy – bless him, he really was lost. Like a puppy trying to find its feet. He was genuinely trying.

'Show her the person you showed us just now in the cemetery,' Sumaya said. 'Lose the male bravado. Be vulnerable. She needs to know that her feelings and thoughts are valid. *Listen*.'

'I want to, I just . . . she won't even talk to me . . .' Imran whined.

'Take your phone out now and send her a message,' Sumaya said. 'Don't tell her you want to speak. Tell her you want to listen. Whenever she's ready. She can name the time. The place. You're ready to open your ears.'

And so, that's what Imran did.

Chapter 23

Imran

Fahima replied to his message the next day. She simply texted him a time and location: *6pm, Tower Bridge*.

The significance wasn't lost on him; when they had first started dating, it was on the bridge that Imran and Fahima had rendez-voused for weekend dates, him cycling from Bow and her taking the train from Maida Vale to Tower Hill. This was where their worlds had united. Where east met west and two hearts became one. It was on that very bridge that Imran had promised Fahima the world if she married him. And where, shutting out the opprobrium she would receive from her parents, she had agreed.

Regret clawed at Imran's chest. Ten years of marriage, and could he truly say he had fulfilled his promise of giving her the world? One thing or another had always seemed to get in the way of their relationship, and he realised now that he had selfishly put his own feelings above her own. The pressure at work, Amma dying, then Baba, the miscarriage, and now the attack. Even when it wasn't about him, he'd retreated into himself and made it so. He'd never realised before how he'd taken her for granted, how he'd assumed she'd always be there. He'd leached off his wife's compassion and failed to notice the heavy toll it took on her; she had been slowly disappearing by his side. He had to make it right.

As he walked along the bridge, he spotted her. Fahima was already there waiting for him, deep in contemplation as she looked out over the Thames, the breeze from the water gently fanning the wisps of brown hair that peeked out of her hijab. His heart swelled. How beautiful she looked tonight, and how much he yearned to be reunited with her, to take his wife home with him and put this all behind them. She spotted him as he approached, and he noticed how her expression changed from serene to stony. Taking her home and drawing a line under this whole debacle wouldn't be so easy, he realised.

Imran opened his mouth to speak, but Fahima interjected. 'You said you wanted to listen, so listen,' she said determinedly.

Imran was taken aback by his wife's forwardness. He had rarely ever seen her this way. She had always been so sweet-natured, kind – deferential even. But Fahima looked at him with steely eyes and he couldn't discern what was going on in her mind, or fathom her next move.

'I've been doing a lot of thinking,' she said slowly, turning her body back to face the river.

The water below them seemed to crash in waves, as if moved by his wife's emotions. He could only imagine what she felt inside, but he pictured a roar like the water moving beneath them.

'All my life I've tried to please others. My parents, your parents . . . you,' Fahima said, as they both faced the river. 'Even when I went against my parents' wishes and married you, I always tried to placate them. To make them see you how I see you. I've always made myself smaller, weaker even, because I thought that was who I needed to be to make others happy. I let other people's happiness be my happiness. But the truth is, I have never felt as happy as I did those few precious months I was with child. Finding out that I would be a mother . . . I didn't know how much I wanted it until it happened, and it was ripped away from me.

'These last few years I have tried to make myself happy. I fooled myself into believing I was happy, that I had a blessed life and a good husband. There would be other chances to have a child. But that day . . . when that man reached out and grabbed me . . . I suddenly found myself relieved? I didn't know what he was going to do. I didn't know if he would pull out a knife and stab me. Leave me for dead. But deep down, I felt relief. That I wouldn't have to pretend anymore. That I wouldn't have to fake the happiness anymore. If that was it, then I would have gone peacefully.'

Imran turned to his wife, and from the placid expression on her face he could tell that she was deadly serious. A jolt ran down his spine. What was she saying? How could she even think like that? He wanted to grab her by the shoulders and shout, 'Enough!' It took everything in his power to temper his emotions and let her speak.

'In that moment, I saw myself as everyone else sees me – a dutiful wife, a disappointing daughter. I thought, would these people actually miss *me*? Or would they miss me out of obligation? How well do they truly know me and what is in my heart? How much do they really know or care about the pain I have carried for my lost child? How I would have given anything to swap places with them. I have carried a void in me for so long that it has become part of my very essence, who I am. I look in the mirror and I see only sadness. When was the last time you noticed that, Imran?'

Imran tried to speak, but again Fahima cut him off.

'And then, I saw myself as the world saw me – another girl in a hijab. I was everyone and no one to that man. I know it was just sheer bad luck, but to me, it almost felt like fate. It was like Allah presented me with an ultimatum – do I live or do I give up? These last few weeks, I have felt like giving up—'

'Fahima! No!' Imran cried. No longer able to restrain himself, he tried to reach out to his wife, to take her in his arms, but she simply held her hands out in front of her, halting him.

'Please. Let me finish,' she said curtly. 'That day when you were arguing with your sister. What she said about that girl. The baby. At first, I could only think of what I had lost. How easy it was for you, a man, to have a child and not even know, or care. I think I resented you more in that moment than I ever have. It wasn't fair that you got to have two chances. I know, it doesn't sound logical, but that is how I felt. I had to get out of there. I couldn't stand to be around you.

'And then, it was only at Mum's house that something else occurred to me. I could blame you for the pressure I felt to be a Stepford wife. I could blame my parents for never truly accepting my choices. I could blame that man for making me feel scared. But I was also responsible. I allowed other people to make me feel smaller. To take away my voice. My agency. I allowed other people to put me into whatever box suited their needs, without argument. But it's funny, because hearing your sister shout and swear and stand up for herself, and hearing what your mum did for you . . . it made me realise that the woman I thought I had to be doesn't exist. Our mums' generation, they didn't have the choices that we have. I have my own education and my own money. Why, instead of moving with the times, do we try to uphold standards that just don't make sense in this day and age? Look what your mum did for you, Imran. She had to adapt to the times she was living in. Can you imagine how scared she must have felt? There was no rulebook for her to turn to. We're all just making it up, and judging others for the way they're making it up. I'm done with that.'

Fahima turned to her husband, locking eyes with him.

'From now on, you must take me as I am. I am not perfect. Or weak. Or a victim. I will do what I want to do, say what I want to say, be who I want to be. Why do I have to be one thing? Maybe I want to be a mother and have a full-time career. Maybe I won't do anything at all. But it'll be me deciding for myself. If you don't think you can handle that, Imran, then—'

'Yes,' Imran said without hesitation. 'I can handle that. Anything except losing you. I thought you were gone, jaan.'

The sudden understanding of how close he had been to losing her hit Imran.

'I'm sorry . . .' he said, his voice quivering. 'I never meant to make you feel smaller. Please believe me. I can't say how sorry I am if that is what I made you feel. I have been soul-searching a lot, too, jaan. I realise now I have made mistakes – big, colossal mistakes that have affected everyone around me. I am far from perfect myself.'

'I know that,' Fahima said. 'I've been thinking a lot, too, about that girl. How I would have felt if I were in her shoes . . . I can't imagine how frightened she must have been.'

Imran felt a crack in his chest at this confession about Sophie. Even when she had been through so much herself, Fahima still had so much compassion for others.

'Now that you know, do you regret it?' Fahima probed him.

'Yes,' he replied unequivocally. 'Thinking about what I've done – it haunts me, Fahima. I wish I could change my past, but I can't. All I can do is pray that she has moved on, that she has a good life. That what I did . . . that I didn't scar her too much.'

Imran reached out and held on to the edge of the bridge and let out a sigh. 'I haven't always been a good man, I know that. After losing Amma and Baba, I thought, now I had to step up, I had to be better. I felt responsible for everyone in this family. I thought I needed to be the man of the house, but . . . I realise now that I did everything all wrong. That what I thought was being a man and taking charge just drove people away from me. I was selfish, I didn't listen – I pushed you away, and Majid and Sumaya. Amma and Baba would be ashamed if they could see me now. I have let them down. I really tried to be a good man . . .'

Fahima laid her hands atop Imran's. 'It sounds like we both need to let go of what we think of as "good" or "perfect", Imran. Because the more we try to live up to these imagined expectations, the crazier we will drive ourselves. It doesn't matter what Amma and Baba would have done – what would *you* do? We can do things differently, Imran. We don't have to emulate our parents.'

'I just wanted to make them proud . . .' Imran said, his voice barely above a whisper.

'And you can still,' Fahima consoled him. 'We are only human, at the end of the day. You have made mistakes with your brother and sister, in your past . . . but the best thing you can do is show them that you are trying to learn from those mistakes. The man I fell in love with was warm and funny. When was the last time you loosened up around your siblings? Just had a normal conversation instead of trying to be a substitute parent? I get it. You lost both of your parents and I feel sad for you – *all* of you – for having to experience that, but you need to see your siblings as the adults they are. They're not kids.'

Imran felt a jolt of optimism, as though an electrical current ran through Fahima's fingertips into his own hands. His wife always knew just what to say to make him feel better. She was his biggest cheerleader and motivator. And yet . . . beneath that momentary elation, he also felt a tinge of shame still.

'Fahima,' he said, clasping his hands on either side of her cheeks. 'I'm truly sorry. It's not just Majid and Sumaya I've let down. I feel like I'm not worthy of you. Everything about you is so good and pure . . . and I don't feel like I deserve you. And then I don't know what to say or do when I see you upset, because I just feel like I'll never be good enough. You are the best part of me,

Fahima. I wish I could change the past and take away your pain. I wish I could go back to when we lost the baby and be more attentive. I wish I had handled it all differently. I should have stayed by your side, I should have asked you how you were.

'These last few weeks, I shouldn't have left your side or left you to wallow by yourself. I realise now that I buried my head in the sand. I didn't show up for you as I should have. I guess I still struggle to express my feelings with you . . . it's something I need to work on. I *will* work on. I don't want you to feel smaller or lesser, or feel like you have to be perfect. To me, you already are. I just want you as you are.'

Fahima looked her husband in the eye. 'I want to be an equal,' she said. 'Fifty-fifty. Both of us. It's the two of us against the world, or nothing at all.'

Imran smiled. How beautiful and bold his wife was with this new-found confidence.

'Equals,' he said, reaching out his pinky finger.

Fahima twined her pinky finger around his, and then she leapt forward, wrapping her arms around her husband. Imran held on tightly to his wife.

They stood there silently for a moment. Relieved and grateful for a second chance, and filled with hope.

Chapter 24

SUMAYA

Sumaya saw her family walk into the auditorium, and sprinted towards them. They had all turned up to support her, Seema and Haroon in the short documentary competition at the university.

Seeing Fahima again for the first time since she had inadvertently dropped the bombshell about Sophie's pregnancy struck with her fresh guilt. She wrapped her arms around her sister-in-law.

'I'm sorry—' she began, but Fahima interrupted her.

'It's okay,' Fahima said, squeezing her tighter. 'I love you.'

Relief washed over Sumaya. This was the last piece that she had left unresolved before her flight to New York, but now she had closure with her sister-in-law too, as well as her brother and whatever it was she'd had with Neha.

'The screening is about to start; I saved you some seats with us at the front,' Sumaya said, directing Imran, Fahima and Majid to the second row. In the front row sat the three judges who would decide which of the seven films won the competition. Sumaya had helped produce a live daytime television show in New York, had produced two feature-length documentaries, but this, right now, felt more important than all of that. The film she had helped Haroon and Seema make didn't feel like it was just a silly ten-minute student film. It was personal, to all three of them. They'd all laid themselves bare on camera.

The previous night, Haroon and Seema had come round to Majid's flat to finalise the edit. When Sumaya saw herself onscreen, vulnerable, exposed, her body language awkward and her eyes barely able to meet the camera, she knew that this was something special. The beauty of documentaries was to show the real, unvarnished truth. In herself, she saw a woman who seemed so unlike her – the perfectly crafted facade was gone. In its place was the real her, as she was. More than a little scarred by her past, maybe even a bit broken by the perfect illusion she had tried to maintain, but still standing. Still fighting. Still longing to *live*.

As Sumaya, Imran, Fahima and Majid filed into their seats in the second row, sitting beside Haroon and Seema, Sumaya was struck by the implausibility of this motley brown crew. If only the other people in the auditorium knew the secrets and hurt they had all had to overcome to be sitting here together. She couldn't recall the last time the four of them – her, Imran, Fahima and Majid – had done anything together as a family, not since Amma and Baba were alive. But after everything they'd been through, all the pain they'd accrued individually and collectively – and even inflicted on one another – they were still standing. Together. A family. With Haroon and Seema, too, she felt kinship. They were at least a decade younger than her, the most improbable of friends, but they each understood each other implicitly. They may have been divided by generations, but they were united in lived experience. They each knew the struggles of being migrant, Asian and queer – and that, that was a kinship that transcended generations and brought them together. Only a small minority in the world would ever truly know the skin they lived in. She finally felt like she wasn't alone.

The half-full auditorium clapped politely through the first four films. But when the fifth film – their film – was introduced by the vice-chancellor of the university, there was an inordinate amount of hooting and hollering, concentrated mostly in the second row. Sumaya covered her face in feigned embarrassment as Majid began whistling through his index finger and thumb, but deep down she was touched by her family's overt show of support. Dysfunctional as they may be, they were there for each other when it counted.

Sumaya locked arms with Seema, who in turn locked arms with Haroon in the seat next to her. 'Whatever happens, I'm so proud of you,' she told them.

The film began, and Sumaya felt tension in her chest. What would Fahima and Imran think, hearing her being so open about the secret she had kept buried, the consequence of Amma's promise? Sumaya held her breath, looking tensely around her as the film played, trying to catch a glimpse of Imran and Fahima to deduce the expressions on their faces, but it was too dark and Majid blocked her view.

First came Seema's story, her conversation with her mother. And then Haroon's story. Sumaya heard a restrained sniffle coming from Haroon's direction as the conversation with his uncle played, and as they discussed how he hadn't felt accepted by his parents. Sumaya leaned forward in her seat and looked across Seema in his direction. 'You're amazing,' she mouthed. Haroon smiled back at her.

Finally, the third act played. Haroon, Seema and Sumaya sitting in conversation on Majid's couch. Last night, she had barely been able to watch without the raw emotion of seeing herself clawing at her. Now, however, she fixed her eyes on the screen, trying not to overthink her brother and sister-in-law's reaction. Would she cause another rift by opening up so publicly about their family life? Would her detente with Imran suddenly cease because of her honesty?

The screen turned black. The film ended. There was scattered applause from the hotchpotch of people that filled the auditorium. Once again, the loudest cheers, and wolf whistles, came from the second row. A well-to-do white judge in the front row turned to Majid with a surly look on his face.

'It's not a library, bro,' Majid shot back in response. And then, suddenly realising he was talking to one of the documentary-film-making lecturers: 'Sorry, Professor Collins, sir.'

As the vice-chancellor came back up on stage to introduce the next entry, Sumaya felt a tap on her knee. Imran and Fahima were crouching in the aisle beside her.

'Amma would be proud,' Imran said. 'I'm sorry it was so hard for you, Sumaya. You never need to be afraid to be yourself. Not with us.'

'That was beautiful, Sumaya . . . I had no idea,' Fahima said, squeezing her sister-in-law's hand. Sumaya could see that she had been crying. 'This will *always* be your home.'

Sumaya felt tears prickle her own eyes. She had spent so long afraid of home, and now she realised it had been irrational. Amma's fears were her own.

She was safe, and she was loved.

'Actually,' Fahima said, interrupting her train of thought. 'I have an idea, and I wonder if you can help me . . . Let's talk after.'

◆ ◆ ◆

'And the winner is . . . *Brown and Queer: Stories across the Generations*!' the vice-chancellor announced after a short interval following the final film.

Majid jumped out of his seat, his whooping and hollering filling the entire auditorium. Sumaya turned to Haroon and Seema, teary-eyed, and the three of them held each other.

'Guys, you've got to go up on stage,' Fahima interrupted them.

They watched as the vice-chancellor delivered the judges' verdict: 'Our judges unanimously said that *Brown and Queer* was heartrendingly open and honest, and offered perspectives that we haven't seen before. Judge Sara Issawi, documentary producer from BBC Studios Productions, said: "This is the kind of film that we need. Too often, queer stories are homogeneously white, but here, we are given an insight into the complexities of not only intersectional identity, but intergenerational, too. To say 'brave' would be an insult – too often non-white queer stories are labelled 'brave'. No, this is just the world beyond one narrow viewpoint."'

Sumaya hugged Haroon and Seema tightly before they made their way to the stage. 'This is your moment. I'm just happy to be a small part of it,' she said.

Sumaya looked on proudly as the students, wide-eyed and smiling, had their pictures taken.

'Hey,' said a figure sidling up to her. She turned to her left to see the judge that had praised their documentary so effusively.

'Hi! You're Sara, right?' Sumaya said, extending her hand. 'Thank you so much for your kind words. Those kids are incredible.'

'It seems like they had a really great mentor,' Sara said, shaking Sumaya's hand. 'I have to confess something . . . I've been following your work, actually. You produced that climate film last year . . .'

'Co-produced,' Sumaya replied. 'But yes, that was me.'

'Your work is so needed. I don't know if you'd ever be looking to collaborate with the BBC, but I think my boss would like to meet you . . .' Sara said, pulling a card out of her pocket. 'Why don't you call me sometime?'

As she accepted the business card, Sumaya felt an electricity pass between their fingers.

◆　◆　◆

After the short film competition, Fahima laid out her idea to Sumaya when they all returned to the family home. 'I don't want people to see me as a victim,' she said. 'I don't want to give him power over me.'

'I support you one hundred per cent,' Sumaya told her sister-in-law as they sat at the kitchen table, waiting for Imran to let them know when he and Majid were ready. 'Just imagine the impact this will have, Bhabi.'

In the short time since they'd last seen each other – the night that Sumaya and Imran had laid all their family history bare – each of them had had to dig deep to find themselves again. Sumaya now noticed a considerable difference in her sister-in-law: the way she seemed more confident, unapologetic even, compared to the shell she had been a few weeks ago, when Sumaya first returned to London.

'Listen, I just want to say,' she began to apologise again, 'I never meant for you to get caught up in all the shit between me and Bhaiya. I'm sorry . . .'

'Sumaya, it isn't your fault,' Fahima replied. 'I understand that you were doing what you thought was right – for Amma. And in a way, if you hadn't said anything, would we be here now? Allah has his ways. Perhaps we needed to endure this hardship to realise what we have – what's truly important. I see you and your brother smiling and laughing together today, and you have no idea how happy it makes me. I know he's so proud of you, Sumaya. And so am I,' she added, reaching forward to hug her sister-in-law. 'And we meant what we said,' she added. 'You'll always have a home here.'

Sumaya opened up to her sister-in-law about the dilemma facing her when she returned to New York: breaking up with Jonathan. 'It's been emotional, but I feel like I've learned a lot about myself too these last few weeks. I don't love him, and it isn't fair on either of us to keep it going.'

'Oh, Sumaya,' Fahima reassured her. 'You and me, we've both spent so long letting our past dictate our present. We deserve to be happy and live on our own terms, don't you think? You've always inspired me, Sumaya, with how smart and fearless you are. I believe that you know what is right for you, and if this is what you need to do, I know it's the right decision. I think we just need to make a promise to ourselves and to each other – that we won't hold ourselves back anymore. Promise?'

Sumaya thought momentarily about the shifting dynamics in their family, and all that Amma had done for them in silence. 'Amma may have done things quietly, behind the scenes, but that was *her* time, her generation,' she said. 'I think it's time we step out from the shadows and into the light. I promise.'

Sumaya and Fahima hugged again just as Imran walked into the kitchen. 'We're ready,' he said.

Sumaya had enlisted Imran and Majid to help her and Fahima; they would be shooting the video in the living room, Imran in charge of recording and Majid of editing and uploading it to YouTube.

When the camera rolled, or rather Imran hit record on his iPhone, Fahima seemed to know what to say instantly. Like she had been preparing for this all her life. To break out of the boxes people kept putting her in. To shake off the labels they attached to her.

'My name is Fahima,' she said. 'You don't know me, but you do. A few weeks ago, you probably watched a video of me, shared it, commented on it, wrote about it in the media . . . even joked about it. I am a Muslim woman, and I was attacked by someone I don't even know, because I wear a hijab. I want you to know that behind the video, behind the commentary, there's a real person. Me.'

Sumaya watched in awe as her sister-in-law talked so fearlessly into the camera. She looked around the room at Majid, at Imran, and they seemed equally captivated by her.

'In this world, Muslim women in hijabs are seen as inferior. We are seen as subjugated, we are seen as being in need of saving,' Fahima continued. 'And I'm here to tell you, we're not. Islam isn't about the subjugation of women. In fact, it empowers women. It gives us a choice. And my hijab is a choice. Too many people feel comfortable speaking about what we should and shouldn't do, feel too comfortable policing women's bodies. But I am not something to control or police. I am a living, breathing, thinking human being. Just like you.'

Fahima's determination, the steely, uninhibited look in her eye, hit a nerve in Sumaya; how she wished she had been this assured earlier in life, instead of trying to be someone she was not.

'To my attacker, I want to say,' Fahima said, 'you may have wanted to hurt me, to make me feel so small. You may have seen your actions as a joke, or some political stand, but all you showed yourself to be is a coward. In fact, it's *you* I feel sorry for – for the hate in your heart. For the entitlement you feel but cannot justify. The world doesn't belong to any one race or creed. One person is no better than another.

'Over these last weeks, I've felt the gamut of emotions – pain, anger, depression. But today, I stand firm in what I know to be true. That I have been put on this earth for a reason. That I have a voice.

'My attacker may have wanted to silence me, hurt me . . . I could have lain down and died. But I won't give him that satisfaction. I won't cower. Because to do that would let him and others that think like him win. And I won't let them win.

'We are here, we will always be here.

'You'll just have to get used to it.'

Epilogue

A YEAR LATER

Sunlight poured in through the floor-to-ceiling windows in Sumaya's new flat in Stratford. The open-plan kitchen and dining room was adorned with balloons that she and Sara had spent the last hour blowing up. A sign hastily taped to the bookcase read 'Happy Graduation, Majid!'

'Do you think they'll like me?' Sara asked.

'Of course they will,' Sumaya assured her girlfriend as she removed a roasted chicken, marinated in tandoori spices, from her new oven. It was the first time Sumaya had used the kitchen, and she was anxious to impress her family. Until now, she had mostly relied on takeaways or dinners out with Sara, indulging every craving that she had so sorely missed during her time in New York, from the local fish-and-chip shop to Nando's.

Sara laid out the cutlery on the table and placed a bowl of fatoush salad in its centre. The Emirati woman had taken the care and time to prepare a traditional Arabic dish for her partner's family – anxious, too, to make a good impression. The scent of fresh lemon juice, mint, feta cheese and olive oil perfectly complemented the zingy aroma of Sumaya's chicken.

Sumaya had left New York permanently six months ago, ending her relationship with Jonathan and moving her business over to London. 'I can be based anywhere,' she told her brothers and sister-in-law. 'Besides, I want us to be a family again. A real family. We've lost too much time in each other's lives.'

The split with Jonathan had seemed to signal not only the end of her relationship, but also a natural conclusion to her life in New York. She knew it was time to go home, to put aside the woman she had tried to be and embrace who she really was. To be back in her home town, with her family, on her own terms, just felt right.

Sumaya and Sara had reconnected shortly after she moved back. Sara had introduced her to her boss at the BBC, as promised, and Sumaya left the meeting with a first-look deal for three feature-length documentaries.

Their first date was at a Lebanese restaurant in Edgware Road. They had laughed and bonded over how they each subverted the traditional role of women in their different – but not wholly dissimilar – cultures. At the end of the evening, time running away from them, they'd split a hot, syrupy dessert of knafeh, clinking their spoons before diving in. Now, they were one of those couples who always split desserts.

Majid was the first to arrive for the dinner in his honour. Sumaya hugged him as he crossed the threshold and practically yelped, 'Happy graduation!'

Majid had achieved a first in his studies, exceeding the 2:1 degrees of both his siblings. Imran, Sumaya and Fahima had all attended his graduation ceremony, and as he crossed the stage, Imran and Sumaya had exchanged a look that they both immediately understood. Their younger brother, who had lost both his parents at such a young age, was the best of them, and they were proud of all that he had accomplished. He would burn the brightest of them all.

Imran and Fahima were the last to arrive. Imran's new business was experiencing expected first-year teething pains, but his family all agreed that they had never seen him more fulfilled in his work. Fahima, too, had taken steps to pursue what had once been her dream career in social work, by enrolling in a refresher course.

'Bhaiya, Bhabi, meet Sara,' Sumaya said, reintroducing Sara to her brother and sister-in-law as her partner.

Although her brother had assured her that he was fully supportive of whoever she wanted to date, Sumaya still felt a prickle of apprehension as she introduced a woman to her family. And yet, from the way that Sara and Fahima instantly embraced, she knew her concerns were unfounded. And in her heart, she could feel that introducing Sara felt more natural than it would ever have been if she'd been introducing Jonathan.

Once they had all sat down around the table, Imran cleared his throat loudly, waiting until all eyes were on him before he spoke.

'We also have some news . . .' he said, placing a hand on his wife's stomach.

The room erupted in a chorus of gasps and cheers.

All three siblings simultaneously had the same thought: if Amma and Baba could see them now . . .

They were three branches of the same tree, each extending in their own direction.

But bonded by their roots.

Read on for an extract from Tufayel Ahmed's debut novel, *This Way Out*.

Available to buy now.

Prologue

This is not a love story . . . is what I would probably say if I were a middle-class white woman.

It sounds clichéd, doesn't it? But I guess it's true.

I wasn't planning on falling in love.

I was too consumed by grief to even think about it.

It was a year after Mum died that I met Joshua. A year after the greatest tragedy of my life came the greatest blessing.

Funny how life works like that. It can completely knock you on your ass, like you've gone twelve rounds with Tyson, and then lift you up and dust you off, as if to say, *We cool now?*

No, life, we definitely are not cool.

But as far as reparations go, Joshua coming into my life was acceptable compensation, though I'd still give anything to have Mum back, too. Maybe I was being greedy, thinking I could have both.

After she died, I was living in pain on a daily basis, unmoored from the world. Life was a haze. I was existing, not living. Where there used to be love, there was now a void. All the love I had ever known was from Mum. How could I continue without her? Sometimes, I blamed her for leaving me behind. For leaving me to navigate whatever was left of this life without her – her voice, her touch, her smell. I blamed her for being so fucking selfish. And then I'd cry for ever thinking so ill of her. Of course she wasn't being selfish. It wasn't her choice to leave. She would have stayed if she could have.

Every day was a struggle, but the nights were the worst. I held myself as I slept, whimpering like an injured baby animal. I tried to keep my cries to acceptable decibels – too loud, too untamed, and the world would know the broken human being I had become.

I tried to keep it together.

Until I couldn't.

My world unravelled quickly after that.

Within four months of Mum dying, I was completely wrapped in my cocoon of grief and misery. I barely left the house, stopped returning calls and texts, and tried to sleep my way through the darkness that had embedded itself in my brain.

At first, my manager at the advertising firm I worked for was understanding when I needed to take a week off, which turned into two, then three. Once I'd exhausted the compassion in compassion-ate leave, I just stopped turning up. They held a disciplinary meet-ing in my absence. Then, a month later, they fired me *in absentia*. I was asleep when HR called and left the voicemail message: 'We're really sorry but we have to let you go.' I didn't care. I had taken on a new full-time job: mourning.

Six months after Mum's death, I was more like a zombie from *The Walking Dead* than a human. I hadn't been outside in so long that I was starting to look wan and lifeless. My hair and beard were overgrown. I had even resorted to eating Pot Noodles.

If it wasn't for Malika, my best friend, insisting I get out of the house and re-engage with life and the living, I'd never have ended up working with her at Whitecross Street Bookshop, a quaint little indie near Moorgate station run by her gay friend Elijah.

More importantly, I'd never have met Joshua.

My early shifts at the bookshop were easy enough that I could hit pause on mourning for a few hours – and besides, few things give me joy like discovering a good book and talking about it with Malika.

Huddled behind the till, I read classics I'd never read before – *Norwegian Wood*, *To Kill a Mockingbird* – and new releases, all under the pretence of working. Elijah didn't tell me off or push me to do more work, for which I was grateful. He gave me the breathing room to re-enter society at my own pace, book in hand like a security blanket.

A few months after I started working at the bookshop, on a particularly slow trading day, I noticed him.

Tall, blue-eyed, bespectacled, handsome Joshua.

A strange sensation came over me, one that I thought I'd lost in my grief: attraction.

Watching Joshua browse books, my libido spluttered into action like a long-abandoned, dusty power station that had finally turned on. I surreptitiously followed him around the shop with my eyes, and was surprised to see him pick up a book I'd just finished reading, his forehead wrinkling as he considered the blurb on the back.

A Little Life, Hanya Yanagihara's desolate tome about the trauma of abuse, self-harm and suicide, was not exactly light reading in the midst of mourning, but it had appealed to my maudlin sensibilities. Dubbed 'the great gay novel' of our times, it was displayed prominently on the shop floor in solidarity, and it sold well.

'That's a great book,' I called out to Joshua. 'I just finished it.'

'Oh, yeah? My friends keep talking about it,' he replied.

We spent the next ten minutes talking about the dearth of gay literature and Yanagihara's adroit dissection of modern masculinity.

Joshua left with a copy of *A Little Life* and my phone number, and we promised to meet up when he finished reading it.

◆ ◆ ◆

I fell for Joshua somewhere between our third round of drinks and second straight hour of talking. When we kissed at the end of that first date, the rest of the world fell away. It was just him and me.

We continued to bond in the weeks to come, over books we'd read, embarrassing holidays and food-related innuendos. He was a chef, he said. And I was starving.

The rapport between us was natural, and our conversations flowed without those dreaded awkward silences I'd become so familiar with. He made me feel at ease in a way I'd never experienced before. How does the cliché go? It was like I'd known him for ever.

Joshua was like a rope lowered down into the well that was my grief. Little by little, he helped me to smile again, to stop feeling so apathetic about life, and to allow myself to fall in love. The sorrow, as well as the worries I'd carried for so long, quietened.

I wondered sometimes about the cruel irony of this great love after such loss. What if it was necessary to lose Mum, I asked myself, so I could move forward with my life and meet him? One guardian passing the torch to another. I wanted to believe perhaps she had pulled some strings to engineer this from above.

We knew we wanted to live together almost immediately and ended up jumping at the first place we saw: a cheap, ground-floor flat with a leaky kitchen tap and too-narrow bathroom. The bedroom barely had enough space for a large wardrobe and a bed, and the kitchen and living room were open plan. Less than ideal for cooking curries, but there was a charm to our shabby fixer-upper. And it was in our modest – mostly thanks to me – budget.

While the flat itself was tiny and we could entertain only one person at a time, around us, London Fields was a thriving area just far enough from Central London to be considered bohemian and yet still well connected. Artists and creatives flocked there to use the lido or to buy artisanal bread and cold-pressed juice from Broadway Market. We never had to go too far out the door for decent coffee.

But it was the mundane things that couples do together at home that gave me the most joy: preparing dinner together, a cup of tea on the sofa and a movie, debating whose turn it was to do the laundry.

The world outside ceased to exist. We became each other's world.

It's been three years since Mum died.

I've been with Joshua for two years now.

Two weeks ago, Joshua proposed. I said yes, of course.

Now I have to do the hardest thing I've ever done.

Come out to my family.

Maybe this is a love story after all.

A beautiful, fucked-up story about love.

ACKNOWLEDGEMENTS

Well, here we are again. I never imagined that I had one book in me, let alone two. Writing a second novel, I was warned by my agent and editor, is the hardest thing a writer will do. And, boy, were they right. But I have loved creating these characters just as much as I did Amar in *This Way Out*, and I hope you love them too.

First, I want to say a big thank you to you, the reader. The out-pouring of love and support for *This Way Out* was overwhelming. The emails and direct messages from readers who related to the story in some way meant so much to me, and really shored up my confidence while writing this one. Thank you for taking Amar and Joshua into your hearts.

To the dream team of Victoria Oundjian, my editor, and my agent, Cara Lee Simpson, once again this has been such a magical experience. I am eternally grateful for your continued belief in me, my characters and my words.

It's only when you publish a book that you realise just how much work goes into it and how many people it takes to bring a book into the world. I want to say a big thank you to all who have worked on *This Way Out* and/or *Better Left Unsaid*: Salma Begum for her expert developmental editing, Amit Malhotra for designing the gorgeous covers for both books, the amazing publicity team at FMcM – Emma Mitchell, Chloë Rose and Rhiannon Morris – for making me feel like a very minor celebrity, and everyone at Amazon Publishing and Brilliance Publishing.

A big thank you to all of the family and friends who have supported me through the publication process of *This Way Out*, strategically namedropped my book in conversations with family, friends and colleagues, and listened to me say 'I can't do this!' a million times while writing this one. What fun we had celebrating in Shoreditch. Here's to the next one!

Finally, Francesco and Gigi, thank you for being my constants.

ABOUT THE AUTHOR

Photo © Robert Greene

Tufayel Ahmed is a journalist and lecturer who proudly hails from the streets of Tower Hamlets, East London. He has written for *Newsweek*, *Vice*, CNN, the *Independent* and more. This is his second novel. To find out more, visit his website, tufayel.co, or find him on Twitter @tufayel and on Instagram @tufayelahmed.

Follow the Author on Amazon

If you enjoyed this book, follow Tufayel Ahmed on Amazon to be
notified when the author releases a new book!
To do this, please follow these instructions:

Desktop:

1) Search for the author's name on Amazon or in the Amazon App.
2) Click on the author's name to arrive on their Amazon page.
3) Click the 'Follow' button.

Mobile and Tablet:

1) Search for the author's name on Amazon or in the Amazon App.
2) Click on one of the author's books.
3) Click on the author's name to arrive on their Amazon page.
4) Click the 'Follow' button.

Kindle eReader and Kindle App:

If you enjoyed this book on a Kindle eReader or in the Kindle
App, you will find the author 'Follow' button after the last page.